GLASS ONION

DAVID YURKOVICH

DEDICATION

This book is dedicated with love to my sweetgirl, Dianne. *Glass Onion* would not exist were it not for Di's brilliant edits, ideas, suggestions, encouragement, and fine judgment.

TABLE OF CONTENTS

ACKNOWLEDGMENT

A special thank you to my friend and colleague, Pratima, for sharing her knowledge of Thai culture and language.

I would also be remiss if I did not tip my hat in gratitude to Mr. Lennon.

1 Philadelphia, January 27, 2009: Otis Atop the Ben Franklin Bridge

Contrary to what you might think, the pedestrian walkway of the Benjamin Franklin Bridge has never been a popular platform for suicide. Beautiful bridge, great view, but few suicides, perhaps because very few know of the walkway, and fewer still know its access points. Or perhaps it is more practically because that, from a suicide perspective, the distance from the walkway to the Delaware River (less than 42 meters) is not considered a fatal drop. Those seeking a fast and dramatic death fare better in San Francisco where the famous Golden Gate Bridge has played host to more than 1,200 suicides since its 1937 opening. But one of the first things people on the onion hunt learn is you work with what you've got, which is why Otis Oppenheimer found himself on the pedestrian walkway of the Benjamin Franklin Bridge in the early morning hours of January 27, 2009. It was a typical cold, damp Philly winter evening. Oppenheimer chain-smoked and rubbed his hands together for warmth as motorists and PATCO transit cars alike sped by, oblivious to his presence.

"Goddam east coast weather," he mumbled as he fumbled with the tiny recorder, which he wore like a necklace. "I'll have to assume this is working," he said pointedly toward the small microphone on the recorder's side, "though honestly I've never much trusted technology. Where was technology on Nine Eleven? On a fucking vacation is where."

Otis paused to light another Camel. His shadow stretched across the length of the walkway, lit by the overhead gantry lights. He counted the remaining cigarettes. Along with the unopened pack, they totaled thirty-three. It would be enough; it would have to be.

"The thing about it," he continued, "the thing is, you just never know. No, that's not it. You do know. You fucking know and you still carry on. Out of loyalty. Out of a naïve sense of honor. Out of belief. That's what pulled me in; I think it's what pulled all of us in. Belief."

The cold wind whipped up and down the Delaware River. It stung his eyes and ear lobes. But it would be okay now. Oppenheimer sat down on the walkway and leaned his back against the concrete railing. He stared down at the river and watched as the Spirit of Philadelphia sailed lazily toward its berth at Penn's Landing.

"Maybe I can impart a bit of wisdom to you—three rules that I've learned. In my 45 years I've come to live by these rules. Always figured they'd serve as the foundation of a self-help book I planned to write in the retirement years, but let's be honest, there won't be any retirement years. Anyway, maybe they'll do you some good, help you to attain the good life—socks and sandals and a lawn chair by the barbecue.

"Okay, so, first rule: trust no one. A total shocker, I'm sure. But believe me, it's not as easy as it sounds. The truth is, we want to trust. We want to believe in our friends, our lovers, the government. Don't do it. Resist the urge, because you're going to get fucked regardless, so you might as well be fucked with your eyes open.

"Second rule: Build a solid social network. I admit that my career path hasn't enabled me to follow this one. It's been a problem. Nothing that a 10-year antidepressant prescription and a slight addiction to gin can't help overcome, but that, in its own way, is part of the problem. We should need people more than we do. Barbara Streisand was right, dammit. And I admit, I freely admit, that building a social network while trusting no one sounds like an oxymoron. But it's important, trust me.

"Final rule: If you're going to be working in the north east during winter, bring along a decent coat. The fucking east coast winters are brutal."

Otis stared into the evening sky. It was dark, but the nearness of the Philadelphia skyline kept it from ever being too dark. A jet thundered overhead en route to Philly International.

"Boeing 238-passenger jet model 747-200M; one of 43 currently in use by major carriers. Various accidents and incidents plague the 747 series, among the most notorious is Korean Air 007 which was shot down in by the Soviets in 1983 and—"

He paused.

"You see, this is what happens. It's what happens when you choose a life like I've chosen. Too much down time and nothing to do with it but memorize stupid shit that at the end of the day doesn't fucking matter. I probably know more about Boeing than most Boeing execs and engineers. Christ.

"What I'd really like, what I need, is a time machine. I need to go back to 1986 and do one of two things—stop me from signing on to this piece-of-shit Holy Grail assignment, or kill myself. Simple."

2   April 5, 1986: Reagan's Dream

The lights in the West Wing of 1600 Pennsylvania Avenue NW burned brightly at 3:00 a.m. President Reagan and First Lady Nancy were seated at a round oak table. Draped in a black, custom-made silk robe specially designed by Antonio Versachi, the leader of the free world resembled an aging cultist. Seated between the Reagans was Julia Copeland. Copeland was no stranger to the First Family, having been summoned to the White House on no fewer than 36 occasions since Ronald Reagan's ascent to the US Presidency on January 20, 1981.

Under typical circumstances Copeland's attire would have more closely resembled her profession; she was especially fond of wearing brightly colored silk paisley garments for meetings such as this. But the Secret Service arrived unannounced at her Bethesda home at 2:08 a.m. rousing Copeland from a deep sleep. The agents had insisted that she dress with haste and accompany them.

Seated between the Reagans, the 27-year-old Copeland (wearing faded jeans, Nike high tops, and a Foreigner t-shirt) looked less like an internationally renowned psychic and more like a vacationing waitress. She'd at least had the good sense to place a kerchief around her head to downplay the recently dyed hair.

Nancy sat quietly and sipped tea from an ornamental cup of china so thin she could almost see her fingers through the design, while actor-turned-politician Ron sipped bourbon from a thin metal flask. The flask was made of platinum, a gift from Nancy that bore an inscribed testament to Ron's prowess in bed. It was a private token that only a very select few had ever seen. Copeland busied herself with a Tarot deck as she struggled to maintain a calm demeanor. The Reagan's were not known for this impromptu behavior; something was up.

"Do you remember what you told me in February 1981?" Reagan asked.

"Yes," Copeland answered. "I told you an attempt would be made on your life."

"That's right. You told me I'd be wounded but not fatally."

Nancy said nothing but refilled her teacup with Earl Gray poured from a teapot as gossamer as the cup.

"In 1983 you advised me on the Grenada situation. Do you remember what you said?"

"I said the Grenada invasion would succeed with limited loss of life. There were 19 American deaths, if I recall correctly."

"We prefer 'casualties' to 'deaths' dear," Nancy said softly.

"Well," Ronald Reagan said soberly, "those brave men and women made the ultimate sacrifice for liberty, answering freedom's call."

An awkward silence followed and Copeland found that her palms were sweaty.

"How may I help you this morning, Mr. President?" she asked.

Ronald Reagan didn't answer. He seemed troubled.

"Ron's been having the dream again," Nancy said.

"The glass onion dream?"

"Yes."

"I see. Tell me about your dream, sir."

"Well," Reagan said, "It's round. It's glass. It's a bit larger than palm-sized."

"No. I'm sorry. I don't mean the physical appearance of the onion. Describe what happened in the dream."

"It's the same dream as always. The glass onion is at my side. It...reveals information. I'm shown the future. I visit with Gorbachev again. We meet for a summit in Moscow. The Soviet Union collapses in 1989."

"Since we last discussed this, I've been researching the object. This glass talisman you dream of exists, or at least is rumored to once have," Copeland explained. "It is mentioned in several nineteenth century texts—hinted at, really. Philosopher Nils Boman wrote that the onion could not be kept by any mortal, and that it appears only when it wants to be found; it reveals itself selectively to certain individuals."

"It wants me to find it?"

"I believe it does, though honestly, how such an undertaking could be achieved escapes me."

"My dear," Nancy said, "my husband is the President of the United States of America. He can pretty much make everything and

14

anything happen."

****

There's a joke known to DC espionage insiders and few others. It goes like this: Two CIA staff members (call them Agent Red and Agent Blue) meet at a local bar. They begin a clandestine conversation.

Agent Red: This job is taking its toll. I suspect my wife is having an affair.

Agent Blue: She is.

Agent Red: From the moment I first banged her, I knew she was not to be trusted. I swear I'm gonna plant hidden cameras in the bedroom.

Agent Blue: Be sure to hide them on the right side of the room. Maybe on the bookcase adjacent to the mini-bar.

Agent Red: Why on the bookcase adjacent to the mini-bar?

Agent Blue: It's my better side. By the way, you're low on martini mixer.

Agent Red: I just hope I find out who the bastard is.

A dumb joke for sure, but it summed up government intelligence and espionage of the late 20th century. An inability to spot the obvious coupled with a healthy dose of dissatisfaction with the status quo were the status quo.

But the dozen agents who arrived for debriefing in the White House garden on May 17, 1986 were new to the agency. Eyes bright, faces innocent, hearts filled with hope and confidence. They were ready to change the world (or at least die to keep America safe).

The recruits wore tacky, light-colored polyester suits, though not by choice. It was part of the CIA hierarchy. The dark silks of designer attire were reserved for experienced personnel and deep undercover operatives. The twelve rookies who stood on the lawn were still years from Armani. They were the new kids on the block, so new in fact, that the imitation-gold foil on their badges still reflected against the afternoon sun. Low-clearance rankings. Low pay. Low everything. They were lacking in all arenas except self-esteem. The twelve were agency newbies with aspirations for greatness. The combination of no experience or clout and great ambition made them perfect candidates for the task at hand.

Twenty-two-year-old Otis Oppenheimer was perspiring from the DC humidity, but his enthusiasm was unbroken. He understood the politics of the agency enough to realize that something unusual was happening here. Newbies weren't invited to the White House on a sunny afternoon—or any afternoon—for a meet-and-greet with the Commander in Chief.

Oppenheimer, like his eleven contemporaries, knew they were being reassigned. Beyond that, he hadn't a clue. But they were all weathering bad assignments, drone-type desk work mostly, so any change would be a change for the better.

"Well, this is different," Oppenheimer said.

"You must be Otis Oppenheimer," the man standing to his right said.

"Yes. How did you know that?"

"You're wearing a name badge. We all are."

"Oh, uh, I see, Reilly."

"I'm not Reilly; I'm Billings. He and I switched badges, just to fuck with the rest of you."

"Very clandestine I'm sure, Mr. Billings."

"Billings is my first name. I'm actually named Smith; can you believe it? Really. Guess my parents wanted to jazz it up with Billings."

"Smith. Right."

Reagan appeared moments later, flanked by a half-dozen Secret Service agents, most of who were with him on the day of Hinkley's botched assassination attempt. He was smiling, but it was tight lipped. There was no physical contact, no handshakes or pats on shoulders. Most of the newbies were, nonetheless, star struck.

Reagan stopped about twelve paces away from the recruits. He looked them over and spoke in his soft, fatherly voice: "Thank you for coming here today. Whether you realize it or not, you twelve are embarking on a mission of national security. It will likely be the most important assignment of your life. You're all agency men and women, so I won't bother to explain that this project you've been assigned to requires the utmost discretion and absolute professionalism, or what an honor it is to have been chosen, by me, for something special. It is vital, vital that you succeed. You all know Denton Chambers. Mr. Chambers will provide you with the full details. I envy you, actually. If I was half my age, I'd be joining you. Together this mission will be our legacy to these blessed United States: actual peace on earth. Good luck. Godspeed."

Reagan smiled an impish smile and nodded at each of them, one at a time. Then he turned and began the walk across the lawn and toward the White House, never once looking back.

3 March 1987: Singleton House

Far from the bustling London streets is the quaint Nickleborough, known affectionately by locals as Pastryborough. The alluring scent of hot scones or a sack of warm pecan tassies serve as an unobtrusive early-morning wake up call to the neighborhood working class. Certainly it's far more pleasant to the nose than the diesel smoke that pours from the exhausts of commercial truckers cruising along the interstate just a few kilometers to the north.

Toward the southwest corner of Nickleborough is Bristol Way. It's a narrow, cobblestone land bordered by a select handful of cottages. At the end of the road is Singleton House, a three-story stone edifice built in the late 19th century, with a modest façade that does not reveal to the average resident that in its 100-plus-year history, Singleton House has been many things to many people, and least of all a home.

Initially built as a seaside estate for the Singleton family during the turn of the century, Singleton House was formally adopted by the Secret Intelligence Service during World War II to serve as a briefing ground for counter-intelligence agents working to infiltrate the German Navy. Dunkirk Singleton, Lord of Singleton House and a former member of British Intelligence, was more than happy to offer his estate if it helped to thwart Germany. Although Dunkirk tried to shelter his daughter from the realities of war, eighteen-year-old Sarah did not want to move from Nickleborough and soon discovered what the goings on at her home were related to. She was eager to contribute to Britain's cries of defiance against the Nazi war machine. Miss Singleton proved to have a keen mind, and soon was working directly with agents of the Government Code and Cypher School, and her efforts, instrumental in the decryption of numerous Nazi code books, earned her the nickname Cypher Sarah.

Years after Germany's defeat, Sarah continued to work with the SIS, though she soon lost interest in the espionage game and graduated to diplomacy, working as an ambassador to visiting foreign delegates. She collected works of literature. Her fascination with the printed word was boundless. Lady Sarah had no interest in turning Singleton House back into a mere home and instead converted many of its rooms into an extensive library. It wasn't until the early 1970s when Singleton House would again see a boarder besides herself and her volumes of books. The circumstances were such that Lady Sarah could hardly refuse in good conscience.

Thus it was that Sarah met Archie Huntsman.

Huntsman was a thin, quiet man with an adherence to routine and a schedule so rigid the most senior operators of the London Underground would have bowed in envy at his precision. Each morning at 8:00 a.m. the forty-four-year-old Huntsman arrived at Singleton House. He passed by the kitchen and presented Lady Sarah with a cup of black tea and a bag of warm crumpets. He then walked to the small office on the third floor, unbolted the door, entered the room, and locked the door behind him. There he remained until 5:00 p.m., at which time Archie Huntsman packed up his briefcase, threw on his overcoat and derby, and quietly descended to the first floor to bid Lady Sarah "a fond farewell until tomorrow."

While she never violated Huntsman's privacy, Lady Sarah, even if she hadn't been specifically asked by SIS to provide him with "lodgings," would have been aware that he was involved with SIS. There were signs; some more obvious than others. Huntsman's unflinching punctuality. An influx of telephone technicians who dutifully replaced "bad" wiring in and around Singleton House on a monthly basis. The assortment of seemingly random letters and numbers circled in red ink on the front page of his morning newspaper each Friday, newspapers that he asked her to burn when she lit her fire for afternoon tea. She concluded that Huntsman was either very stupid or that he wanted Sarah to be in the know, if only peripherally. Huntsman was many things, but he was far from stupid.

On March 23, 1987, when Huntsman entered Singleton House per his usual morning routine, Lady Sarah was seated in the conservatory reading the morning financials. Huntsman placed a cup of tea and a bag of crumpets on the table beside her.

"How kind," she replied, as she did every morning. "Mr. Huntsman, do you know what day it is?"

"I believe it's the twenty-third of March, M'lady."

"Today, Mr. Huntsman, is the tenth anniversary of your arrival here."

"I wasn't aware of that," he lied.

"Ten years. I believe a celebratory lunch is in order."

"Can't today, M'lady. I'm meeting with an associate from the head office."

"What do you do for the service, exactly?" Sarah asked.

"Surely you know. I'm in the insurance racket. Life, accident, and such. It's all quite humdrum I can assure you."

"Yes, I'm sure it must be. Did you know that Newkirk Barnaby passed away last night?" Sarah asked.

"I don't know who that is."

"Ten years ago Newkirk contacted me and asked if I'd let a room to you. He and I go back a ways, back to the war against the Nazis. Newkirk was an old campaigner with Section D and the SOE. I always assumed you knew him."

Huntsman's eyes met Sarah's. He smiled politely.

"It's quite possible I did," he said. "I meet a lot of people…in my line of work."

"Yes, I'm sure you must."

"Yes. By the way, at 11:35 this morning I'll be meeting with a client. It's a rather sensitive account, so I'd appreciate it if we weren't disturbed. I'll come down to let him in; no need to trouble yourself. I like to give the personal treatment to my accounts." His left eye seemed to have developed a tremor.

In ten years Hunstman had never "given the personal treatment" to anyone before.

"But of course," she said.

Huntsman nodded and left Lady Sarah to her breakfast.

At precisely 3:00 p.m. Reginald Middleton arrived at Singleton House and was greeted by Huntsman.

"You're looking well, old boy," Huntsman said.

"A daily nap and a spot of tea can resolve most of life's problems," Reginald replied.

"No time for a lie-down, I'm afraid. But there's tea aplenty."

The two men quietly retreated to Huntman's office and locked the door.

"How much faith do you have in this dossier you've procured, Reginald?"

"I have all the faith in the world."

Huntsman studied the documents again. It was the fourth time he'd reviewed them in the last hour.

"I stopped believing in crystal balls a long time ago," he said.

Reginald Middleton shook his copious bald head disapprovingly.

"I realize that this sort of thing isn't within your domain of excellence, Huntsman. Quite frankly, I suggested to McColl that this assignment be given to someone with, how do I say this tactfully, a bit more field experience."

"Yes, perhaps that would be in everyone's best interest."

"Yes, well, unfortunately the organization is strapped for resources at the moment. Too many Soviet-related directives. That seems to be the main area of concern these days as far as SIS is concerned. Not that I'm telling you anything you don't already know."

"Reg, with all due respect, you can't seriously expect me to oversee a taskforce whose goal is to scour the earth in search of..."

"A glass onion. Yes, that's the long and short of it."

"Fuck. How many on the taskforce?"

"Five, I think. Naturally you're welcome to hand pick your squad. But I'd like it to include Tad Dewhurst."

"Why Dewhurst especially?"

Reginald's voice tightened. He was a large, government man who had long ago mastered his emotions. But Archie's question touched a nerve that he realized, too late, was best left alone.

"The bastard broke my sister's heart. My sweet, dear sister. The bastard. Send him to fucking Siberia, Tehran. I really don't care provided it's fucking miserable."

"Blimey. Couldn't we...couldn't we just finance the US effort?" Huntsman asked. He fidgeted with a pencil and began doodling.

"In theory, I suppose that's a realistic option. Unfortunately, we have reason to suspect that the operative who leaked the dossier may have also offered it to other nations."

"A scavenger hunt of global proportions?"

"Quite possibly. Assuming this...talisman exists, I'd rather not see it in the hands of a hostile nation. Of course if you feel otherwise..."

Huntsman was silent. Reginald Middleton stood up and approached his junior colleague. He extended a large, meaty hand in Archie's direction.

"Then we're agreed. Very good, Huntsman. Very good indeed."

"Of course, sir."

"I always enjoy the completion of business. Onto leisure. What've you got to drink here? I'm positively parched, and I'm afraid I'll be needing something with a bit more kick than Earl Gray."

Huntsman removed a bottle of Beefeater and two glasses from a cabinet drawer.

"I forget you're not much of a drinking man. Well, it'll have to do I suppose," Reginald said. "Cheers."

He downed the beverage and gathered his coat and hat.

"You'll want to hold onto that dossier, Archie. I'll have the boys at Lambeth wire you a few other documents."

Reginald stared down at the pencil sketch which depicted a stick figure in a noose.

"If you don't mind my saying," Reginald said, smiling, "illustration really isn't among your assets. Don't want to let your mind give itself away like that."

"Yes," Huntsman said, picking up the sketch and enveloping it in his fist, "I can see you're in right there."

"Right. Yes. We'll be in touch then. Just for the record, everyone in the agency admires your service record. We're all expecting great things from you, Archie. I'm sure you won't disappoint."

Reginald Middleton departed, his massive form barely squeezing through the door opening. Alone, Archie stared at the open bottle of Beefeater and then pressed it to his lips. His disgust and skepticism remained, but the liquor took the edge off of it, if only slightly.

4   March 23, 1989: At the Darby

The Darby Diner, located at the intersection of Madison Street and Blair Avenue, is among the oldest eateries in St. Louis. Built in 1903 by restaurant entrepreneur Henry Darby, the diner officially opened to coincide with the 1904 World's Fair. In the years that followed, the diner became more than a business to Henry Darby; it was as much his child as his own living children were.

The business survived the Great Depression, and although it struggled during that and World War II, Darby's return from the war as a naval hero solidified the business in the community. As the years passed, the diner's care was left to Darby's aforementioned children and, later, to his only grandchild, Jackson. Jackson Darby had little regard for the food-services industry. A twice-convicted felon, he assumed ownership of the diner at age 32 when his father dropped dead of a heart attack one Christmas morning. Jackson regarded the Darby as little more than an effective location for trafficking stolen merchandise. The eatery's once-bright interior had become overrun with grime and neglect. The veneer of the dining tables had long since faded and peeled. And the black and white ceramic tile floor was chipped, cracked, and stained.

The sorry state of the Darby Diner didn't escape the notice of Otis Oppenheimer, who sat in a corner booth eating fried cheese sticks and sipping ginger ale. It was late morning, after the breakfast rush, and aside from the staff and handful of counter-side patrons, the establishment was empty. Oppenheimer was unaware of the illegal activities Jackson was perpetrating in his grandfather's diner on a daily basis. Had Otis known, he might have intervened. The distraction would have provided a few minutes of stimulation in what was fast becoming a mostly unwelcome assignment.

Flo Beasley, a slender fifty-ish waitress with poorly dyed jet-black hair approached Oppenheimer.

"Refill your drink?"

"Sure. Thanks."

"Refills cost a buck twenty-five."

"It's okay."

She returned a moment later from the drink station with a fresh soda.

"Not from around here are you?" she asked.

"No."

"I could tell. People around here don't typically dress like you. I mean, black suit, black tie. You work for a limo service?"

"Something like that," Otis said, wishing his work offered as much diversity as a chauffer's.

"I'm Flo."

"Otis."

Outside, Billings Smith frowned as he parked his Lexus and walked across the parking lot of the Darby Diner. His eyes were drawn to the loading area at the rear of the building. He walked into the diner and spotted Oppenheimer in the distance, still chatting with his waitress.

"Jesus Christ," Billings said under his breath.

He approached the booth, sat down, and listened as Flo Beasley described her sad transition from a 1960s B-movie actress in Hollywood to a St. Louis waitress.

"And so I said to myself, 'Flo, you've got to facilitate this and do what's best for you.'"

"I hate to interrupt this fascinating tale full of romanticized self-awareness, but do you think maybe, just perhaps, I can possibly get a fucking cup of coffee? Do you think you could maybe facilitate that, Flo?"

Flo Beasley recoiled as if she'd been slapped, and turned on her heel toward the drink station.

"That wasn't necessary. Or nice," Oppenheimer said.

"You know what's not nice? The fucking Darby Diner in fucking St. Louis. Why do you always choose the most deplorable places for our little tête-à-têtes?"

"It's St. Louis. The gateway to the west."

"This diner is the gateway to intestinal discomfort and nothing more. I've half a mind to bust whatever illegal operations are going on in the back of this shit hole."

"What illegal activities?"

"You're not very observant, are you Otis?"

"A bit. For example, I'm observing that you're dressed rather causal. Since when are jeans and t-shirts standard agency issue?"

"You must'a missed the memo."

Flo returned and slid a cup of coffee into the middle of the table without looking at either man.

"Keep it coming. And bring me a BLT on rye toast. No mayo."

"You seem more bitter than usual," Otis said. "I didn't think it was possible."

"Let's just say I'd rather be in Seattle. Or LA. Or New York. Or Columbus-fucking-Ohio for that matter. You sure this place is clean?" Billings lifted his cup and took a deep swallow.

"It's clean."

"The coffee sucks." Billings said. "I hate this fucking job. I used to think it was an assignment, but it's not. It's a job, and I hate it."

"It is what it is."

"Yeah, thanks Captain Cool. I dunno about you, but when I enlisted with the agency I didn't expect that I'd be on a five-year search mission. I didn't know that I'd be spending my days rummaging through glassware at every decrepit Salvation Army thrift shop in the goddamn world or running to every fucking piddley garage sale in the northeast."

"Life is a scavenger hunt. And we're the scavengers," Otis said.

"That isn't quite what I expected life to be. Have you been inside a Salvation Army? Do you know what they smell like? Old people, death, mold."

"Look, it's exhausting. I admit it," Otis said. "Still, could always be worse."

"Don't try to spin it. This assignment could not be worse. We're five years in. Reagan's out of office but his pet project continues unabated. I don't understand it. I've been denied reassignment twice; Tudor advised me not to request future transfers. Fucking glass onion stupid shit fuck nonsense. We've got a better chance of finding the goddam Ark of the Covenant."

"I know. I know. But when we find it—"

"*If* we find it, which, from where I'm sitting doesn't appear too likely."

"We'll find it. Twelve of us, one planet."

"We haven't found it in five fucking years."

"I guess we'll have to keep searching. Look, there's no way out of this, Billings. You don't just quit the agency. Is that what you're thinking of doing?"

"I hate this bullshit assignment, Otis. It's so fucking… suburban. Fucking desk job with local law enforcement would be more engaging. I mean, I'm no elitist, but this…this mission is an embarrassment to the agency."

"It is what it is, Billings. Nothing either of us can do but suck it up. Do you remember what Chambers said about it? About the onion I mean. He called it an *object of unimaginable power.*"

"Yeah. He also described the odds of our task succeeding as insurmountable. And you know why? Because it's a fucking fairy tale story Otis. There's no fucking onion. There's just this goddamn scavenger hunt dropped on our laps by an old man with Alzheimer's, for fuck's sake."

"Never mind that. I know his mind's not great now, but it was then. No, Billings, no. It's out there…somewhere. And whoever among us finds it is guaranteed one thing."

"What's that?"

"A ticket. A ticket to the world."

5   March 28, 1997: Arnold Dallas Henderson

It is well known that 6900 Georgia Avenue NW houses The Walter-Reed Army Medical Center, a 113-acre facility that serves more than 150,000 members of the various branches within the US military. With more than 5,000 patient rooms and a history dating back to 1909, Walter-Reed's medical care facility is among the most widely recognized medical centers on the east coast.

The dying man in room 2317 was named Arnold Dallas Henderson; those who knew him referred to him as Arnie. His chest, aided by a high-frequency ventilator, reluctantly rose and fell. To his left stood Denton Chambers. Chambers' six-foot-six frame cast a massive grim reaper's shadow across Henderson's bed. Visibly restless, Chambers unconsciously adjusted his eyeglasses mercilessly. Next to Chambers stood the considerably shorter Brad Calloway. Seated and casually turning the pages of a weathered issue of *Vanity Fair* was Emma Johanson. Emma's crimson dress, which matched her shoulder-length hair and complemented her starkly pale skin, was a defiant splash of life in a room largely comprised of neutral colors, cold electronics, and agency-black attire.

"Shouldn't we get started?" Calloway asked.

"We wait until Otis arrives," Chambers insisted.

"I don't think this guy has long to live. And lord only knows what's keeping Oppenheimer."

"Otis will be here momentarily; he's just paying the cab," Emma said. "He was hung up on the runway at Dulles."

"How do you know he…Oh. Oh, right," Calloway said, and quickly fell silent.

A moment later the door to room 2317 opened to admit Otis Oppenheimer. Otis placed his briefcase on the floor and joined his colleagues.

"Sorry I'm late. The flight from Miami was on time, but we were hung up on the runway at Dulles."

"So I've heard," Calloway said.

"I'll bring you up to speed," Chambers said. "You already know agent Calloway. Seated is agent Johanson. She's on loan from the Psychic Division."

"Emma Johanson, yes?" Oppenheimer asked.

"That's correct," Johanson answered.

"I remember reading a spotlight on you in the agency newsletter. Some of your, uh, predictions have been way off."

"It isn't an exact science, Otis," Emma said, flatly. In her profession, skepticism was expected.

"I meant no disrespect."

"The bed-bound patient," Chambers said, finishing the introductions, "is Arnie Dallas Henderson."

"*The* Arnie Dallas Henderson?" Otis asked.

"You know him?" Denton said.

"I was being sarcastic."

"Looks dead," Otis said. "Agency man?"

"Private citizen. Real estate salesman. Not quite dead, but he's certainly dying. Calloway, why don't you take over from here."

"Sure, why not?" Brad Calloway said. He was a small man who appeared even smaller in the towering presence of Chambers. He pushed a hand through a once-full head of brown hair and cleared his throat.

"One week ago, operative Billings Smith was in North Dakota; Devil's Lake. You all know Billings' reputation. Good man; a real agent's agent. On March 22, central received what appeared to be a rather promising albeit brief message from Billings. He claimed to have found the glass onion that we've all been seeking these past 11 years. I was nearest in proximity to Billings and was flown in.

"When I arrived at 221 Windward Way there was no sign of Billings or the glass onion. There was, however, an open wall safe in the master bedroom and a small, empty jewelry box on the floor. Adjacent to the jewelry box was Arnie Dallas Henderson, unconscious and bleeding like a stuck pig. I radioed for air transport and Henderson was transferred here. Doctor's pulled two slugs out of his chest."

"So where's Billings?" Otis asked.

"Well, that's the $500,000 question, isn't it? I searched the area surrounding the house. No Billings. No sign of his vehicle. There's a lake about 100 yards north of the property. A recovery crew is scheduled to drag it tomorrow morning."

"So we basically have nothing," Otis said.

"Not nothing, because our resident psychic, Ms. Johanson, is here, and she's going to help us fill in the blanks."

Emma Johanson tossed the magazine to the floor and stood up. Calloway frowned; she was considerably taller than he'd calculated.

"Do you need the lights down or some candles?" Chambers asked.

"Don't be facetious," Emma answered. "Just…just give me a bit of space. And don't expect any kind of crazy X-Files-speaking-in-tongues shit; it doesn't work that way."

"Oh," Chambers said, looking disappointed.

Emma Johanson pushed aside the cotton blanket atop Henderson's chest. She pressed her right hand firmly against his heart and just above the surgical dressing that covered several dozen stitches. She extended the fingers of her left hand and placed her index and ring fingers on Arnie's temple. The silence was awkward. The three men looked at Emma and then looked at one another. Brad checked his watch several times. Chambers continued to fidget with his eyeglasses. Otis studied the curvature of Emma's body.

After several uneasy minutes, Emma's eyes began to flutter. Her head started to bob wildly.

"Emma," Denton Chambers said, "are you okay?"

A low hissing sound, like the air escaping a punctured tire, crept from Johansson's mouth. Seconds later Emma's body was thrust backward in an involuntary spasm that sent her crashing into the heart monitor before she landed flat out on the floor.

"Jesus Christ!" Brad said. "That was seriously fucked up!"

"Are you alright?" Otis asked.

"That…wasn't typical," Emma said, and struggled to her feet. "It was, nonetheless, productive."

"Tell us," Denton said.

"Billings is dead; I don't think that's coming as a surprise to anyone."

"How?" Brad asked.

"Billings was following a lead. It brought him to 221 Windward Way in Devil's Lake, the property that Mr. Henderson here was selling. Billings posed as a prospective buyer and met Henderson at the house. During the tour of the house, Billings and Henderson split up. It was during this time that Billings discovered the wall safe, which he soon opened. When Henderson discovered Billings with his hands in the safe, Billings took the steps necessary to contain the situation."

"He shot Henderson," Otis said.

"He tried, but his gun misfired. He resorted to fists, but in the ensuing fight took a nasty tumble down a flight of stairs and broke his neck. Henderson panicked. Brad's divers will indeed find Billings and his vehicle at the bottom of the lake by the house. After disposing of the body, Henderson returned to the property and cleaned up the mess. At this point his curiosity got the better of him. He looked in the safe and discovered the glass onion inside a jewelry box. And, he made the mistake of removing our highly coveted onion from its protective wrapper. As soon as Mr. Henderson's skin made contact his mind was flooded. Lost in the onion's visions, he never heard her coming."

"Wait a minute. Never heard *who* coming?" Brad asked.

"His assassin, of course."

"Who was she?"

"I don't...I don't know. But Reilly does."

"Reilly? Key Reilly?" Denton asked.

"Yes."

"Key Reilly is a neurotic drunk."

"You wanted answers. You got answers," Emma said. "If you'll excuse me, I need to rest before I collapse."

"Wait a second," Brad said. "This guy, Henderson, he held the onion?"

"Yes."

"What did he see? What did it show him?"

"Even if I told you, you wouldn't understand," Emma said, and left the room.

The three men stared first at one another then turned their gaze to Henderson. The dying man was still unconscious. He was also smiling.

"How does she know what I would and wouldn't understand? Fucking psychics. Am I right?" Brad turned to the men. "Jesus, so what now?"

"We talk with Reilly?"

"What about him? What about Henderson?"

Chambers placed a hand on the ventilator and switched the power buttons to the off position. The LED numbers that glowed bright red slowly faded to black along with the green power-on light. "Now you can check that box Brad. How does she know? Even I know Boy, and I'm not psychic."

Arnie Dallas Henderson, real estate agent, never sold the property at Windward Way. The remote lot had been given to him as a challenge by his manager at Oxford-Quinn Real Estate. It was a challenge his industry colleagues preferred not to have. They knew, not unlike Arnie, that the place was Oxford-Quinn's cross to bear, and that none of the team's star performers would ever be tasked with the estate. He'd been given the property as a result of a year-long shoddy sales record.

But Arnie was okay with that. He never expected to excel at real estate. He'd lived most of his 52 years with scant financial ambition and little understanding of the real world. He never married, never knew the love of another in the flesh. Arnie, however, lived quite happily in the pages of books. "Avid reader" was not a strong enough description for Arnie. The printed word was his alcohol, and he was a blissful drunk. He loved reading regardless of genre, regardless of subject matter, regardless of author, as long as it was fiction. Arnie kept the local library in business, and was there with his savings when any bookstore had to close its doors. He always felt that as long as he had a book by his side, he was never truly alone. But sometimes, between books, he'd wonder. Sometimes, while driving, or walking, or taking a shower, he'd wonder. Sometimes, when his eyes folded down the last time at night, he'd wonder.

Arnie never expected to succeed at real estate, and was quite terrified to find himself standing in the old place looking down at a dead body. He didn't know who would believe him. He knew nothing of the stranger, aside from his name. He had no idea why Billings Smith had attacked him. Arnie felt as if one of his more lurid reads had suddenly come to life around him, and he was desperate to think who would defend him, who would vouch for his character. His parents were gone; he hadn't spoken to his sister in Sarasota in years; he had no friends; his landlord was no more than a P.O. box. He found himself wondering if they had libraries in prison; if the other men would let him read or if they'd hurt him. He ran to the back door, and remembered the pond. The pond. Arnie's mind raced toward a dark corner as he formulated a plan. Billings Smith, his felled attacker, had never been to the real estate office; he'd only phoned in to request a viewing. Arnie ran to the body, grabbed the dead ankles, already cold, and pulled . He averted his eyes and heaved Smith's body into the water. The pond swallowed up the body like a hungry child. It was happening so quickly, and so easily, like a chapter in a dime-store detective novel.

His mind raced and he dashed back to the house, smashed a window, and recalled the wall safe. The wall safe that neither he nor his colleagues at Oxford-Quinn knew existed. He ran the stairs 2 at a time, body pumping with adrenaline. Arnie never felt so alive. He thrust his arm into the opening in the wall, and retrieved a large wooden jewelry box. Within the box was a velvet bag. And within the bag…He tugged at the chords of the bag and the palm-sized orb slid out and onto his bare fingers. And Arnie sank to the floor, his eyes slid sideways, and he smiled. He slid into a comfortable faraway place, oblivious to the stranger who silently crept up behind him.

Arnie died on March 28, not surrounded by friends, but by strangers in a military medical hospital thousands of miles from his home. Arnie died with one click of a little switch on a machine. Nonetheless, Arnie died happy. The onion, the strange little glass talisman that continued to elude an entire squad of agents charged with its finding, had found Arnie and had given Arnie the great gift of showing him that his life, however imperfect, had in fact been rather nice.

6   March 29, 1997: A Visit With Reilly

There was a moment when it appeared that the game would be concluded without incident. Maximillion Stoddard was losing and losing badly. Most of his game pieces were gone and downfall seemed all but certain. The black and red checkerboard was being dominated by his much-younger opponent. It was unprecedented, and Maximillion Stoddard was dumbfounded.

"Crown me," Key Reilly commanded, as he moved a playing piece forward. It was the sixth time he'd made the demand in as many minutes.

With defeat on the horizon, Max opted for an unorthodox gaming approach to achieve a stalemate and, thus, maintain his undefeated status within the home. In an instant he shoved the game board off the table. The game pieces scattered across the floor in all directions. Max then tipped over the card table. He sprung at Key Reilly and uttered a primal, savage cry. Reilly was knocked to the floor and Max began choking him. An orderly raced toward the men while others in the room stared with rapt fascination.

The snap of breaking bone and cartilage was followed by a scream. Maximillion released Reilly from his grasp and staggered backward.

"My face! You broke my fucking face!" he screamed, before blacking out.

Reilly stood up slowly and stared at Maximillion's broken nose. The blood was intense, as always with a nose wound, but there was minimal damage. Reilly was a shadow of his former self, but some skills were more easily retained than others. He still knew how to drop a man when necessary.

"I need you to move toward the corner and have a seat, Key," the orderly said and phoned for a medic.

Moments later, Brad and Otis arrived. Key stared at the men with little more than vague recollection.

"Reilly. You're looking well," Brad said kindly, as they walked toward Reilly's room and shut the door.

Unshaven, and dressed in green sweat pants and a t-shirt, Key Reilly sat on the edge of his twin mattress looking a decade beyond his 36 years. He had difficulty maintaining eye contact, but, still somehow, he remained as handsome as he had been as a young recruit.

Otis Oppenheimer stared at the four walls that defined Reilly's universe. White walls. Drop ceiling. Wall-mounted television. Industrial gray vinyl flooring. An 8 x 10 laminated poster with large type that read "Montgomery Rehabilitation and Correctional Center: Client Rules of Conduct."

Reilly had been the first to crack. The isolation, long hours, and monotony of the glass onion assignment left him feeling alienated. He turned first to the comfort of prostitutes and alcohol. Stronger stimulants followed. Recreational drug use became full-blown abuse. Twice he overdosed and twice he was brought back from the abyss. When his third overdose occurred in January 1993, Key's body eventually recovered. His mind, however, was less fortunate. The neurologic damage was irreversible. A few months later, agent Reilly traded his badge and revolver for a pair of fuzzy slippers and three squares per day.

"He doesn't remember us," Brad said.

"I know you," Reilly said, struggling to recognize his former colleagues.

"Of course you do. I'm Otis, this is Brad."

"Yes. Yes, of course."

"Reilly," Otis said. "We need your help. Do you think you might be able to help us?"

"Why would I want to do something like that? I don't even know you."

"Yes you do. You know us." Reilly looked at Otis, searching for recognition. "Key, before you…before you left the agency, were you dating anyone?" Otis asked.

"I…you know, I really enjoy it here. Sometimes I imagine that I'm outside, just outside, walking barefoot on the grass. Do you ever do that? Walk barefoot, I mean."

"No. Not often," Otis said. "Not often enough. Key, we need to know this."

"I'd like it so much, but I won't be going outside for a while. Not after today and even though I was acting in self-defense. You don't cheat at checkers—you just don't. Still, I can walk barefoot in my room; pretend I'm outside."

"For Christ's sake," Brad said, "we just need to know who you were fucking back in '92 or so. You think maybe you have any recollection of that."

Key's eyes focused. "You shouldn't speak to me like that Brad, you little pisser. I can break you in eight places in without trying."

"Yeah? Good, please try," Brad said, and pressed the barrel of his revolver against Reilly's forehead. Reilly's pupils went to outer space once again.

"You're not helping," Otis said.

He placed a hand on Brad's weapon and moved it away from Reilly. Reilly fell back onto his mattress and began softly singing over and over, "When the boys came out to play, Georgie Porgie ran away."

"Fuck," Brad said, and holstered his gun. It angered him to see his former colleague in such a pathetic condition. More, it frightened him. Too often he'd thought about crawling inside a bottle and not coming out. Seeing Reilly in his damaged mental state curbed that temptation, but it didn't change the reality of his assignment. He leaned in close to Reilly and spoke with restraint.

"We need the names of any women you knew when you were active with the agency. Anything you can recall will greatly help."

"I don't know," Reilly sobbed. "I don't remember. I don't remember anything."

Brad was tight lipped as he leaned in even closer to Reilly's ear. "Think about it for a moment. It's extremely important."

"I just don't know!"

Reilly curled into a fetal position and began Georgie Porgie again..

"Well?" Brad asked.

"We should have brought Emma."

"Maybe this will help," Brad said, removing a small paper bag from his inside jacket pocket. "Hey Reilly, I brought along an old friend of yours."

"Don't," Otis said.

"You have any better ideas?"

Brad tossed the bag onto the bed. Reilly studied the wrinkled brown paper. He knew it well. With trembling hands he grasped the bag and slowly peered inside.

"We shouldn't be doing this," Otis said.

"Relax. It's just a little something to help jumpstart the memory, isn't that right Reilly?"

"I haven't…I haven't had a drink in five years, twenty-seven days, 17 hours, 57 minutes."

"Then you're long overdue, my friend."

Reilly twisted open the cap. The smell of Tennessee whiskey crept into the air like honeysuckle on a warm spring night. Without a word he pressed the bottle against his lips. His head sprung back like a jack-in-the-box. The bottle was small, but it was large enough to do the job. He switched on the TV and randomly surfed. The alcohol burned his throat and made his eyes tear. Before long he was sounding like his old self, the Agency Reilly everyone liked.

"There were….a lot of women. I can't say that any of them were more than one-night stands. The ladies always liked me. Still do, even now the nurse occasionally slip me someone else's meds. It's not so bad here, really."

He started to fade.

"Key," Otis said, " We need to know. Anyone you might have talked shop with?"

"Of course not."

Key blinked. He was aware that his lucidity was improving. This was better than the neuroblockers he'd pilfered from the staff nurse.

"Listen, you didn't by any chance slip a little something extra into that bottle?"

"Concentrate for a minute," Otis said. "You spent a considerable amount of time in the northeast. Connecticut. Maine. Vermont. And in the southwest. I understand the isolation and loneliness, better than you can imagine. Christ knows the agency's help line is anything but helpful. Was there someone you might have confided in? Hotel clerk. Waitress. Letter carrier. Barkeep."

"I don't know. What does it even matter?"

"Billings is dead. Murdered. We think he found the onion."

"You have it?"

"No. But we think that someone you know—someone you knew—might."

"Christ."

Key hung his head. Even in this lucid state the past was little more than faded chalk on the blackboard of his mind. He stared at the infomercial airing on the television. A nurse and doctor eagerly advocated the latest miracle weight-loss pill. The engines of recollection began to slowly turn in Key's head.

"There was one woman. A nurse. I've always liked nurses you know. My mother was a nurse."

"Were you close?" Otis asked.

"Close?"

"Were you close?" Brad repeated, his patience nearing exhaustion. "Did you spend time together? Were you fucking her? Did you share a bedroom and, by association, bedroom secrets?"

"She'd visit me after her shift, usually late at night."

"Where was this?"

"Vermont. I think it was Vermont."

"You see, Otis, we don't need Emma at all. We're looking for a nurse who once resided in Vermont."

Otis Oppenheimer nodded.

"This is good, Key. Now think. Think and think and think and see if you can recall a name."

Night was approaching as Brad and Otis left the parking lot of the Montgomery Rehabilitation and Correctional Center. A light rain fell. The interior of the car was silent but for the hum of intermittent windshield wipers. Otis cracked the passenger window and lit up.

"Jesus Christ," he said, and dragged deep. "You think we'll ever end up like Reilly?"

"I fucking hope not," Brad said.

He grabbed the open pack of Camels from the dash.

"Do you mind?"

"Help yourself."

"I don't know how he can live like that," Brad said. "And that fucking smell—ammonia, urine, and cafeteria food. It's disgusting."

"It's not a life, that's for sure. Though I don't suppose he's altogether cognizant most days."

"Dark already. Won't be back to DC until well past midnight."

"That's optimistic."

"Fucking Reilly. If he'd kept his goddam mouth shut we'd have the onion right now. You realize that, right? I mean, Billings would still be sucking on pond water. No changing that. I'd have gone to Devil's Lake. I'd have found Arnie Dallas Fucking Henderson with the glass onion. I'd have had it in my possession at this very moment. We could all get back to having lives again."

"At least he remembered the woman's name."

"Yeah, well, it'll be a miracle if the lead is legit," Brad said, and pulled onto the rain-soaked interstate.

"Why wouldn't it be legit?"

"Oh, I dunno. Maybe because Key Reilly is a crazy motherfucker."

"Myrtle London. Sounds legit."

"Yeah. Yeah, it does. Though if it's not, I may need to pay Key another visit."

"To try again?"

"No. To put him out of everyone's fucking misery."

7   March 31, 1997: Run Myrtle Run

The sidewalk of the Vegas strip was littered with colorful business cards and flyers, each belonging to pretty girls who survived by selling sex. Each evening, thousands of cards were handed to passersby young and old. Most of these ads ended up discarded on the sidewalk. When the sun rose at dawn the streets looked as if they had played host to an X-rated ticker-tape parade all night long. Each morning, men with long-handled brooms swept up the mess and tossed the cards into the garbage. It was a cycle that repeated daily, 365 days per year, and fueled a multi-million dollar industry.

Initially shocked by the crude adverts, Myrtle London became quickly desensitized to their presence. She even stopped wondering whether pornography would be the only print media to survive. She found it far more difficult to tolerate the smell of old tobacco that reeked in each of the city's glimmering, tacky structures. No matter which building she entered, the stale undercurrent of nicotine was present. Her hotel room was on the fourteenth floor of The Mirage. A nonsmoking floor. Yet the smell was there also. It crept in during the late evening, and each morning as Myrtle awoke she gagged in the bathroom sink for several minutes. Three days into her stay Myrtle was convinced that Las Vegas was determined to kill her.

Nothing, she discovered, ever goes as planned.

After fleeing Devil's Lake, Myrtle had stopped for the night in nearby Bismarck, North Dakota, where she checked into a twenty-dollar-per-night EZ Stay motel. Myrtle's exhaustion was all consuming, fueled by the reality of her actions and the small, glass object that she held onto tightly even while asleep. The following morning, fully rested, Myrtle London had driven 23 hours straight from Bismarck to Las Vegas, stopping only to refuel her car; her body could wait. Despite the distance,1,500 miles, Myrtle completed the trip (the majority on Interstate 15) with ease. She felt safer being far away from North Dakota and the house at Devil's Lake. Far away from the crime she'd committed.

An ambulance raced by as she walked along Frank Sinatra Drive. Myrtle paused. She thought about the life she had before. Before. She wondered if she'd ever see her family, Greater Eastern Memorial, or Burlington, Vermont ever again. The walk back to The Mirage was long and the desert winds blew hot. Three days in Vegas though it felt like thirty. Myrtle longed for a relaxing bath that would soothe her aching body and give her a moment to weigh her options.

The elevator ride to fourteen was crowded with tourists aspiring to leave Vegas with casino gold. Myrtle pressed a hand against the back of her neck. Vegas was too hot and her hair too long. She would cut it. Myrtle recognized this as a good idea for several reasons, particularly if they were searching for a brunette with shoulder-length hair. And they were surely searching for her.

She closed the door and dropped the AC to 61 before running a bath. The room phone rang as she disrobed.

"Hello."

"Myrtle London," a man's voice said calmly, phrasing the words as a statement, not a question.

"No, sorry."

"Listen closely. We aren't going to dance around the facts, Myrtle. You know who you are. I know who you are. Now do we cut out the bullshit or do Mr. 357 Magnum and I head over to Turtle Drive and pay a visit to your granny at the Glydewell Senior Center? The choice is yours. Today being Thursday, I believe we'd find her at the Bingo table."

"Who is this?"

"My name is Otis. Otis Oppenheimer. I'm an associate of Key Reilly. You remember Key, I'm sure. Tall, thin, drank a lot, talked too much. What sort of secrets did Key share with you, Myrtle?"

"None. No secrets."

"I disagree. I think Key talked with you about some very special things. Secret things that were clearly not meant for your or anyone else's ears. Did he tell you about the GO Project? I'm almost certain that he did."

"Where are you?" she asked.

"Me? I'm in Washington, DC. Or maybe I'm on a westbound jet. Quite possibly I'm standing in a phone booth across the street from your granny's social club. Though perhaps I'm at the concierge desk in the lobby of The Mirage. You know The Mirage, right

Myrtle?"

Myrtle stuck the receiver between her shoulder and her ear, picked up the phone and with her free hand she began packing her shoulder bag frantically as she circled the room. Random objects. The big suitcase would look too conspicuous even among Las Vegas' sea of inhumanity. Myrtle had driven to the gambler's city to pawn the glass onion. She initially thought about contacting Reilly, but Reilly was useless. She'd seen his once-sharp mind reduced to rubble through his own vices. Besides, if the U.S. government knew of the onion, then doubtless, so did other political entities. The challenge lay in finding them.

But there was a greater problem. Myrtle was forming an attachment to the glass onion. Like Tolkien's ring was to Frodo, the artifact seemed drawn to Myrtle and she to it. It seemed to instill in Myrtle a confidence she'd lacked since an ankle injury in 1982 shattered her Olympics aspirations. Myrtle kept the glass onion close to her always. During sleep, she held the onion like a child holds a security blanket.

"I know what you're thinking," Otis said. "You're thinking that you're simply one in ten million people. You're thinking you can blend in. Hide in plain sight. Not so. And more importantly, no need. I'm authorized to negotiate a purchase price."

"You want to buy it?"

"That's why you're here, isn't it? Myrtle, you must realize the considerable financial resources that have already been invested in this project, to say nothing of the toll it's taken on those of us involved in the onion's pursuit. In many ways you've done us a service; it's only fair you be compensated for it."

"Provided I give you the onion."

"That's typically how a standard business transaction works. One party compensates the other for goods or services provided."

Myrtle paused. It seemed a reasonable exchange. And she knew from her time with Reilly that those assigned to it absolutely loathed the GO project and its seemingly impossible objective. It seemed logical to believe that she would receive restitution for her efforts. And yet, she couldn't help but recall the stories Key had shared during his spirited moments. Men like Key Reilly and Otis Oppenheimer killed without hesitation, and double-cross was as much a part of the business as the façade of the respectable suit and tie. She felt like a plastic game piece poised on the middle of a board game. There little option but to move one space ahead. Myrtle inhaled the stale hotel room air deeply and slowly began to exhale.

"Okay," she said. "Let's talk terms."

Myrtle and Otis agreed to meet at the very public, very crowded Viva Las Vegas Diner on the south side of The Strip. Otis arrived at 6:00 p.m., a full two hours early. He handed the waitress a hundred-dollar bill.

"Keep the coffee coming and take it easy on the chit-chat," he said.

By 9:00 p.m., Otis was shaking from the caffeine and Myrtle London was nowhere to be seen. Brad Calloway, seated outside the diner in a jet-blue Subaru chain smoked while skeptically watching for Myrtle.

"Can you say 'no show'?" he asked Otis through the wireless transmitter.

"Yeah, looks that way, doesn't it?" Otis said. He finished another cup, headed outside, and stepped into the car.

"Finally decided to break down and buy a pack, eh?"

"It's not so much the cancer that attracts me; it's the flavor I love. Christ. The ball has been dropped and dropped hard."

"I believe the words 'fucked royally' are apropos in this particular situation, as in we are fucked royally," Brad said.

"It's my own fault. I overestimated Ms. London's sincerity."

"Try explaining that to Chambers."

"The situation is still under control. Her assets are frozen. Every piece of plastic she owns has been red-flagged. Myrtle will surface again soon, and when she does, we'll be there."

His confidence notwithstanding, Otis realized he'd made a rookie error. He was experienced enough to know better. They visited Myrtle's hotel room, but house cleaning had already done its worst. Otis spent the rest of the evening in a hotel room at the Golden Nugget reviewing Myrtle's phone records and banking history dating back five years. Brad, meanwhile, did his best to break even at the blackjack table but, like so many, lost it all. He returned to the hotel room shortly after 2:00 a.m., drunk from bottom-shelf complimentary scotch and soda. Otis was still buried in work.

"I just dropped fifteen-grand to a stunningly gorgeous dealer named Alexis. The bad news is, she refused to sleep with me. The good news is, it all goes on the expense report."

"God bless the USA. Are you interested in more good news?"

"Possibly."

"It looks like we're headed west," Otis said.

"West is okay. I can do west, as long as we're talking San Diego or San Fran and not LA. Are we talking San Diego or San Fran?"

"We're talking LA."

"Goddammit."

"What's the matter with LA?" Otis asked.

"Another time," Brad said. "Got to lie down now before I fall down."

He staggered onto the bed, kicked off his shoes, and collapsed.

"Fucking Los Angeles," Brad mumbled, and fell asleep almost instantly.

Two-hundred-sixty miles southwest, Myrtle London arrived at 509 California Avenue in Santa Monica and rang the front bell. Dorey Hill awoke from a sound sleep, swayed down the stairwell and across the living room floor before peering through a side window. She recognized her friend and unlocked the door.

Myrtle collapsed into Dorey's arms and began to cry.

8   January 1992: Tip-Top Secret

In a small stifling bedroom in a small ramshackle apartment in the middle of a quiet street of a middle-to-lower class neighborhood they rested naked on the bed. They rested atop exceptionally soft 500-thread count cotton sheets woven in Malaysia. Soft like pink cotton candy. Soft like childhood nursery rhymes told just before bed. Soft like dry February snow in the Pennsylvania mountains. Outside the thermometer swelled past one hundred and five while the radio deejay announced that the heat wave would likely continue into the weekend.

"Phoenix in the summer. What the hell am I doing in Phoenix in the middle of summer?" Myrtle London said, wiping the back of her right hand against her forehead.

"Getting drunk off your ass," Key Reilly replied.

"No, that would be you."

"I'm not drunk."

"Hell if you aren't."

"Hell if I am. You don't get drunk on Milwaukee's Best, which is, if I might add, the biggest fucking oxymoron since the original ad campaign for Lite Beer from Miller. It all tastes like warm piss."

"You need to refrigerate it..."

"Yeah. At least then it'll taste like cold piss."

"...or switch to a beverage more befitting a man of your refined quality."

Key chugged what little fluid remained before tossing the can onto the pile already amassed on the floor. He toppled out of bed clumsily, stepped onto the empty aluminum cans and subsequently lost his balance. He landed clumsily on the hardwood floor, twisting his ankle.

"Fuck!"

"You're an absolute Flying Wallenda—I mean, except for the grace and coordination."

"Regular comedian today, aren't you?" he asked, rising slowly and favoring his right ankle. "Tell me, Myrtie, could it be any fucking hotter in here?"

"I told you the building doesn't have central AC and my window unit is on the fritz. And do not call me 'Myrtie.' How many times do I have to tell you that?"

"Right," Key said, and belched loudly. "Gonna grab me that bottle of Jim Beam in the kitchen cabinet, Myrtie."

"The one you finished last night?"

"Christ. You got anything else to drink around here?"

"There's a bottle of raspberry schnapps in the cabinet beneath the stove. Go nuts."

"Raspberry schnapps from a strawberry blonde. Lovely."

Forty-five minutes later Key swallowed the last of the schnapps. Myrtle, dressed in a tank-top and a pair of low-rise briefs, played with the remote control. She channel surfed mindlessly, stopping suddenly to stare with no small consideration at the screen and a duo of sports commentators.

"...as we look forward to watching these young hopefuls, who will compete in these upcoming Goodwill Games."

Myrtle's sad, lazy eyes widened with interest.

"Hey!" she yelled, as Reilly pulled the remote from her hand and switched off the set. His eyes were glazed, bloodshot, and his grin smug.

"Wanna—wanna do it again?" he asked.

She looked at him pathetically.

"I was watching that."

"C'mon. Bunch of gymnasts jumping around on vertical bars."

"Parallel bars."

"Whatever."

"It's exciting."

"Christ. I'd rather watch my own piss dry."

"That's because nothing interests you. You have nothing," Myrtle replied quietly.

"What did you say?" Key asked soberly.

"I said nothing interests you. No passion about anything."

"You have no idea how wrong you are, little flower."

"Right. Tell me."

Key paused a moment, waiting for the statement to filter its way to his inebriated mind. He staggered onto the bed and crossed his legs as if sitting next to a campfire.

"Alright," he said, and waved a cautionary finger at Myrtle. "But this is tip-top secret. A-1 Classified. That means, shhhhhh."

"Right."

"I'm fucking serious. Look at me, Myrtle," he said with profound sobriety. "I'm serious."

"You're drunk."

"Maybe. Maybe not. But this—what I tell you—stays in this room."

"Right."

"Seriously," he said, grasping her wrists a bit too tightly.

"Okay, Key!" Myrtle said, wrestling free of his grip. "Christ."

He stepped out of bed, careful to sidestep the empty beer cans and bottles. He dressed in a pair of boxers and walked toward a bureau atop which sat a combination-lock black briefcase.

"How well do we know each other?" he asked.

She hesitated before answering while Key unlocked the attaché.

"You and me? Not too well."

"Tell me about me," he said.

"Okay…um, sure. Age 33. You have a rugged, Sean Conneryesque face, circa *Thunderball*, that's often eclipsed by your alcoholic overindulgences. Long-distance blueprint courier. Born and raised in West Palm Beach. Two brothers and one sister. Your dad was shot to death in robbery attempt when you were nine. As a result you have a strong dislike of firearms. Your mother recently remarried; she lives in Atlantic City."

"Ocean City," Key said. "What else?"

"Excessive alcohol consumption—did I mention that already?"

"Yeah."

"Favorite soup is lobster bisque. Favorite band, The Smiths. That's it."

"That's it?"

"That's it."

"That's a lot. Don't you think it's a lot?"

"Maybe. I guess."

"It's a lot. It's also all a goddam lie."

"Uh-huh."

"It's all a lie, Myrtle. Everything you know about me is fodder for Mister Rogers Neighborhood. It's all make-believe."

"You've been lying to me? So what, you're married? Goddammit. Are you fucking married?"

"No. Nothing like that."

Key removed an object from the attaché and turned slowly to face Myrtle; he clutched the object in his right hand as the color vanished from her face.

"Do you know what this is?" he asked, pointing the gun in her direction.

Myrtle held her breath and made no reply.

"This is a Smith & Wesson N-Series 10 millimeter automatic firearm, specifically, the 610. The N-Frame series is nearly a century old, dating back to 1908 when the company introduced the New Century Hand Ejector revolver—which doesn't quite roll off the tongue, does it? "

"You're...you're a serial killer. Oh...oh God, please don't..."

"Don't be ridiculous," Key said.

"Who are you?"

"Don't interrupt; it's rude. The production run of the Smith & Wesson 610 was limited to 5,000 units, an amazingly small number given the popularity of handguns in the United States. The barrel length is five inches, though it was also manufactured with a 6.5-inch barrel; both feature adjustable sights and combat wood grips. The cylinder holds six rounds, and is typically loaded with full- or half-moon clips, which hold three and six rounds, respectively. Feel the weight."

Key casually tossed the weapon toward Myrtle, instinctively she tried to catch it, but fumbled with the weapon and it bounced atop the bed.

"Who...are you?" she asked, terrified.

"I'm Key. Key Reilly," he said, and walked toward her to the bed.

He dropped belly first onto the mattress, the firearm mere inches from either of them. His breath a toxic mix of schnapps, whiskey, beer, and cigarettes. Myrtle's gooseflesh betrayed any attempt to feign calm composure. She considered reaching for the gun, but the questions plaguing her mind rendered her body inert. What if Reilly was faster? What if it was precisely what he wanted her to do?

"Don't worry," he said, propping his head onto a pillow. "You're not in any danger, little flower."

"What are you? Police? FBI?"

"Do you like old movies?" he asked.

"Yeah. A few I guess."

"I thought you might, seeing as we're close in age. The younger generation couldn't care less about vintage cinema. They believe...they believe if it wasn't recorded in Technicolor with Dolby sound it's not worth viewing. Fucking ignorant misanthropes."

"I like old holiday movies," Myrtle said, anxious to keep Key on topic. "*Christmas in Connecticut. A Christmas Carol*—the one with Alistair Sim, not the Reginald Owen version. *The Bishop's Wife* with Carey Grant and, um—"

"David Niven."

"Right. Oh, and anything starring Bogart—*African Queen, Casablanca, To Have and To Have Not.*"

"*Maltese Falcon*, with Sydney-Fucking Greenstreet. My life...my life is the *Maltese Falcon*, Myrtle, I swear to God."

Key rolled onto his back and stared at the ceiling.

"You know, a skylight would be a welcome addition to this place."

"I'm not sure the tenants above us would want us looking up and into their apartment."

"To quote Bogie in *Treasure of the Sierra Madre*, 'Fuck 'em.'"

"He never said that."

"Maybe it was *Maltese Falcon*. Tell you, I used to love that goddam movie. Now it's my fucking life."

"You keep saying that, but I don't understand."

"Christ. I should not be...I should *not* be telling you this. But you know what? Fuck it. I'm sick to death with the horse shit cloak and dagger routine. But it stays here, in this room. Do you understand?"

"I understand."

"I'm fucking serious, Myrtle."

"Are you fucking serious, Key?"

They both glanced at the firearm on the bed.

"I'm fucking serious, Myrtle."

"I understand. It doesn't leave this room. You fucking psychopath."

Key smiled.

"Long time ago this stupid-looking naïve kid fresh out of junior business college joins the FBI. Although he's looking for a steady, high-paying job in the Bureau's accounting offices, he ultimately becomes an agent, learning every rule, regulation, and guideline in the Bureau's field manual. Later, he's transfers to the CIA where, along with eleven others, he's assigned to the GO project."

"What's the GO project?"

"Don't interrupt me. GO is a simple assignment: find a needle in a fucking haystack. No transfers to other assignments. No end to the assignment, not until the needle is found."

"But what's GO?"

"GO is dossier file name for the onion assignment; the glass onion. The needle we've spent the last five years of our lives trying to find. Fuck. I don't even like onions."

"That's your mission. Find a glass onion."

"Yes."

"And twelve of you have been searching for it."

"Yes."

"For five years."

"Yes."

"Why?"

"I don't know."

"You don't know?"

"No. I mean, it's allegedly a, 'source of unimaginable power, able to shape dreams into reality' or some such bullshit."

Myrtle's mind flashed back several minutes to the images of the many hopeful gymnasts who danced confidently across the television screen and recalled once having dreams.

"So, what, you travel around the country scouring the bric-a-brac sections of curio shops?"

"Something like that," Key said, yawning.

"Sign me up."

"It's a shit assignment, Myrtle. Trust me. Fucking thing probably doesn't exist."

"You've never even seen it?"

"There's one photo in an old book on myths and legends, kind of a grainy black and white. Fucking Loch Ness Monster's photo has more clarity and authenticity."

"Can't you be reassigned?"

"Were you listening? No reassignments. Ever."

"Are there, you know, other people—private citizens—or other governments searching for it?"

"Probably. Maybe. Fuck, I have no idea."

"Your own personal Dead Sea scroll. Lucky you."

"Lucky me," he said softly, and passed out.

Myrtle slowly picked up the handgun and stepped across the floor. She returned the weapon to a velvet-lined tray containing two additional firearms.

"Jesus," she whispered, and closed the attaché.

Later, with sleep on the horizon, Myrtle switched on the television and watched the remaining gymnastic preliminaries. She stared for a moment at the two diminutive scars on her right knee and wondered what her life might be like were she to possess an onion made from glass, an onion that could shape dreams into reality.

Key woke the following day just before noon. His head throbbed. The night before was little more than a distorted blur. Increasingly it was becoming like this. A night of binge drinking followed by memory lapse. Key considered it a small price to pay for a brief escape from consciousness.

He read Myrtle's brief note announcing that she'd be back soon with lunch. Key poured a cup of coffee from the pot. It was cold but he'd drunk worse. He then pulled the journal from his attaché and sat down to study his upcoming agenda.

Myrtle returned with two bags of food and a bag of hard liquor. She sat the groceries down atop the smoked-glass kitchen table and walked into the bedroom expecting to find Key asleep.

"What's going on?" she asked.

"It's time," Key said, zipping shut a nylon suitcase.

"Time for you to fly, REO Speedwagon?"

"Bingo."

"You're leaving?"

"Yup."

Myrtle frowned.

"I don't pick the hours, Myrtie, they pick me."

"So," she said, "Where to this time?"

"Long drive. Chicago and Kansas. Reichenbach contracted for a new high-rise project with designers in both cities. I'll be gone a few weeks. Try to have something worth drinking when I return. I left you a note on the bureau, along with an obscenely large roll of bills."

"I don't care about the money. You were…you were just going to leave without saying goodbye?"

During his five years as one of the agents assigned to the GO project, Key enjoyed a near-unlimited spending account courtesy of the tax-paying public, as well as the company of several women from the Atlantic to the Pacific coasts. He maintained a comfortable emotional distance from each of them, and when things got too personal, drugs and alcohol were available to assist with the detachment. Myrtle was simply one of the crew. Just another band groupie. The blueprint courier cover afforded Reilly a quick out—it provided a reason to be gone and usually he needed to be gone.

"It's not like I want this," Key said.

Though of course he wanted to leave. His freedom was tied to a talisman that he was charged with finding. The sooner it was retrieved, the sooner he'd have a life again. His female acquaintances were mere diversions to help facilitate his sanity. There were no conversations of substance with these women, for his life had no substance.

He realized that if there was one individual in whom he felt he could bridge a gap of trust, it was Myrtle. Upon deeper reflection he noted that their association was based mainly on alcohol and sex—was only as deep as the bottom of a gin bottle and as solid as the springs of a worn-down mattress. Yet Myrtle was also kind to him, and that of itself was a comfort he'd not felt before.

"At least stay for lunch," she said.

"I'm late already," Key said, trying not to notice exactly how good Myrtle looked standing before him in cut-off faded denim shorts and the white cotton tee-shirt two sizes too small. "It's business."

"Just stay a while," she said. "You can do that, can't you?"

Key looked hungrily at the curvature of her inner thigh, the definition of her calves and ankles. He needed to go. He needed to follow-up a lead—a bartender named Buss McGuire in a jerkwater town 475 miles north of Phoenix. Myrtle undid the top buttons of her shorts. Her delicate fingers pushed the fabric down below her waist, revealing a low-cut panty.

Key watched anxiously and weighed several factors. The McGuire lead would almost certainly produce no results; the leads never produced results. He knew where Buss McGuire lived and worked; Buss wasn't going anywhere, so whether Key rushed made little difference. Lastly he thought of his humanity. Despite how much of it he'd sacrificed, despite the killing, depression, and his growing addiction to narcotics, he was, in fact, still a man.

"Can't you stay?" Myrtle asked again, and rolled the fabric of her shirt above her naval in a slow, titillating fashion.

Key pulled Myrtle close. As his right hand slid beneath her tee-shirt and exposed the soft flesh of her shapely back, his lips pressed against her cheek. The familiar smell of her sweat was like wine, and he licked the nape of her neck softly, savoring the taste of her salty skin. Myrtle's slender fingers tugged at his belt and she undid the metal clasp while her tongue, snakelike, pressed against his. The familiar aroma of whiskey was still heavy upon his breath. Myrtle undid the top button of his trousers and slowly opened the zipper. He pulsated expectantly against her waist and Myrtle acquiesced by squeezing firmly through his boxers with her right hand. Abruptly, Key grabbed her wrists and raised Myrtle's arms above her head. He tugged at the fabric of her tee shirt, and when it failed to yield, he tore it open, exposing her soft breasts.

"Naughty girl. I forget that you sunbathe topless," he said, noting the lack of tan lines upon her sun-brown flesh.

"Not just topless," she replied, glancing seductively toward her waist.

They tumbled onto the bed, two lovers straining against maddening passions, not bothering to completely disrobe. For the first time in longer than he could recall, Key felt completely engrossed in the present. All thoughts of the onion, the agency, the leads, the killings, McGuire—all such thoughts were lost, however momentarily, replaced by a lust and rapture they both shared as a stifling hot Phoenix apartment became ever hotter.

Later that afternoon the apartment swelled to an uncomfortable 89 degrees. Myrtle stepped out of the shower and wrapped herself in a white and orange-striped beach towel. The water glistened on her lips. Key followed closely behind her. He toweled his back dry and stepped into fresh boxers. Myrtle fell onto the bed as her towel dropped to the floor.

"Still thinking of leaving?" she asked.

"No choice in the matter," Key said, and continued dressing. "Besides, it's too fucking hot in here."

"Surely not too hot," she replied, parting her legs.

Key moved toward her and leaned forward, kissing the toes of Myrtle's right foot.

"I have to go."

Myrtle frowned with disappointment.

"Following up on another hot tip?" she asked. She sat up and began dressing.

"What…what did you say?"

"Another tip. Another hot clue that's going to lead you toward that glass vegetable you longingly crave."

He moved with stunning quickness and the pain washed across her as Myrtle was pulled by her hair from the bed and tossed to the floor. Her head slammed against the wooden bureau. Key knelt beside her and asked the question a second time. He held her chin in his hand, and accentuated each word slowly.

"What…did…you…say?"

"Key, what the fuck? Let go of me!"

"Tell me what you know."

"What I know?"

"Yes, what you know. About the onion."

"I…I only know what you told me."

Key pulled Myrtle across the room by the hair and released her like so much dead weight. He placed the briefcase atop the bureau and Myrtle's eyes widened. She was already familiar with the attaché's contents.

"What did I say? What did I tell you?"

"You don't remember?"

"Let's pretend I don't."

"You told me…about the onion…your job."

Key slapped his palm against his forehead a half-dozen times, angered by his own carelessness.

"Fuck! Fuck! When? When did I tell you this?" he asked, removing the Smith & Wesson from its case.

"Last…last night. You were drunk. Don't you remember?"

"Of course I don't fucking remember!"

On the brink of hysteria Myrtle began crying. Key leaned down, close to her and stared into her frightened eyes.

"Listen to me. Listen to me! You were told things that were not intended for your ears. Important, secretive things. Do you understand?"

"Tip-top secret," she said, and nodded her head slowly, nervously, as the barrel of the handgun loomed ever closer.

"I need to know whether you discussed this information with anyone—with anyone at all."

Myrtle said nothing.

"Did you discuss it with anyone?" he asked again.

"No—no one."

"Are you quite fucking sure?"

"I swear to God," she replied with quiet, terrified conviction.

"That's good. I'm sorry about this, Myrtle. I genuinely am."

Key rose and stood above Myrtle London like an adult about to punish a child for bad behavior. He grabbed one of the whiskey bottles that Myrtle had purchased earlier and drank deeply. Myrtle glanced up, afraid and confused, with the horrifying realization that her life was over.

"It's just…if you should mention anything I said to you, even briefly—even as a fucking joke—it'd be the death of me. Others too."

"Christ, Key, don't—don't do this. I…I love you."

Key walked across the room and switched on the stereo. He adjusted the volume control to its highest setting. Caravan exploded from the quad speakers. He walked slowly toward Myrtle and extended his right arm. Myrtle stared at the barrel of the weapon through teary, bloodshot eyes.

"Shut your eyes," he said.

"No."

Key hesitated a moment, then continued.

"It'll be easier if you…if you just…put your head down and close your eyes."

"Easier for you."

"Just…please do as I ask."

Myrtle acquiesced, more out of fear than from a desire to ease Reilly's conscience.

He waited patiently. Waited until the music hit a crescendo. Until the drums and horns were at their loudest. At that instant Key fired two rounds from the 10 millimeter automatic firearm. He then placed the weapon in the attaché and shut it tight. He took the briefcase, the alcohol, a bottle of prescription pain killers, and a leather travel bag containing clothes and other belongings. He didn't bother to close the door behind him.

Myrtle lay on the floor, unmoving, naked, and fetal. Her ears were still ringing as she slowly regained consciousness and staggered to her feet. Key Reilly was gone and she was alive. He left behind two bullet-sized holes in the wall an inch above her head.

"Message received, Key," Myrtle said.

She crawled across the floor like an infant and switched off the music. Myrtle then managed to reach her bed, onto which she promptly sobbed hysterically as she collapsed.

9   April 1, 1997: Myrtle and Dorey

"I shouldn't be telling you this."

"Myrtle, we're best friends. We competed together in the Olympic trials. You can trust me."

"I know. It's just that, Christ, it's all such a mess. I've already said too much."

"What I don't understand is why you just didn't let it go. I mean, you were nearly—I can't believe I'm saying this—assassinated. Why did you decide to pursue this…thing? Why risk it?"

Dorey Hill and Myrtle London were seated at the breakfast table of Dorey's cozy Santa Monica home. Myrtle sipped coffee while Dorey, having just returned from a jog along the beach, sipped a bottle of filtered water with a lime twist. Outside, a heavy marine layer produced a thick fog that eclipsed the morning sun.

"Well, yeah, I wish I had an answer. The truth is I don't know. I mean, after Key attacked me, I fled Phoenix. I didn't want to take a chance that he'd have second thoughts and return to finish the job."

"You don't think he could have found you? I mean, given his profession."

"Of course, but I tried not to think of it. I decided to return to my roots—to nursing. But I'd burned too many bridges when I first followed Key west. Besides, I didn't exactly miss the east coast."

"You met this Key creep while you were at St. Francis?"

"Yeah, in the ER. He staggered in one evening. Immaculately dressed, exceptionally stylish, and bleeding from the gut. He said he'd been robbed. Lord only knows what really happened. We clicked. He's a persuasive man. It wasn't long before I followed him to Phoenix where, well basically, I dropped out. I didn't need to work. There was always plenty of cash. I should have asked. I should have asked how a blueprint courier had so much disposable income."

"I still don't understand," Dorey said. "I mean, you found this thing—this onion—that an entire team of federal agents has been seeking for years. It strikes me as more than, well, just coincidence."

Myrtle clutched the onion tightly with her left hand.

"I can't explain it either. After that whole incident with Key, I found work at an emergency care center in Briswold. Time passed and I forgot all about Key and his special assignment.

"Two weeks ago I woke in the early morning and felt this compulsion to drive north. When I arrived at the house at Devil's Lake I honestly had no recollection of driving there. I mean, we've all had moments where we've checked out behind the wheel for a moment or two, but this was ridiculous. I parked far away from the property. It was late. Sunset. Inside I heard two men arguing. I watched through one of the living room windows. They were fighting near the top of the stairwell. I'd never seen either of them before. There was a loud crash, as one of the men tumbled over the railing and onto a dining room table. He was dressed in the same jet black that Key used to wear, and for a moment I thought it was Key. Unfortunately it wasn't."

"Jesus."

"The guy who survived, well, his name was Arnie Henderson. Arnie Dallas Henderson. I noticed his photo on a couple of real estate billboards on the way to Devil's Lake. Smallish fellow; older. Not an attractive man. Anyway, he pulled an Anthony Perkins. Wrapped the body up, put it in the trunk of a car, and shoved it into Devil's Lake. He staggered back to the house and walked upstairs. I followed. Henderson reached into an open safe, and there was the glass onion, on the palm of his hand."

"And he just, what, handed it over to you?"

"No. Not exactly. I think I shot him."

"You think you shot him? You're not sure? What the fuck, Myrtle."

"I found the gun in the back of a closet in Phoenix; something Key left behind, I guess. Anyway, Henderson left me no choice. But he was alive when I left the house with the onion; I swear it."

"Did you phone 911?"

"No. I just...I just drove away."

"So was it worth it? Did you have a...a vision?"

"No. Not a goddam thing. And I…I…"

Myrtle began to shake as a deluge of tears rained down her cheeks.

"It's okay," Dorey said.

Dorey stepped toward her friend and forced a hug.

"I thought it would show me something or somehow make everything okay. But it's useless. It's just a stupid piece of glass. I thought maybe I could sell it in Vegas; sell it and get away. But they found me. I don't know how, but they found me, and it's only a matter of time before they find me and kill me."

"Did anyone follow you here?"

"No. I was hyper-paranoid about that. I wasn't followed."

"Okay. No one is going to find you. You'll be safe here, at least for a while."

"I don't want…I don't want to put you in any danger."

"I don't want you to put me in any danger either," Dorey said. "You look exhausted. Rest for a while and we'll think this through later."

Dorey escorted Myrtle to the guest room and pulled back the blankets from the bed. Myrtle stumbled onto the mattress and her head sank into the soft pillow. She quickly yielded to sleep, and the glass orb that she'd been clutching gently slipped from her fingers and rolled onto the bed. Dorey knelt down and stared at the strange object. She cautiously extended her fingertips toward it the way a child might test whether water from a spigot was too hot to touch. Finally, she grasped the glass sculpture with both hands, expecting nothing would happen. She was not at all surprised when nothing happened.

"There's no such thing as magic," Dorey said.

Still, she held onto the object for several minutes and found herself lost in thought about Myrtle and her perplexing story. It occurred to her that there was more to Myrtle's tale than she had been willing to reveal. Perhaps it was all fiction. Dorey was determined to learn the truth.

While Myrtle slept, Dorey drove to the Santa Monica Public Library. Minutes bled into hours as she searched for information to substantiate the onion's existence. Dorey knew and trusted Myrtle, but they were by no means close. She also knew that if there was truth in Myrtle's tale, she was, technically, a fugitive. So she searched. Books. Web sites. Reference materials. The search yielded no results that weren't related to John Lennon and The Beatles. Lastly, she ran a web search of Arnie Dallas Henderson. The search yielded dozens of links to residential and commercial real estate properties under his representation. Though the most compelling link was from the Chiyoke County, North Dakota, police department web site. Arnie was the most recent entry on the county's missing persons report.

Dorey returned home and found Myrtle asleep. She thought about Myrtle and their time together years earlier during the Olympic trials. Myrtle's desire to succeed was strong, her mind sharp and focused. Myrtle had been destined for greatness before the accident that, while not entirely robbing her of her athletic prowess, had nonetheless eliminated her from serious competition. In the years since they had first trained together, Dorey and Myrtle kept in touch, if only briefly. Dorey realized that, beyond the superficial details, she knew very little about Myrtle London.

Dorey grabbed her cordless phone and stepped onto the patio.

Special agent Enrique Valdeza of the Los Angeles FBI Field Office at 1100 Wilshire Boulevard was finishing an expense report when he received the call.

"I'm trying to reach…do you have an agent Reilly, um, Key Reilly."

"One second. Sorry, no agent Key Reilly. Can I help you?"

"Can you check your other offices?"

"One second. Can I get your name please?"

Dorey hung up the phone.

As it sank slowly over the Pacific, the evening sun appeared to melt into the water, creating a blue orange pool of liquid color.

"It's beautiful," Myrtle said.

She and Dorey sat on a bench at the Santa Monica pier as Myrtle mindlessly threw crackers to appreciative seagulls. The pier was its usual crowded mix of locals, transients, young lovers, fitness enthusiasts who weaved in and out of the masses, and wide-eyed tourists.

"I never get tired of this view," Dorey confessed.

"You're fortunate to live here. It's paradise."

"I wouldn't go that far. LA has its pluses and minuses like any other city. Have you thought about what you're going to do next?"

"No. I mean, I know I can't stay here. I'm actually thinking I should try to contact him and arrange another meet."

"Another meet with who?"

"Otis Oppenheimer. The agent I dodged in Las Vegas," Myrtle said. "I mean, I'd rather not, but if we met in an open area like this, well, what could possibly happen?"

"Depends on your outlook. It sounds dangerous."

"I wish I'd never gotten pulled into this."

Myrtle's face tightened as she started to cry.

"Sometimes," she said, "sometimes I really resent the life you have, Dorey."

"It wasn't handed to me on a silver platter."

"I know," Myrtle said. "But I worked really hard, too. Years of competition and sacrifice laid waste by a stupid accident."

"I'm sorry, Myrtle."

"You know, after drifting along on a wave of self-pity for more months than I care to remember, I entered the nursing profession. It seemed like a decent career move and I actually had aspirations of helping others. It worked out fairly well until the day I met Key."

"What can I tell you?" Dorey said. "Men are assholes."

Several blocks south a black Corolla pulled up to 509 California Avenue. Otis Oppenheimer and Brad Caloway stepped out of the vehicle. Their clothes dripped nicotine. The drive had been far too long, courtesy of LA's crowded freeways. But it was okay. The car in the driveway belonged to Myrtle London. This was more than okay; it was almost too easy.

"I fucking hate Los Angeles," Brad said, dusting the ash from his jacket.

"Yeah, I know. You've reminded me of this fact for the last ninety-seven minutes. You realize that, technically speaking, we're in Santa Monica."

"You realize I don't give a flying fuck?"

"You got any gum?" Otis asked, and involuntarily rubbed an index finger along his lower gum line.

"You thinking of asking this chick out on a date or something? Big ol' make-out session for Agent O?"

"Have you any gum or not?"

Brad handed Otis a pack of Wrigley's.

"Go nuts. And technically, Santa Monica is part of LA county, fucko."

"I really don't understand the hostility," Otis said.

"I'm not hostile. Just not a fan of LA."

"Maybe someday you'll tell me why."

"Maybe someday I will," Brad said, "though right now we have a more pressing engagement."

After knocking for a minute, Otis forced the front door and the men slipped inside. The house was dark but for a 60-watt hall light that hummed softly.

"No one home," Brad said.

He opened the fridge and removed a half-empty bottle of chardonnay.

"What are you doing?" Otis asked.

"I'm fucking thirsty is what I'm doing."

Brad pulled the cork loose with his teeth and finished the bottle while Otis did a quick room-by-room search. He stepped into a bedroom and switched on a lamp. An open suitcase sat on a dark oak bureau. A green duffel lay sideways on the floor.

"'*Someone's been sleeping in my bed*,'" Otis said.

Brad entered the room and searched both bags.

"No onion," he said.

"That would have made this business easier and so much less nasty."

"You expect it'll be nasty?" Brad said.

"Always is. No exception this time."

"Good."

They searched the rest of Dorey Hill's home and Myrtle London's car, which was parked in the garage. No Myrtle. No onion, glass or otherwise.

"Get comfortable," Otis said.

He gently removed his suit jacket and hung it on the back of a dining room chair. Brad inspected the refrigerator, but his search for additional spirits proved fruitless.

"Look at this," he said, removing two boxes of soft tofu from the fridge. "This isn't food. This is wall spackle. I mean, who eats this shit?"

"I've had it in stir-fry. It's okay."

"Seriously? Christ. I'd sooner eat waxed paper. Not a goddam thing worth eating or drinking here."

"We're not here for the buffet. They could return any moment."

"True, or they might be gone for hours. And I'm fucking hungry now."

Brad rummaged through the kitchen drawers and pulled out a stack of restaurant menus. He grabbed Dorey's phone and tapped the redial key.

"FBI. Special agent Valdeza. How may I help you?"

"Just wanted to say, you're doing a bang-up job there," Brad said and promptly hung up.

"What was that?

"Just thanking the local law enforcement for the hot tip that brought us here."

"Good deal."

"Yeah, so what'cha want on your pie?" Brad asked, and phoned the Old Original Santa Monica Pizza Factory.

"Ham and pineapple."

"That isn't a pizza," Brad swore under his breath. "It's a god damn monstrosity. You're getting sausage."

"Look at this," Brad said.

He and Oppenheimer had eaten an entire pie and were waiting patiently in near darkness for the return of Dorey Hill and, they assumed, Myrtle London.

"Look at what?" Otis asked as he mindlessly channel surfed.

"This," he said, and pointed at a frame on the living room wall, "this is an Olympic gold medal."

"Serious?"

"Yup."

"Kind of explains the swank digs."

"You think the Olympics paid for this?"

"Commercial endorsements."

"Oh. Right. Listen, I'm officially bored," Brad said.

"You really have to learn to relax," Otis said. "Find a hobby. Bird watching. Stamp collecting. Maybe you'll find an elusive inverted Jenny."

"Who the fuck is Jenny and why is she inverted?"

"The Jenny was the first US airmail stamp ever issued. It featured a red, white, and blue design with a Curtiss JN-4 airplane in the middle of the design. There's one at the Air and Space; classic airplane. Anyway, because color printing was in its infancy, the guys at the Bureau of Engraving and Printing had to run the sheets through the printing press twice."

"Sucks for them," Brad said.

"Yeah. It's the reason most stamps produced prior to World War II were issued in a single color. Multi-color printing was a pain in the ass. Anyway, someone at the Printing Bureau fucked up big time and fed a few sheets through the printer backward. End result was—"

"The upside down airplane stamp. Yeah, I've heard of that."

"Only one of the sheets ever reached the public, and it was snatched up by a single collector."

"Greedy fucking bastard."

"Well it got sold a few times and the sheet was eventually split up among philatelists," Otis continued.

"What the fuck is a philatelist?

"Know what a stamp collector is?"

"Yeah."

"Then you know what a philatelist is."

"Oh."

"You find one of those inverts, Brad, you can retire tomorrow."

"How come you know so much about this shit?" Brad asked.

"Because I don't spend all my free time reading porno."

"I don't spend all my free time reading porno either. I also happen to watch porno."

"My mistake. I—quiet."

Outside the faint sound of rubber tires on concrete signaled a vehicle's arrival. Dorey Hill dropped her car into park, switched off the engine, and stepped out.

"Lemme grab my other shoes then we'll be off," she said.

Dorey raced into the house, oblivious to the fact that she'd opened the front door without unlocking it. She shot down the hallway to her bedroom and switched on the light. With practiced ease, she kicked off her sneakers, which had accumulated too much beach sand, and she stepped into a pair of comfortable sandals. Dorey paused and quickly checked her appearance in the mirror and adjusted her hair. She caught Otis' reflection a scant second before he grabbed her arms.

She squirmed loose with an agility that surprised the seasoned agent. Dorey raced back down the hall toward the door but was shoved to the ground by Brad, who leapt from the shadows like a hungry panther.

"What's the rush, Ms. Hill?" Otis asked, as Brad grabbed hold of Dorey's wrists.

"Never mind the small talk," Brad said.

Otis unholstered his revolver and stepped closer.

"Where is she? Where's Myrtle London?"

Since first winning Olympic gold, Dorey trained daily to maintain her strength and stamina. She also taught a women's self-defense class in Marina del Rey. Dorey screamed as she writhed and kicked against Brad. Her left knee landed square between his legs. Brad doubled over in pain as Dorey scrambled to her feet. She was out the door before Otis could get off a shot. She stumbled into the car, switched over the ignition, shoved the gearshift into reverse, and slammed her right foot onto the gas pedal. Otis ran toward the vehicle and fired a half-dozen rounds. Two of the bullets hit the passenger-side door. Another took out the rear passenger window. Myrtle screamed and Dorey raced down California Avenue toward Lincoln Boulevard.

"Jesus Christ!" Myrtle said.

Dorey continued to glance in the rearview mirror as she sped along the avenue. She caught a green light at Lincoln and shot through the intersection.

"Where are you going?" Myrtle asked.

If Dorey heard the question, she didn't bother to acknowledge it. She was struck by the realization that, without a doubt, her phone inquiry with the FBI Field Office had brought the agents to her door. It was no longer Myrtle's life at stake, but her own as well.

"What happened?"

"I don't think your pal Otis is interested in negotiating at this particular juncture. Don't worry. I have some friends in Pasadena. We can lay low there for a while. Just need to reach the 405."

"But they'll follow us."

"You haven't been on the 405."

She took a right onto 10th Street before turning left onto Wilshire Boulevard.

"I told you I'd find them," Otis said, gunning the accelerator to close the gap. "She's trying to make it to the expressway."

"Just don't lose them," Brad said, "I got a bullet she won't be able to outrun."

"Is that some kind of sexual reference?" Otis asked. "Cause if it is, it's a bit weird."

"What? It's a reference to my fucking gun!"

"Oh."

Dorey became aware of Otis and Brad's presence as the agents' car raced through a red light at 20th Street, nearly clipping an ambulance that was pulling into St. John's General Hospital.

"Christ," Dorey said.

"Drive faster!" Myrtle insisted.

"I'm trying. I shouldn't have taken Wilshire."

Otis continued to press forward.

"Hold on," he said.

"Why?" Caloway asked.

"Just do it."

He ran the light at 26th Street and sent pedestrians scrambling. Seconds later came the sound of metal on fiberglass as the sedan's grille impacted with the back bumper of Dorey's vehicle. Dory gripped the wheel tighter and swerved into the oncoming lane of traffic.

Both vehicles blew the light at Barrington. The 405 expressway, though still distant, was finally visible. Otis continued to ram Dorey's car and both women braced against the impact.

"They're going to kill us!" Myrtle cried.

"We'll make it. Just hang on."

Dorey was unusually calm and focused. Her competitive instinct was in full throttle. The 405 onramp was simply another finish line, and she was determined to reach it intact and ahead of her would-be assassin opponents. Her confidence was as high as it had been during the 1984 Los Angeles summer games. It was a confidence and assurance Myrtle had never known, not during her childhood, and certainly not during the Olympic trials. Even before the injury that ended Myrtle's dreams of Olympic gold, Myrtle knew that Dorey's athleticism and self-assurance placed her on level of excellence reserved for the likes of Jessie Owens, Olga Korbit, and Mark Spitz.

Dorey surged ahead and swerved toward the outermost lane of Wilshire. The green and white metal signs suspended on the overpass indicated certain victory. But Dorey's euphoria quickly faded as she approached the onramp and saw the LA-DOT trucks and work crew.

"The ramp's closed," Myrtle said.

"I can see that."

"Got a back-up plan?"

"No. But I'm quite good at improvising."

Dorey sped past the onramp and across Sepulveda. Fifty yards back Otis Oppenheimer remained calm and collected behind the wheel. Brad Calloway was less composed.

"Goddammit Otis. You're going to lose them!"

"Not going to lose anyone," Otis said softly.

"Fucking LA traffic!"

"Technically we're in Westwood. Have a cigarette. Try to relax."

"I'll relax, Otis. I'll relax when you stop driving like a goddam grandmother on life support."

"Now see," Otis said, swerving to avoid an oncoming bus, "you're simply perpetuating a false stereotype. Honestly."

Ahead of her pursuers, Dorey turned off Wilshire Boulevard and drove toward the parking structure of the New Millennium Mall in Century City. She crashed the ticket gate and kept going.

"Why are you bringing us here?" Myrtle asked.

"Trust me."

She took the corners hard and fast, tires squealing in protest on the concrete.

"How far up were you planning on going?"

"Rooftop."

She reached the roof level in sixty-four seconds and jumped on the break.

"What now?" Myrtle asked.

"Get out."

"What?"

"Get out. Run to the elevator and head into the mall. It's huge. They'll never find you."

"What about you?" Myrtle asked.

"Better that we split up. I'll lead them away from here."

"Maybe we've already lost them."

Even over the sound of her car's engine she could hear the sedan as it raced through the parking lot in hungry pursuit.

"Not likely. Go. Get out of LA. And take this."

Dorey handed Myrtle an ATM card.

"The PIN number is my birthday. Do you remember my birthday?"

"October 10."

"Right. Just don't wipe out my checking account. Good luck."

Myrtle ran toward the elevator and hit the down button as Dorey headed toward the exit signs. She sped past Otis and Brad as their vehicle reached the roof.

"Goddammit!" Brad shouted at Otis. "She just passed you."

With machine-like quickness, Otis locked the brakes and his vehicle skidded to an exasperated halt. He dropped the gear shift into reverse and slammed both feet onto the gas pedal. As the sedan shot backward Brad braced his hands against the dashboard.

"Otis, what the fuck?"

Otis glanced over his shoulder and continued to pursue Dorey's vehicle. The devastating impact occurred within a few seconds. The agent's car shattered Dorey's already compromised rear bumper, and the crash sent her vehicle fishtailing into two parked SUVs. Dual car alarms echoed across the vast parking structure. A second crushing blow shattered the left rear axle and Dorey's escape vehicle was suddenly little more than scrap metal.

Brad was out of the car within seconds. He dragged Dorey from her vehicle by the hair and shoved her to the ground.

"Where is she?" he asked.

"Where is who?" Dorey said.

Brad kicked Dorey in the face. He kicked her hard enough to fracture her jaw but in such a fashion that Dorey did not lose consciousness. She screamed.

"Do not fuck with me," Brad said.

"Leave her; it's Myrtle we're after," Otis said, and ran toward the stairwell.

Brad kicked Dorey a second time, a hard precise blow to the trachea. She was dead in seconds. He followed Otis to the stairwell where, one flight above, Myrtle stepped into and then back out of the elevator. She did not want to be trapped in a metal box and she doubted that the mall would offer camouflage or protection. Her best chance of surviving, Myrtle believed, was to remain outdoors. She began sprinting across the length of the parking lot. Otis reached the landing and saw Myrtle in the distance, nearly lost in shadow.

She reached the south end of the structure and realized there was nowhere to go but down. There was, however, one other option. An adjacent rooftop to her right, approximately fifty yards away. It would be a long run, and an even longer drop if she took a misstep, but it was her only choice.

Otis approached with a firearm in each hand. Brad was a few steps behind, weapons drawn. Myrtle held up her one bargaining chip.

"I wonder what would happen if I smashed it to the ground. I imagine it would shatter into several hundred little useless pieces."

"Don't kid yourself," Brad said.

"You think I'm bluffing. I'm a trigger finger away from death. You know it. I know it. The fuck do I care if your precious glass ball is destroyed? It's your decision to make, Otis."

"Set it down, gently, and you can walk away from this alive," Otis said.

"You didn't say 'I promise,'" Myrtle said.

"I promise."

"Fuck you. I learned long ago that promises aren't worth the paper they're written on, and yours isn't even written on paper."

"I'm not going to stand here and debate you," Brad said.

He was hot, tired, and anxious to have the whole business at an end. He took a step forward, but stepped back as Myrtle feigned a throwing motion.

"Don't! Just fucking don't," he said.

"What do you suppose is going to happen here?" Otis asked.

Otis and Brad lowered their weapons.

"Do you think this standoff will have a happy ending?" Otis asked.

Myrtle didn't answer.

"Maybe...maybe you think a good Samaritan will help out? Is that it?" Brad said.

As if part of an elaborate stage performance, the doors to the nearby elevator slowly opened and Henry Burbank emerged carrying several department store bags. Henry had spent the better part of the evening in search of the perfect pair of frames for a new eyeglass prescription. At 42 years, his eyes were beginning to weaken from excessive computer use. He settled on red plastic frames. Cherry red. The same color of his Stratus. The path to his vehicle brought him directly into the presence of the estranged trio's standoff.

"Is everything okay here?" Burbank asked.

He stared at Myrtle, puzzled by her odd stance and the glass object that she grasped in a strange, foreboding fashion. Henry clicked the alarm on his key ring to disable his vehicle's alarm system.

"Is that a Stratus?" Otis asked.

"Yes. Um, what's going on here?"

"Good mileage and performance?"

"Reasonably good."

"Well, here's the situation, mister, um…"

"Burbank. Henry Burbank."

"Henry Burbank. That's a good name. Very charismatic," Otis said, in a calm and collected fashion that belied the situation. "Here's a rundown of the present state of affairs, Mr. Burbank. The woman is named Myrtle London. My associate and I are trying to procure the object you see in Ms. London's grasp. Ms. London does not want to surrender this item, because she believes that in so doing, my associate Brad and I will terminate her life, i.e., kill her. Ms. London has an overactive, some would say unhealthy, imagination."

"I don't understand," Burbank said. "Miss, do you need me to get the police?"

Myrtle offered no response. Her pose remained unchanged, but her eyes looked glassed over.

"This is all easily resolved, Mr. Burbank," Otis continued. "Ms. London will provide us with the object we desire. You will provide us with your shiny red Stratus—our vehicle was, unfortunately, damaged in this evening's unanticipated antics."

"I don't understand any of this," Henry said as he continued toward his vehicle.

"For fuck's sake!" Brad said, and fired two rounds into Burbank's head. He snatched the dead man's keys from his hand as Burbank slumped to the pavement. "Sometimes, Otis, your boy scout routine can be a total fucking pain in the ass."

Brad returned his attention to Myrtle who was too mentally drained to scream.

"You know what? Fuck this. I don't care if you drop it. I don't care if it shatters into a hundred-thousand tiny pieces. You know why? Because intact or otherwise, my assignment ends here tonight."

Myrtle stared past Otis and Brad. In truth, she no longer saw the agents for who they were. She was no longer standing atop a parking lot roof in Century City next to a dead stranger with new red glasses. Without her realization, the glass onion was transforming Myrtle's reality. Space and time were reshaped before her eyes and her eyes alone. She stretched her calves as, nearby, Dorey, along with Myrtle's other fellow Olympic teammates, began cheering her name. On the sidelines an official fired the start gun into the air, and Myrtle began to run, determined to bring home Olympic gold.

"Look, there's nowhere for you to go," Otis said, though all that registered in Myrtle's mind was *"Go!"*

Brad and Otis gave chase, but Myrtle was already ten yards ahead of her competition and gaining speed. She reached the end of the lot within seconds and focused on the jump that lay ahead. Her spine arched and twisted in a manner that was both beautiful and grotesque. Myrtle glided through the air toward the adjacent rooftop and saw not ducts, air-conditioning towers, antennae, or PVC pipe. She sailed ever closer to a soft bed of sand where her landing would be carefully scrutinized by an international judging committee.

Myrtle's landing was flawless. She hit the sand with an incredible force but was unfazed by the impact. Without a moment's hesitation, Myrtle brushed the grains from her knees and rose from the ground. Moments later she, along with Dorey Hill and a sprinter from Kenya named Wangari Nbereba, stood before an awards committee and received the gold, silver, and bronze medals. The stadium erupted in applause and lit up with a thousand camera flashes as Myrtle London stood and smiled, her eyes tear stained, her heart swelling with pride.

"Jesus Christ," Brad Calloway said.

"Jesus Christ, indeed," Otis said.

Both men stared at Myrtle. Myrtle, her body broken and twisted on the asphalt four flights below, stared back. Blood flowed freely from her mouth, nose, and eyes. Even as death swept down to claim her, Myrtle held onto the glass onion. Her dreams would follow her into the unknown beyond.

"That was fucked up," Brad said. "I mean, she can't possibly have thought she could make a leap like that."

"True."

"Look at her mouth. She's smiling. She looks happy. What the fuck is that about?"

"Never mind," Otis said, and ran toward the elevator.

"I don't think she's going anywhere."

"It's not her that concerns me at this point."

They reached the street in less than a minute and pushed aside a dozen curious gawkers. As Myrtle's life ended, her hold upon the glass onion relaxed. It dropped softly to the pavement and began slowly rolling toward the curb. Brad moved to snatch it but tripped on a slick of engine coolant. The onion continued to wobble ahead, dangerously close to a storm drain. Brad scrambled on hands and knees in desperation that bordered on comical. A second later the onion was gone. Swallowed up by the Los Angeles sewer system.

Brad plunged his arm into the narrow grate but found only refuse.

"Fuckfuckmotherfuckerfuckfuckerfuck!" he screamed.

Otis opened his phone and stepped away as Brad continued a primal scream. One of the onlookers, a chubby teenage boy with curly orange hair largely suppressed beneath a Beastie Boys cap, chuckled as Brad's outbursts continued. Without saying a word, Brad clocked the boy with a right hook that knocked him to the ground. He removed the pistol from his shoulder holster and aimed it at the crowd.

"Everybody get the fuck out of here. Now."

The onlookers quickly dispersed and Otis returned a moment later.

"What's the story?" Brad asked.

"Crew will be here in 20 minutes. There's a man hole about a half block from here. We'll go down and find our prize."

"Fuck that. I'm not crawling around in no goddam sewer."

Otis looked at his colleague with doubt.

"No. Of course you aren't."

The cover-up was easy enough. When local authorities arrived, Otis explained the situation, insisting on absolute discretion and describing the incident as a matter of national security. It was a preposterous tale of murder-suicide that involved an estranged Myrtle killing both Dorey Hill and Henry Burbank in a jealous lover's rage after which she leapt to her death. The LAPD investigators didn't even blink.

Otis watched as Myrtle's body was placed inside the 36" x 90" vinyl body bag. As she was carried into the ambulance, he noticed two small fragments of glass on the ground, each no larger than a pebble. He placed the glass on his palm. Ordinary glass; nothing more. Most likely the remnants of a shattered beer bottle.

Except there were no other shards to be seen.

He placed each shard in a small evidence bag and zipped them shut.

"What'cha got?" Brad said.

"Nothing. Probably nothing," Otis said.

He handed one of the bags to Brad.

"But it could be important," he said. "Keep it safe."

An LADWP crew arrived. Two trucks; five men. The foreman, a short, squat Hispanic with a razor-thin black moustache approached Brad and Otis.

"Estoy buscando a Otis Oppenheimer," he said.

"Yes," Otis said, "I'm Otis. And this is Brad."

"Me llamo Rojo."

"Rojo?"

"Sí. Rojo Pimienta."

"Red Pepper," Brad said. "That's messed up."

"Vamos bajo tierra," Rojo said.

"Yes, we're going underground."

"Sí."

The agents followed Rojo to his truck. They stripped down to their undershirts and slacks and donned vinyl waterproof hip boots, long-sleeve denim shirts, gloves, and flashlight safety helmets before descending a twenty-two foot ladder that dropped them into the Los Angeles sewer system. Rojo and his crew accompanied the men. A string of fluorescent lamps were lowered down and strung along the top of the tunnel. They walked through eighteen inches of sludge water toward the storm drain that had swallowed up the onion. More lights were carried into the tunnel to aid in the search.

"Señor," Rojo asked, "Qué estamos buscando?"

"I don't...I don't understand. No entiendo," Otis said.

"Me perdone. Qué...what are we look for?"

Otis described the object as simply as possible, aware that anything but the most rudimentary of explanations would likely be lost in translation. Rojo nodded in acknowledgment and spoke briefly with his crew.

"Mire a su alrededor. De cebolla de vidrio. Buscarlo. Puedes buscar ahora."

"A twenty-foot drop into less than two feet of water," Brad said. "It must have shattered. Goddammit."

"Maybe," Otis said. "But let's hope not."

They searched for twelve hours. And then twelve hours more. Exhausted, the men emerged from the sewer. Rojo and his crew sealed the manhole, packed up their gear, and departed.

"Well, we're fucked," Otis said.

"Maybe. I need a goddam drink and a cigarette," Brad said.

They walked a block to an upscale 24-hour gentlemen's club on the corner of Wilshire and Barrington, but both men stank and the bouncer refused to let them enter.

"You know," Brad explained to the bouncer, "if I wasn't so goddam fatigued right now I'd break your mother-fucking arm in six places."

Across the street the agents noticed an all-night liquor store. A short while later, they were back in the parking structure and seated in the front of the red Stratus that had belonged to Henry Burbank. They drank scotch and whiskey straight from the bottle and went through two packs of Marlboros. By 4:00 a.m., Otis was asleep and snoring lightly. Brad continued drinking and smoking, and he sang along to a 70s FM station he found at the end of the dial. As the sun rose over east Los Angeles, he threw open the passenger door and vomited wildly.

"I fucking hate this city," he said, shutting the door and promptly passing out.

10   April 15, 1999, Pittsburgh, PA

It was raining in Pittsburgh. Otis Oppenheimer crawled along the Parkway West toward downtown. The morning rush was over but weather conditions and a jackknifed semi had extended the usual morning delays into early afternoon.

He arrived at 12700 Fifth Avenue nearly an hour late. It didn't matter. He stepped through the security checkpoint.

"No weapons," the guard said.

"Right."

Otis removed the firearms from his shoulder and ankle holsters. The guard processed the items, placing them into a lockbox, and presented Otis with a receipt. He was also given a visitor's badge, which he affixed to the lapel of his jacket.

A narrow hallway lead to the reception desk and Dr. Mosby Jefferson was paged. He arrived within a few moments. Jefferson was a young man, obscenely tall. His complexion was dark but only slightly. Brief introductions were made. Jefferson's accent was vaguely South African.

"Welcome to the Kensington Institution for Mental Health, Mr. Oppenheimer. I trust you checked your weapons with Mr. Swanson."

"Didn't have a choice."

"It's not for their protection, you understand, but for yours."

"Right."

"Five, six years back, a criminal profiler with the Akron Sheriff's Department was here conducting a routine interview with one of our residents. Nice man. It ended very badly for him. Policy changed shortly thereafter."

Otis followed Mosby toward a bank of elevators. The men ascended to the fourteenth floor. As they approached room 1420, the duo was greeted by a large intern dressed in hospital white.

"This is Mr. Piranha. He'll be outside the door should you need anything."

"Is that really your name?" Otis asked, closely observing the intern.

"Yes. Yes it is."

"What's your first name?" Otis said.

"Zachery."

"Zachery Piranha. Nice. Anyone ever fuck with you about it? Your name I mean."

"Sometimes. Not often."

"It's nice to meet you, Zachery Piranha. Dr. Jefferson, you were saying?"

"Yes, well, I doubt you'll have much to worry about with Carrington. He's quite mad, of course, but he doesn't say much. Not the emotional type; at least not now."

"What do you mean?"

"Mr. Carrington is given an uncharacteristically high dose of fluoxetine, an SSRI class drug, daily. It levels his mood while decreasing libido. You've read his work?"

"I've studied it."

"I assume you're familiar with his sordid past," Mosby said.

"If by 'sordid' you mean the fact that in 1967 he butchered eight people, including three women and children, with little more than a set of house keys, then yes, I'm familiar with Mr. Carrington's sordid past."

"There is, of course, much more to the man's life than that unfortunate moment of unbridled violence."

"Perhaps," Otis said, "though I think you'd agree it's become the defining moment in his life."

"Yes. Well, I'm sure you're anxious to get started. If you don't mind my asking, what's the nature of today's interview with my patient?"

Otis said nothing and turned his head away from Jefferson's gaze.

"I see," Jefferson said. "National security. Classified information. Something like that?"

"Yes. Something like that."

Mr. Piranha fumbled with a large key ring for a moment before finding the correct key and unlocking the door to 1420.

"Just knock when you've finished speaking with Mr. Carrington," Piranha said.

"Right."

Otis stepped into the room and found Karl Carrington seated at a small wooden desk. Atop the desk sat an antique Remington Portable and a ream of paper. Otis was familiar with the typewriter. In his collection of essays published in 1961, Carrington often praised the Remington Portable series of manual typewriters and chastised writers who succumbed to the technology of the moment.

Carrington, round and wrinkled, was seated at the desk. He wore an orange pullover sweater that stretched around his fat midsection like a fitted bed sheet. His chubby, pasty fingers danced along the keys of the machine with dizzying speed. Every few seconds he'd slap the vertical return bar to begin a new line of type. Otis sat and faced Carrington. An aura of kinetic current seemed to surround the old man, and Otis was suddenly nervous at the thought of breaking Carrington's concentration. Finally he cleared his throat and spoke.

"You look…different from what I expected," Otis said.

The clack-clack-clacking of the keys against the paper abruptly ceased. He brushed a hand over his thick silver hair and stared at Otis with skepticism and annoyance.

"You were expecting someone taller?"

"Younger. The last photo I saw of you was from the *On the Precipice of the Comet's Tail* dust jacket. Jet-black hair. Smooth complexion."

"Christ, kid, that was 1964. I was a young, well, reasonably young, man. I remember that photograph. It was taken by my ex-wife, my second ex-wife, Cheryl, on Christmas day in 1962. My agent and publisher both hated it. Said I looked arrogant. Goddam Philistines."

"There is a definite self-assurance in the photo."

"I fucking hope so. I'm a goddam writer, at least that's what my WGA card says. Without self-assurance, without that arrogance, there's nothing. Any writer is only as good as he believes he is. Trust me, there are plenty in this world who will try to rip and pull apart any sense of identity you or I might have. They exist only to eviscerate those who, let's be brutally honest, reside on a higher plane of existence. People like Asimov, Herbert, Sagan."

"You," Otis said.

"Well, yes, goddammit. The destroyers will take aim like ancient Rigvedic archers and their arrows will cut through to your psyche. It's up to each of us to stare naked into the mirror and mend those wounds. Eventually, if you become a tough son of a bitch, the archer's arrow bounces off."

"Tough skin," Otis said.

"Man is the cruelest animal."

"Kierkegaard?" Otis asked.

"Nietzche. You have a tough skin, you survive. Um, who the fuck are you?"

"You mean in a meta-physical sense?"

"No. I mean what's your name, dipshit."

"Oh. Otis. Otis Oppenheimer."

"And what brings you here today, Oh Otis Otis Oppenheimer?"

"Just Otis."

"Gotta be quick when you're around me, junior."

"I'll try to remember that. Allow me to explain my raison d'être, Karl. I'm one of several agents with the company who are on a sort of, well, quest I suppose. I think you may be able to help me."

"I seriously doubt it, kiddo."

"Tell me about the onion."

Otis knew that from his silence Carrington was shaken. Men like Carrington were seldom at a loss for words.

"I'm not crazy," Carrington said, abruptly.

"And I'm not an analyst. I'll be blunt, Mr. Carrington. I realize I'm probably wasting my time here, but I have a job to do. Find the glass onion. It's a simple job, really, and to date it's consumed thirteen years of my life."

"Keats once wrote 'My imagination is a monastery and I am its monk.' You know, I used to feel that way. That fucking onion ruined me. If you read the dust jacket copy on any of my novels and collections, you probably know that I grew up in a shit-hole Virginia town called Huntington. Couple hours west of Richmond and in the middle of fucking nowhere. I spent most of my youth indoors—at matinees or in my room reading Mark Twain, Dickens, even Jane Austen. By age 7, I knew I wanted to be a writer. My friends, the few friends I had, were reading comic books. I read comics too, of course, but then I discovered Steinbeck—*Cannery Row, Grapes of Wrath, Tortilla Flat.* Literature became like junk-food to me, and Steinbeck was a bag of Cracker Jack."

Otis realized the futility of trying to direct the interview. Carrington's mind resembled that of a methodical serial killer who always considered himself the smartest one in a crowd. Carrington's ego could not permit a direct Q&A session. He needed to be in control, to maintain an air of substance to his audience, whether it was an audience of one or one-thousand. And it had been so long since anyone had taken an interest in anything Karl Carrington had to say. He was like a vampire that had been denied blood for many years, and Otis was a welcome plasma-fresh victim.

Otis arched his spine and repositioned himself in his chair, prepared for a long afternoon. He already knew many of the details of Carrington's life, but he played along. There was little else he could do.

"How did you get out of Huntington?"

"I ran away. Christ, I was always running away starting at the age of six. When I turned fifteen I ran away for good. Hopped a freight train bound for New York and success. But success, I discovered, would take time. I showed up on the doorstep of a guy named Jerry Hale, who was living in a rat-infested studio apartment on the Upper West Side of Manhattan. We belonged to the same science fiction fan clubs, so we'd previously corresponded through the mail. Anyway, he let me crash with him for a while and I found a job. I found lots of jobs, actually. Office stuff, custodial work, whatever. One of the worst jobs I ever had was stuffing envelopes for one of the first direct-mail agencies. It was a soul-sucking experience, and I quit after two days."

"You went through a lot of bullshit jobs?" Otis said.

"Yeah. And I loathed each new work experience more than the one prior. Either quit or got fired from them all. I was miserable. I hadn't a pot to piss in, and worst of all, I couldn't write.

"Jerry used to kick my ass about it. He was pulling in decent money writing short stories for the pulps. It was hack work— *Amazing Stories, Wild Western, The Shadow*, even romance shit— but it paid the bills.

"One night I took a late walk to do a bit of soul searching and was jumped by three punks. They promised not to kick my ass if I handed over my wallet, but I didn't own a wallet. I considered giving them my cash—all of ninety-seven cents. Instead I gave the middle finger salute and sucker punched one of 'em. Well…they beat the shit out of me and broke my nose in several places. I staggered back to Jerry's place and pulled out my Remington—this very one—and typed out a 5,000 word short, *Apocalypse Dancer*, before sunrise. I was actually less upset about getting mugged than I was about being so fucking destitute. From that moment I wrote every single day of my life."

"I assume everything worked out after that?" Otis said.

"What are you, fucking stupid? When does everything just work out? I wrote that first piece in one evening. Jerry read it. He liked it, so the next day he introduced me to his editor, Mort Silverman. Morty read the first page then skipped to the last page—that's how Morty worked, crazy bastard. He bought the story, changed the name to something dreadful like *The Mechanism and the Madness*, and I got paid fifty bucks."

"That isn't much money," Otis said.

"No, but it felt like a goddam fortune at the time. We were paid by the word back then—a penny a word. Over the next few years I wrote five, six-hundred stories. I would sleep during the day, go into the city at night—bars, restaurants, night clubs—then return home late and write until dawn."

"You largely write science fiction stories?" Otis said.

"I swear to God, every fucking literary critic who ever took basic writing class at a community college and thinks Gustave Flaubert is a pastry chef labels me a science fiction writer. It's like classifying John Craig Venter as a genome-only researcher for Christ's sake. The fact is, I write fiction that includes elements of science."

Otis shrugged.

"Progressive fiction, dickweed. Anyway, after cutting my teeth in the pulps for a few years I began to concentrate on larger stories. The debut novel was *Collateral of the Nebula*. My agent got me a five-book deal with Scribner's. It was a decent deal. I don't think anyone expected the first novel would succeed as well as it did. Book-of-the-Month selection. Glowing reviews. *Collateral* remained on the best-seller list for two fucking years. It was nominated for a Hugo, but the award went to Heinlein for his brilliant, character-driven novel, *Double Star*."

"It was around that time when you began to isolate yourself from the outside world?" Otis asked.

"The thing is, after *Collateral* I couldn't write. There were many reasons, but I realized that the greatest detriments to progress were the constant distractions that kept me from developing my craft. Little by little I took measures to reduce the daily intrusions upon my work. The radio was the first to go. Shortly thereafter, I had my phone disconnected. My world fell into systematized organization. I eliminated banal tasks like grocery shopping, opting instead to have a list of items delivered to my door each week. These efforts succeeded beyond my wildest imaginings. Two-hundred-sixty-three short stories in 1957 alone! I had to publish under multiple aliases to avoid oversaturating the market.

"In June 1958 I was living in a modest mid-century in Sunnydale. That summer I had a six-foot wrought iron gate installed around the property and wooden shutters added to all the windows. Fewer distractions meant more productivity. But still there were annoyances. A neighborhood dog barking; kids playing on the street; cars and motorcycles roaring by. In September of that same year I had the house soundproofed. We're talking decades before consumer soundproofing was mainstream. By January of '59, I was stockpiling canned goods; the visits from the grocer were cut to twice a month. Around this time I hired a third-party confidante to perform menial tasks—bill paying, tax preparation, mundane fan correspondence. All nonessential mail was returned to sender. By mid-1959, there was just me; the outside world and its distractions was no longer my concern."

"You didn't miss socializing? You didn't miss going out for a meal from time to time?"

"All that mattered—all that matters—is the work. Anyone who is serious about their craft knows this. Eventually…eventually I had the skylight covered over so that not even the seasons could distract me."

"You were, in effect, completely isolated from the rest of humanity. A bit of a Howard Hughes complex. Two years was it?"

"Exactly."

"And it was during this period that you penned *They're Here?*"

"Among other work, yes, but *They're Here* was the bread and butter," Carrington said.

Otis studied the room. Bared windows. Blank walls. Virtually no personal belongings. Institutional white, floor to ceiling. It reminded him of Reilly's isolated existence. The main difference was the typewriter and the piles of paper neatly organized in rows in each corner of the room. The paper was all of the same variety, standard 8.5 x 11 inch 20 lb. stock. The stacks were nearly collated and ranged in height from one inch to more than a foot. Some of the piles were yellow with age. Otis pointed in the direction of the paper and fashioned a guess.

"Manuscripts?"

"Of course they're fucking manuscripts! I've got nothing but time; time, paper, my Remington, and an overactive imagination."

"Tell me about *They're Here*."

"You've read it," Carrington said, "You tell me."

"Well, it was partly autobiographical wasn't it?"

"That wasn't the plan, but certainly Anton's self-imposed isolation mirrored my own. The book was intended to be a metaphor, a cautionary tale against blind trust and the dangers of burying your head in the sand, so to speak."

"But isn't that exactly what you did, in a matter of speaking?" Otis asked.

"That was different. It was necessary."

"And killing eight people, was that also necessary?"

"Look, goddammit, that wasn't supposed to happen."

"You're an intellectual. You know there are published studies on the dangers of prolonged isolation. Need-induced fantasies often distort perceptual judgment. Isolation is also linked with impoverishment of imaginative and ideational output. In your book, in *They're Here*, Anton spends five years in a life-supporting isolation chamber. He then finds that everyone he knew is gone. Later he discovers that he is the last survivor of the human race. Do you ever feel like Anton?"

"I thought you said you weren't an analyst. Listen, fucko, I'm not crazy. All that razzmatazz during my trial—the psychoanalysis, the expert testimonials—that was all bullshit."

"When Anton makes his discovery—that he is the planet's sole survivor—he's startled to find a colony of odd-looking alien life forms. He concludes that earth has been invaded and he begins savagely killing the aliens. Later Anton discovers the truth. He learns that a plague had destroyed all life on the planet. The isolation chamber had been his salvation. Those he slaughtered were actually researchers from a pacifist galaxy reporting on Earth's demise for historical purposes of a cosmic nature. Anton is tried for his atrocious acts and is sentenced to death, thus ending the race of man."

"You overlooked the subtext, but that's the basic gist of the tale," Carrington said.

"Tell me about September 25, 1967."

The writer took a deep breath.

"The manuscript was done. Scribner's fast-tracked it into production. I'd seen galleys a week earlier and signed off on the final edits. I felt invigorated and was suddenly desperate to escape the confines of my home. Jerry Hale, my old roomie, was living in Manhattan and freelancing for *Worlds of Science Fiction, Esquire, Gent*. Anywhere he could sell a story. I decided to phone him up for dinner. But as I didn't have a telephone, I walked to 34th Street to use the public phone in front of Caselli's Bakery. The aroma of that bakery was amazing. 34th was a busy street. Couple families stood waiting for the metro. Lots of window shoppers. Cop on the beat. Kids walking to school. Old Polish women with carts on their way to Galinski's Deli."

Carrington paused. The color faded from his already pale complexion.

"The rest," he said, "well, obviously you've read about the rest."

"I have," Otis said, "but I'd like to hear it in your words."

"It looked like an ordinary paperweight. Nothing more; nothing less. Just sitting there on top of the white pages. I didn't think much of it. Just a glass novelty someone had left behind. I held it in my hand, remotely curious, and the world I knew ceased to exist. I won't say I heard voices, because what is that anyway? Lunatics hear voices; all I had were visions. Christ."

"And the visions lead you to murder eight strangers."

"Yes. It was...necessary. Each of them, in their own way had done, or would have done, something unspeakable."

"You experienced second sight?"

"Yes. Or telepathy or clairvoyance or whatever psychobabble label you'd like to paint on."

"You killed three children."

"Its influence is palpable."

"The glass onion's influence."

"Yes."

Otis was familiar with the onion's powers of persuasion. He'd seen Myrtle London leap to her death under its sway. Arnie Dallas Henderson, who briefly possessed the onion, killed Billings

Smith, a connoisseur in the art of self-defense. Otis was not a religious man. He believed in neither heaven nor hell, but he was beginning to think that dark forces had been involved in the forging of the glass onion.

"Do you remember the murders?" Otis asked.

"Just random flashes. Blood caked beneath my fingernails. The sound of cracking bone. Screaming. So much screaming and shrieking."

"What became of the glass onion?"

Carrington's face wore the strain of a man who'd lost a life-long partner.

"Fuck. I wish I knew," the aged author said. "At one point I remember seeing it on the ground and speckled in blood. Following the killings I searched for it. I was crawling on the ground, frenzied, when the police arrived and beat me unconscious. For all I know, one of the cops snagged it, or perhaps a bystander procured it. I was comatose for three months before awaking in a hospital prison ward."

"It all worked out quite well for you, I guess. No death sentence. No hard labor. Man like you wouldn't have survived state prison," Otis said.

"Don't be so sure. I have a mercenary quality that would mesh nicely with the prison system."

Otis walked toward a corner of the room.

"I'm a bit of a writer myself. I find the creative process fascinating. Do you…do you mind if I peruse your work?" Otis said, picking up one of the dozens of manuscripts that lined the edge of the walls.

"Please do, just don't fuck with the order of the pages," Carrington said.

Otis flipped through the manuscript. He glanced at several before walking back toward the old man.

"You do all your work on this?" he asked, brushing a hand against the Remington Portable.

"Of course. Listen, all this technology—electric typewriters, Dictaphones, word processors, laptop computers—it's all bullshit. I've typed with a manual Remington Portable all my life. I use two fingers and I type 120 words per minute, error free. Fuck spell checker."

"What are you, uh, currently writing?" Otis asked.

"This," Carrington said, "this idea has been germinating for approximately two decades. Ideas are like that sometimes. They sit and stew in the subconscious like a seed in the earth, waiting for that moment when they burst from the ground and sprout upward."

He handed Otis the most recently completed pages.

"Yes. This is…very interesting," Otis said, glancing over the work.

"I'm sorry I wasn't any help to you, Otis Otis Oppenheimer. I hope you find your glass talisman; just don't underestimate it. It ruined me. My literary career has essentially been over since 1967. I'm a pariah as far as the publishing community is concerned. A leper."

"I'm sure it's only a matter of time before you're back on top," Otis said.

"Time is the one thing I have in abundance. Perhaps," Carrington said, dropping his voice to a whisper, "perhaps that was the sole reason I was instructed to…to do what I did to those folks. So that I'd gain the solitude I desire and the time necessary to perfect my craft. If that's indeed my punishment then, well, it's not really punishment at all, is it? My literary return may be on the horizon."

"Perhaps," Otis said.

"Yes, I'm sure of it. America loves to forgive its villains—hell, even Nixon was exonerated. Compared to him, I'm a fucking saint."

Carrington looked around the room at manuscripts he'd spent most of his adult life composing.

"All of them," he said, "ready to catapult me back onto the national literary scene like the phoenix arisen from the flames."

"Like Sodom rebuilt from the dust of the wicked," Otis said.

"All in time. Wait and see."

Carrington smiled a confident smile and slid a fresh sheet of paper into the Remington and resumed typing. Otis watched for a moment as the older man's fingers rapidly darted back and forth across the keyboard. He then turned away and proceeded to the locked door where Zachery Piranha was waiting. The door slammed shut; the click-clack of the keys was reduced to a faint whisper.

"Thank you, Mr. Piranha," Otis said.

Piranha nodded.

Otis returned to the elevator bank and pressed the down button. Mosby Jefferson approached from the opposite end of the hall.

"Dr. Jefferson," Otis said. "Good to see you again."

"I trust your interview with Mr. Carrington was a success," the psychoanalyst said.

"Insofar as Carrington and I spoke, yes, it was a rousing success."

"So glad to hear it."

The men stepped into a descending elevator car.

"Did Carrington ever discuss his thoughts...feelings with you?"

"Of course," Jefferson said. "Many times."

"Did he discuss what prompted him to attack and kill eight people on September 25, 1967?"

"Again, the answer is yes."

"What did he tell you?" Otis said.

"You're certainly aware that patient-client confidentiality prohibits me from discussing the details of any dialogues between Carrington and me. I'm sure you can appreciate the delicateness of that situation."

"Of course."

"I'm also certain that you could arrange to have my offices searched; however, I can assure you it would be time ill spent. The specifics of my conversations with Mr. Carrington are stored in an offsite lock-box; even I don't know its exact location."

"I do," Otis said.

He pushed the emergency button on the elevator panel and the car stopped abruptly.

"How long?" Otis said.

"Sorry?" Washington asked.

"Don't be aloof. Carrington's room is lined with dozens of 'manuscripts.' Thousands of pages. Each of them blank because his typewriter has no ribbon."

"Let me tell you about Karl Carrington, Mr. Oppenheimer. Karl arrived at this facility in 1974. Aside from a few toiletries, the typewriter was the only personal belonging that accompanied him. As far as I know, it's never had a working ribbon. Ten, eleven years ago, I actually tried to find one; but after several months without success, I learned that Remington had ceased their manufacture in the 1950s."

"You're telling me he's sat there, day after day, composing novels on a typewriter with no ribbon?"

"For nearly 25 years. As I said earlier, he's quite mad. Quite."

"And your rehabilitative ability sucks," Otis said, restarting the lift.

Moments later the elevator doors opened and Otis walked briskly to the security desk to collect his firearms. He spent the evening in his room at the airport Hilton accompanied for several hours by a red-haired Polish Yugoslavian named Brandy Klausjankovitz and a bottle of Jacob's scotch. Neither soothed his palette nor eased his troubled mind. He later phoned Elise, but she didn't answer.

Otis scribbled notes onto a pad of hotel stationary. Karl Carrington. Arnie Dallas Henderson. Myrtle London. Had they chose the onion or had the onion chose them? If the former, then why? If the latter, then also why? Henderson died in a military hospital bed, alone and far away from loved ones. Comatose. Yet he was smiling. What was in his mind as death extended its hand? Myrtle London leapt to her death, yet it wasn't a death plunge. Even from a distance Otis could see the confidence and determination on her face as she approached the impossible chasm. Even in death there was no fear upon her face. Karl Carrington. A reclusive novelist whose career ended with the slaughter of eight strangers in 1967. A man who spent eight hours each day typing tales no one would ever see. Was there a connection? Was it merely random?

Otis did not believe in magic or the supernatural. They were the stuff of illusions. But this only led him to more questions. If not magic, if not supernatural, then how could the glass onion be explained?

There were few options open to him. The first and most obvious—find it. An unlikely possibility, given that the onion was lost deep to the sewage system of Los Angeles. The second option was to continue seeking out others, like Carrington, whose lives were unraveled by the strange talisman, in hope of finding a common bond. The idea sickened him, though he realized that the scotch and the lingering smell of cheap perfume weren't helping.

He staggered toward the window of his fourteenth-floor suite and watched the jets on approach to Pittsburgh International Airport in 90-second increments. Brad Calloway once expressed his contempt toward Los Angeles to Otis. At the time he didn't understand how a person could despise a city. Otis caught a glimpse of his reflection in the glass and realized that his face was lined with resentment.

Unable to embrace sleep, Otis sat on the edge of the king-sized bed. Two years earlier he'd found a glass fragment and was certain it was of major significance. A fin belonging to a much greater fish. At least once every week he'd remove the glass shard from its cellophane prison, always mindful to handle it with great care. He'd sit and press the glass against the palms of his hands, attaining a meditative state in an attempt to gain insight into the mysteries of the glass onion. These sessions always ended in frustration and disappointment for Otis. Yet his own addiction to routine prevented Otis from abandoning the practice.

Otis opened the plastic bag and the small bit of glass tumbled onto his left palm. He made a fist and enveloped it. Where typically he felt nothing Otis instead felt…something. The images burst in his mind like camera flashbulbs:

A jumbo jet spinning out of control over the Washington, DC, horizon as oxygen bags dangled from the overhead sections like unattended, mad puppets.

His hands fumbling for the seat belt but finding none.

A blinding light followed and he felt the heat of a thousand tons of jet fuel exploding across the sky.

Otis sat, stunned for a moment, attributing the visions to a drunken state of mind. Again he closed his hand over the glass. The same imagery, shorter, yet identical to the first series of visions. He opened his fist and returned the glass chip to its holder.

Within minutes Otis phoned Delta Airlines and cancelled his upcoming flight to Washington, DC, opting instead to fly to Los Angeles. He would not be stepping aboard flight 777.

He wasn't an artist, nor did he consider himself one. Nonetheless, Otis spent the rest of the evening repeatedly sketching an expansion bridge on the pages of Hilton stationary. When he filled up the tablet, he began drawing on the walls of his hotel room. A call to the front desk provided him with sufficient quantities of liquid energy. The alcohol had no effect as long as his pencil moved. He felt incapable of stopping.

Otis woke two days later, having little recollection of the prior evening's events. He flipped through the pages of the stationary tablet and stared desperately at the wall art. Despite the crudeness of the drawings, there was a level of draftsmanship and architectural detail that far surpassed both Otis' drawing acumen and his knowledge of bridge infrastructure. One of the sketches depicted a pedestrian walkway atop which he'd drawn the crude silhouette of a man.

"What does this mean?" he said.

He snapped numerous photos of his impromptu etchings, and tossed the notepad into his carryon. Otis switched on the TV and increased the volume before stepping into the shower. The banal situation comedy was interrupted with a breaking news story.

"Details are still emerging as to what caused Delta Flight 777 to explode mid-air en route to Dulles International. Authorities report it's too early to confirm or deny whether this was an act of terrorism."

Otis slumped against the shower wall as his legs became little more than rubber stubs. He grasped the shower curtain for balance and sank to the tiled shower floor. Warm water slapped against his face as he struggled to push back a wave of nausea. Eventually he was able to stand. Otis stumbled out of the shower and grabbed a towel. He walked into the next room and stared at the images on the TV screen. The still-smoldering wreckage of the DC-9 was strewn across a large grassy field ten miles west of Washington, DC. The unused boarding pass was still in his wallet. Otis scrutinized it.

"My flight. My flight," he said.

Otis retrieved his valued glass fragment and closed it in his fist. But the mysterious talisman had nothing to reveal.

"What does this mean?" Otis said.

It was a simple enough question. He had no way of knowing that a full decade would pass before an answer would emerge.

11   October 1996: Finley Finlay

Finley Finlay never considered herself lucky. Born out of a broken family and shuffled through Chicago's poorly managed foster care system, Finley's childhood was a series of disappointments accentuated by accidents, abuse, and poor health. She grew up without love, without nurturing. Despite these obstacles, or perhaps because of them, Finley excelled in school. She graduated first in her class from Chicago's dismal Mission Central High and received a full scholarship to Illinois State, majoring in linguistics and foreign relations. More than anything, Finley longed for travel. She wanted to be far away from Chicago, far away from the US entirely. She never imagined her dreams would be so easily fulfilled.

There was loneliness, certainly, but Finley Finlay cherished the solitude. Life had taught her that people were worthless and that love was little more than an abstract concept. Her strict adherence to this belief system made it easy for Finley to walk away from romance. It also made killing a lot less complicated.

Killing was as much a necessity as it was an infatuation. Finley's diminutive stature—she stood all of five two—was in opposition to many of the thrill killers she'd known. An unassuming frame merely added to her mystique. Finley was okay with the emptiness within her heart. Though occasionally it became too much. It was during these times when Finley felt most alive, because she knew that killing time was on the horizon.

Her pale flesh burned too easily in the hot Thai climate. Finlay dressed in layers of fine white cotton, always white, to avoid the sun's blistering rays. She found comfort against Thailand's oppressive heat by sipping tea under an umbrella table at one of the cities many cafes. She studied locals and tourists alike with a dim curiosity. They were all potential fodder for boredom and the blade. Except for Dominique.

Finley Finlay and Dominique Hartley first met months earlier. They had little in common aside from their citizenship, but in a foreign land, friendship based on superficial commonalities was better than no companionship at all. The two women sat outside Pantip Plaza in what had become a weekly ritual. Dominique was adorned in a t-shirt and cut-off combination. Her jet-black hair was buried beneath a well-worn Brooklyn Dodgers ball cap.

"Fucking muzak," Dominique said, a cell phone inches from her ear. "Whatever happened to just being placed on hold? When did silence become a fucking crime? If you're going to force me to listen to something, at least make it tolerable."

"Who are you phoning?" Finley asked.

"US State Department. Goddam idiots fucked up my visa. Government ineptitude at its finest."

"You realize there is no such thing as government epitutde, right?"

Dominique switched the phone to its speaker setting and placed it on the table.

"Air Supply? Air Supply muzak?" Finley said.

"Wishing there was government eptitude now smart ass? Well, you can suffer along with me."

"Thanks."

"This call's going to cost a fucking fortune."

"You planning on leaving the province soon?"

"No, but that isn't the point. They fucked up my documentation, and they need to make it right."

"I suppose."

"What sort of delicious deeds have been keeping you occupied today?" Dominique asked.

"Every day is the same," Finley said with a bored tone to her voice, casually glancing at the blood caked beneath well-manicured fingernails.

During the fledgling years of the GO project, Finley Finlay established a smartly devised cover as a world traveler, liaison to an eccentric, reclusive billionaire whose interests in fine art and electronics defied logic. She was careful to divulge as little information as possible regarding her fabricated employer. To those she met, Finley's job was the stuff of envy. She traveled city to city searching for unique, unusual, or state-of-the-art objects. She added credence to her cover story by purchasing the occasional odd treasure—a carved horn ash tray in Madrid shaped like the Virgin Mary, a parrot sculpture from the Philippines composed entirely of dried banana skins, a silver letter opener from Portugal with the words "Kirkpatrick Interiors" etched on both sides, software that back-converted digital files to obsolete analog equivalents. The more bizarre the more convincing, not that she discussed her faux occupation with many. Still, she knew that too much isolation was dangerous. Her relationship with Dominique provided Finley with a much-needed social outlet. Finley's bloodlust satisfied the majority of her other needs.

"You really think every day is the same?" Dominique asked. "Tell that to the guy at the mall kiosk. You know there are people who would kill to have your life."

"I suppose I shouldn't complain."

"Traveling the world and shopping nonstop on someone else's dime. We should all have it so tough."

"Yeah. It's a living. Still, I'd rather be you than me."

"There's nothing glamorous about being the heir to a family fortune. Okay, it's somewhat glamorous, but if I wanted glamour I'd have stayed in New York. Honestly, I don't like people. Present company excluded."

"But what about your entourage?" Finley said, finishing a drink as her pager flashed.

"Entourage is French for leech. Ask that boss of yours; I'm sure he has quite the following."

"I'll do that," Finley said, rising from the table.

"You're leaving me? Leaving me with coma-inducing muzak?"

"Work calls. Anyway, there's enough caffeine in the tea to keep you going. You'll be fine."

The women parted company and within seconds Finley was lost in the massive crowd that walked along the plaza. Hiking through Pantip was less an adventure than a challenge. Narrow sidewalks were crowded with hundreds of vendors offering cheap electronics, music, cameras, DVDs, and software. A sea of people stood at the various taxi stands arriving and departing. A trio of monks, wearing black sandals and dressed in bright orange fabric that extended from head to toe, scrutinized one vendor's assortment of camcorders. Finley side-stepped the clerics and entered the massive IT plaza as she'd done on numerous occasions.

She walked through the food court on the ground floor and rode the escalator to the second level. The plaza contained hundreds of shops ranging in size from a single, small room to thousands of square feet. Visually, the Panthip resembled an amusement park— vivid colors, flashing lights, walls of sound, and massive crowds. Its canvas consisted of brightly lit corporate logos and was dominated by Sony, Canon, and Samsung.

The proprietors of the smaller shops and kiosks were equally present; they moved into the paths of passersby, hands filled with cell phones, memory sticks, or other portables, and demanded to be heard. Some merchants aggressively waved catalogues filled with X-rated films and adult-oriented gaming software. Finley ignored them all and continued her trek through the plaza to the top-most level. Her white, flowing attire gave Finley an unearthly, spectral aura; she moved quickly as if late for her own haunting.

Eventually Finley reached the top floor and disappeared into a small shop that sold cameras. She was greeted by the shop's proprietor, a matchstick of a man in his early sixties adorned in brown linen and thick black eyeglasses. The old man was regarded as a relic by the younger merchants and his shop was seldom patronized. No other customers were present as Finley accompanied the man into a small back room.

"Khun Waen," Finley said, "you paged me. I hope you're not wasting my time."

"Yes, yes, Rutna. Yes. Very important. I not waste your time."

"Why do you always call me that? Rutna. You know my name."

"Yes, but Rutna is precious gem."

Finley smiled, albeit momentarily. She felt a kinship toward the old man, but she knew that kinship and vulnerability were close relatives, so she maintained an emotional distance.

"What did you find?" she said.

Khun Waen retrieved a moderately sized wooden box that he'd carefully hidden between factory-sealed Nikon and Minolta digital camcorders. The box was cherry wood with a dark stain and an ornamental lid containing multiple jewels. He placed the box on a table and pushed it slightly toward Finley. She looked at Waen skeptically and removed the lid.

"This for what you looking ," Waen said.

"I think that remains to be seen; don't you?" Finley said, and began sorting through the box, which was filled top to bottom with dozens of glass objects.

Finley removed the items that were obviously junk—glass trinkets, earrings, marbles—and continued sorting. At last she noticed the glass onion. She studied it closely for a few moments, eyeing the object with a jeweler's scrutiny. Finley opened her palm and the onion dropped to the ground. It burst into several dozen fragments around her feet.

"Worthless," she said disparagingly as Waen hung his head. "Were my instructions not clear?"

"They were most clear. An onion, sculpted in glass."

"I wasn't suggesting that you hire a glass blower and create a forgery. You do realize that, don't you? This object...this item that I seek is old. Very old. It will be of pressed glass, and maybe crudely pressed at that. It will be heavy. Do you understand?"

"Yes, Rutna."

"Stop fucking calling me Rutna!" Finley said, and shoved the box off the table. It crashed onto the tile floor and Wean winced at the sound of more breaking glass.

"One more," Wean said, reaching to try to block the table and its remaining contents from Finley's anger. "One more piece. Would not fit in box. One more. Looks very old."

"Show me."

Waen opened a small cabinet door and retrieved the item, which he'd carefully wrapped in silk cloth. As he unwrapped the fabric the woman in white keenly eyed the object.

"You're good, Waen. You're very good."

She'd given him only a vague description to go on, but he knew value for dollar when he saw it. Waen had considered keeping it, in hopes of procuring a bigger price from another buyer. But Finley's outburst compelled the old man to be rid of it.

"Yes," she said. "This is better. This is much better."

Some part of Finley was unconvinced that she'd found the bona fide product, or that there actually was a bona fide product to find, but she couldn't deny her own eyes. She wanted very much to hold the onion in her hand. She reached toward it, but Waen recoiled from her involuntarily.

"How much?" she asked.

"Two hundred?" the shop owner suggested.

"Every week I come here to your shop, Waen." Finley's voice was clipped, controlled. "Every week I pay you so that you can, in turn, contact others who may have the object I desire. And every week you disappoint me. Today you present me with something that may or may not be authentic and you ask two hundred—and I assume you mean dollars and not baht."

"Dollar," Waen said, quietly.

"I'm not going to pay you two-hundred dollars."

Finley opened her handbag and removed a red leather wallet. The metallic black of a standard-issue .038 reflected the light of the overhead fluorescent lamps across Waen's face. He closed his eyes.

"Open your eyes," Finley said, and plucked the onion from Waen's hand while dropping an envelope on the table.

She left without a word. Waen found that he was shaking uncontrollably. He leaned onto the table for support, and then, after collecting himself, nervously peered into the envelope. His calloused fingers pulled out a single hundred-dollar bill, and then, one by one, 99 of its brothers.

Events in Finley Finlay's life moved quickly following the acquisition. She returned to her hotel room and began packing a regulation-size carry-on. Essential items only; the onion would not be leaving her sight.

Several thousand miles away Denton Chambers sat at his desk mired in paperwork. The day-to-day existence of his GO agents equated to little more than a scavenger hunt, and Denton was charged with the task of coordinating and documenting their scavenging. It was hardly the life he envisioned when he joined the agency in 1983. And while he believed that the glass onion existed, he was far less certain that his team would successfully retrieve it. In many ways Denton envied his agents. They, at least, were not confined to four walls, a desk, and an antiquated computer.

His desk was a cluttered mess. Invoices. Dozens of receipts for reimbursement to be processed. Countless spreadsheets and maps upon maps to log. Far too many paper cups from the café adjacent to the federal building on K Street.

Buried beneath the paperwork were two desk phones, one black and one red. The black phone was used to conduct routine business affairs. The red phone was reserved for a single, higher purpose. Denton prayed daily for the red phone to ring, for it would signal the end of the endless. A call on the red phone meant success and, moreover, it meant closure.

The red phone never rang.

It was nearing 2:00 p.m. Denton had spent the last thirty minutes downloading pornography onto his computer and sipping cold coffee. He alternated between porn and solitaire, neither of which held any particular appeal. The phone rang. And although Denton answered on the first ring, it continued to ring. He stared, unbelieving, as the red phone chimed three more rings. Finally he answered, and the well-rehearsed code (a relic from the Nixon era) sprang to his stunned mind.

"Fra-Diavlo Antiquities," he said.

"Your ad stated that you were seeking odd objects?"

"It would, um, depend on the object," he said, vaguely recognizing Finley's voice. "How odd is it?"

"Quite odd," Finley said. "So odd, in fact, that you would be hard pressed to find another such oddity. You might say it's one of a kind."

"Indeed. I'd be interested in seeing it. Do you have our address?"

"Yes. It will take some time for me to arrive, but I think you'll find it worth the wait."

"Very well. We're always here."

As the call ended Denton realized his palms were cold with sweat. It was the news he'd been waiting years to receive. The Glass Onion file would finally be closed. Though she could be reckless, Denton knew that Finley was highly reliable. He stood and stretched. His life was about to improve in so many ways.

A new assignment.

A promotion and a generous pay increase.

Relocation to a larger office with a view of the Potomac.

"Life is about to get one fuck of a lot better," Denton whispered.

He was tempted to open the champagne he'd been saving in his mini-fridge since 1991, but instead poured a tall glass of scotch. The official celebration could wait another 24 hours for Finley's return.

Finley knew the GO assignment had been little more than a lottery. She scarcely imagined owning the winning ticket. Her years on the project were not bad, but she had suffered from the same mental fatigue as Denton Chambers, Otis Oppenheimer, and the rest of the GO team. Anxious to be back on US soil, Finley was determined to deliver the object swiftly and safely. She envisioned a hero's welcome or, at the very least, a chauffeur-driven ride from Dulles Airport.

Finley stared curiously at the onion from the privacy of her hotel room. As each hour passed, she slowly began to question its validity. Her feelings were uncharacteristic and, she felt, groundless, but nonetheless the doubt remained. The paucity of specifics regarding the glass onion had always been a concern, though only somewhat since, in a decade of searching, none of the agents had identified anything that resembled, even slightly, the highly elusive prize. Finley had scored the jackpot, but she felt concern as to whether the prize wasn't a well-constructed forgery.

She had decided that if she ever did find the onion, she would never touch it. Perhaps she'd read *The Lord of the Rings* saga once too often during adolescence, or maybe she simply felt too touched already by the job. Nevertheless, Finley felt compelled to validate the onion's authenticity. She casually removed the cheap scarf that surrounded it and cupped the onion in her hands while continuing to scrutinize it closely. Finley couldn't deny that the object indeed looked genuine. The onion's creator had been a meticulous glass craftsman, though whether that etching occurred days, weeks, or hundreds of years ago was beyond Finley's expertise to judge. If nothing else, she felt certain the onion wasn't a mass-produced paperweight for the eccentric office worker or rabid collectors of Beatles memorabilia. But this was small consolation in the wake of her call to Chambers. Despite years on the project, she barely knew him. The agency, though, had a well-known reputation; it did not tolerate failure which, by default, meant that Denton Chambers, who whiled away his afternoons engrossed in the collection of pornographic JPEG files, didn't tolerate failure.

Finley considered spending her last evening in Thailand by celebrating. She considered phoning Dominique but didn't want to expose the glass onion to the public any more than she wanted to leave it unguarded in her hotel room. She decided to order in. A light dinner of fruits and vegetables washed down with a bottle of Merlot with a liter bottle of gin seemed the perfect way to bid farewell to Bangkok. Her sobriety slowly slipped away with the evening.

Finley's focus was never far from the glass onion. It seemed an unspectacular thing; certainly not a source of "unspeakable power." And the onion revealed none of its secrets to Finley. This, and an increasing spirit-fed paranoia, fueled the fires of doubt within her heart. She should have never phoned Chambers. She should have just walked in, dropped it on the desk. Bastard.

Several thousand miles away, Otis Oppenheimer slept soundly in the arms of his bride. His dreams, which in recent months had become disturbingly violent, were calm and tranquil. The glass onion no longer occupied his subconscious. At least not as often.

Although he was on a temporary leave of absence, Otis and his mobile were never far apart. He answered its call while Elsie continued to sleep undisturbed.

"You saw it, right?"

"What?" Otis said.

"Two years ago. Santa Monica. You saw it."

"Who is this?"

"Finley. Finley Finlay."

"Finley, it's 4:17 in the fucking morning. What do you want?"

"I found it. I have it with me now."

"Are you serious? Where—where are you?"

"Bangkok. What did it look like? C'mon, just tell."

"Finley, what's going on? Goddammit, are you drunk?"

"I am, perhaps, a teeny-eensy bit drunk. Listen, I think I got it, and I phoned Denton on the red line to tell him so."

"You phoned him on the red line?"

"That's what I said."

"Christ, Finley. How sure are you?"

"I dunno. Seventy percent?"

"Seventy percent? That's not so good. That means you've a three in ten chance of having your ass kicked."

"Christ. Listen, Otis, you've actually seen it."

"Yeah, well, that was 2 years ago. And I didn't exactly have time to take a photo."

"What did it look like? How big was it?"

"It looked like, Christ, I don't know. It looked like an onion. A round onion. Palm-sized. Glass. Kind of ornate."

"What else?"

"It might…it might have a chip out of it."

"A chip?"

"Yeah. Does it looked chipped?"

"I'm not sure."

"It should look chipped. You know it was lost in the LA sewer system, right?"

"Of course I know that. I read the updates, few and far between though they are. What's your point?"

"Nothing."

"You think it's fake? You think the onion is still somewhere in the depths of Los Angeles?" Finley said.

Otis had no doubt that the object in Finley's possession was a forgery.

"Maybe," he said.

"Goddammit."

"Don't worry about it," Otis said, desperate to end the call and return to the arms of his sleeping bride. "It probably is legit. Anyway, we won't really know anything until it's in the hands of the techies or Emma."

"I guess."

"I suppose congratulations are in order. It'll be nice to be reassigned off this godless project. Good work, Finley."

"Thanks. I—"

"I gotta get some rest now. We'll talk again soon," Otis said, and ended the call.

Finley stared blankly at her cell for a moment, unsure whether to feel better or worse. She scrutinized the onion in search of the tale-tell chip, but it appeared flawless. The second bottle of Merlot was mostly gone. She finished it quickly and fell onto her hotel bed.

Finley's decision to kill Dominique Harley was neither impulsive nor inspired by malice. Dominique's demise was business; a necessary evil. As little as Dominique actually knew about Finley, it was too much.

Her flight from Don Mueang International to Washington, DC, was at 2:30 p.m. This left Finley a vast window in which to perform her task. She knew the hotel where Hartley resided. Dominique hadn't disclosed this information; it was Finley's job to know these things. She knew much about Dominique—family history, credit card numbers, senior prom date, known medication allergies.

Finley traveled light. A shoulder bag and carryon would suffice. Her weapons in the carryon would pass through screening undetected as always. The glass onion was secured in her shoulder bag. It took Finley little time to regain her sobriety and pack. At 10:00 a.m. she checked out of her hotel and travelled via taxi to say goodbye to Dominique.

She stood in front of room 1103 at the Hotel Troubadour. No cleaning personnel were present. No maintenance staff. No guests. From within the room, sporadic bursts of laughter shattered the otherwise silent floor. Two voices—one male, one female. Finley knocked at the door. Eventually it creaked open.

"Finley Finlay, the notorious woman in white," Dominique said, and pulled Finley inside.

"Came to say goodbye," Finley said.

She set aside her baggage and stepped further into the room.

"How on earth did you find me?" Dominique asked.

"It's a small town and you don't exactly blend in. I see you're keeping busy," Finley said, glancing at a colorful mountain of narcotics spread across a coffee table.

"The devil will find work for idle hands blah blah blah. And my hands are certainly idle far too often. Why on earth are you wearing gloves?"

"I thought you knew I was a germophobe. Who's your friend?"

"Tacker Something or other. It's Tacker, right? Weird name. Say hello to Finley Finlay, Tacker."

Tacker made two attempts to rise from the orange plush sofa but was unable to stand.

"It's okay. Don't bother getting up," Finley said.

"The universe is so…so fucking vast," Tacker said, his voice soft and fruity. "Our galaxy is like a grasshopper on an elephant leaf by comparison."

"Tacker enjoys hallucinogens," Dominique said. "Personally I never had the stomach for anything beyond cocaine."

Finley sighed at the hand she'd been dealt. A murder-suicide scenario facilitated by excessive drug use. No chase. No real danger. It was, she decided, too easy.

"How do you know Tacker?" Finley asked.

"We don't know each other. Not really. Then again, how much can any person know another person?"

"Fairly well, with a bit of effort."

"Tell me something I don't know about you. I really don't know much beyond your name."

"Well. Okay. I'm a magician. Well, an amateur magician."

"Really? That's brilliant. Show us something magical."

"Um. Okay."

Finley stepped behind the couch, behind Tacker.

"I assume you're aware that magic is considered by many to be evil."

"That's absurd. It's all smoke and mirrors, mirrors and smoke," Dominique said.

"I couldn't agree more. Watch closely. I'm going to make Tacker disappear."

"How utterly delightful," Tacker said.

"Do it!" Dominique said, clapping in encouragement.

"Okay, but only once."

Tacker sat on the sofa and swam along a sea of his own reality. His head bounced to and fro. Finley's hand ran through Tacker's hair and steadied his bobbing head. Tacker felt something small and cold press against the back of his skull. The weapon discharged without a sound, and Tacker's body slumped slowly onto the floor.

"Jesus Christ!" Dominique cried, and backed against a wall.

"I told you. Magic is evil."

"You're a fucking psycho! Who are you?"

"I'm Finley Finlay. Remember?"

Dominique's horrified gaze was strained with defiance as she sprinted toward the door, but she tripped on over an area rug and slammed to the floor. Determined, she edged closer to escape, crawling on hands and knees. Finley made no attempt to stop Dominique; she knew the door wasn't going to open. Finley retrieved a small knife from her jacket pocket and placed her pistol on the floor.

"You asked how much any person could know another person. Actually you know quite a lot about me. My face, for example. My hair color. My complexion. You know that I drink tea and typically dress in white. You know that I'm fluent in several languages. You now know that I'm a magician."

It was still too easy. While Dominique struggled with the door lock Finley tossed her knife to the floor. It landed at Dominique's feet.

"Pick it up," Finley said.

The cab driver's name was Pratimo Bhuttarowa. He'd been a cabbie for 23 years, and the majority of his runs were to and from Don Meuang International Airport. He was a quiet, thin man who worked six-day weeks, twenty-hour days. His cab was his primary residence. When he slept, it was in the front seat of his vehicle for periods of 30 minutes or less. He bathed in restrooms at various gas stations and was fastidious about shaving. Pratimo's face was smooth but for a meticulously maintained paper-thin moustache that stretched across his narrow upper lip. He spent his off day with his daughters. When he was alone with her, Pratimo spent time with his wife making more daughters.

Although Pratimo was fluent in English, in his profession there was little in the way of small talk. Most passengers were tourists, and if they spoke at all, they talked about Pratimo as if he wasn't there. He, in turn, paid little attention to the average foreigner unless he felt it would result in a better tip. But as he raced toward Don Mueang, Pratimo found it nearly impossible to focus on the road.

"Are you sure you do not want be driven to hospital?" Pratimo asked.

"Quite sure."

"I am sorry. I do not mean to question or stare. It just that, you badly injured."

"It's nothing a few adhesive bandages can't handle."

Her forearms were lined with streaks of red and the fingernail gash across her forehead dripped like a slowly leaking faucet. It hurt. Finley smiled not despite the pain but because of it.

Dominique had put up a fight. Not an excellent fight, but a fight nonetheless. Finley respected Dominique's instinct to survive and allowed her prey to score several small victories. With Finley's knife at her disposal, Dominique lashed out with a primal ferocity that belied her character. The blade found its mark several times. Finley refused to defend herself; to her delight the wounds quickly grew in number and severity. As the scuffle ensued, Finley's bags were knocked aside, and the glass onion tumbled onto the floor. It was secured in bubble-wrap, but its presence brought Finley back into the game. She realized that a prolonged fight could easily draw unwanted attention. The altercation ended soon after; Dominique's death was quick and silent.

"I have a first-aid box with bandages. You welcome to them," Pratimo said.

"Khob-khun krup," Finley said.

Her pronunciation was off, but the driver understood. He reached across the front seat, opened the glove box, and handed Finley the medicine kit.

"Where are you travel?" Pratimo asked.

"United States. East coast."

"I been to Washington, DC. See the Washington Monument, Lincoln Memorial, Kennedy grave. You been there those places?"

"No," Finley said. "Maybe someday."

They reached the international departures gate at Don Meuang International Airport and Pratimo parked next to the curb. The airport was a busy blur of cars, vans, buses, Took-Tooks, and the occasional limousine.

"I have only US currency," Finley said, and handed Pratimo a thousand-dollar bill. "Never fear; it's genuine."

"I'm sorry. Cannot possibly break this," Pratimo said.

"Keep it."

"Khob-khun ka," Pratimo said, gratefully. "Khun jai-dee mak mak."

"Thank you for the pleasure of riding in your taxi," Finley said.

Pratimo Bhuttarowa drove away from the airport. He bypassed the taxi stand and the arrivals gates and instead sped toward the center of town. He continued north for thirty minutes before turning down a narrow side street. He parked his cab and raced up the stairwell.

Pratimo's wife was startled.

"What's wrong?" she asked.

"Nothing. There's nothing wrong at all."

Pratimo spent the rest of the day with his family. He enjoyed it so much that his taxi remained parked for the next week. When he finally returned to his cab, Pratimo felt refreshed and content. His moustache, as always, was meticulously groomed.

After departing from Pratimo's taxi, Finley Finlay looked forward to a fast and uneventful journey back to the US. The arrival/departure screens that lined the passenger walkway indicated otherwise. Finley's plane was under a 3-hour delay due to mechanical issues. Her attempts to secure an alternative flight yielded nothing but further frustration. Finley eventually succumbed to the dismal reality of international travel and grabbed a seat at the airport bar. Three hours, she decided, were easily tamed.

It had been Theo West's idea to visit Thailand. Alison, his wife of 25 years, was indifferent to travel. She ran a small mail order tea business out of the couple's Essex cottage and was quite content to see the world through the addressee labels on the boxes she shipped daily across the globe. But Theo had grown increasingly restless following an early retirement from British Copeland Steel. During his tenure with the multinational firm he fostered hundreds of contracts with emerging industrialized nations. His negotiation skills within the industry were legendary. His competition referred to Theo as the original Man of Steel.

Retirement changed everything.

Gone were the flights, the hotel accommodations, the business lunches, corporate dinners, and the shapely and perfumed escorts. As much as he enjoyed a good cricket match, there was only so much television Theo could take and remain sober. He convinced Alison to journey with him to Bangkok, and she acquiesced, leaving her business in the hands of her younger sister, Edna, if for no other reason than to drain dry Theo's bottomless well of complaints.

But it all went poorly for Alison, beginning with airsickness and spiraling downward after an unfortunate bout of food poisoning. She spent two days recovering in a sweltering hotel room while Theo toured the city's seedier corners. By day four she had had all she could take of Bangkok. Theo was reluctant to end the trip prematurely. A compromise was reached, and Alison agreed to remain in Bangkok an additional forty-eight hours provided Theo would agree to a stopover in Washington, DC, to visit Alison's aged parents. Theo agreed and engulfed on a marathon of debauchery while Alison rested in their hotel room sipping tea.

As they sat waiting at the airport gate, Theo questioned whether it had been worth it.

"Goddammit," he said. "We've been waiting for three bloody hours."

"There's no sense in acting out. We'll leave when we leave," Alison said.

"Always the pragmatist."

"That's right, and an optimist. You might consider giving one or the other a go."

Theo frowned and stood up from the plastic chair to stretch. Moments later the boarding call was given for Flight 800.

"Thank Christ. C'mon then, let's go," he said, and the couple walked toward a rapidly forming passenger line.

Finley Finlay also heard the call. She staggered into the line immediately behind the Wests. Half-drunk on bourbon, Finley's breath felt hot like dragon's fire and smelled equally potent. Theo grew up with an alcoholic dad. He recognized the scent radiating from Finley and glanced back in disgust. Though that wasn't why she hit him.

Finley hit Theo because it was the only way she could think of to avoid getting on the plane. Hours later she'd wonder why she hadn't simply walked away. Or simply gotten on the plane, sat down, flown home. Home. Perhaps, she thought, the drama made it all the more real. Like the many outbursts of violence that had defined her life, it happened quickly and without warning. Her eyes looked up and met those of Theo. His eyes were dark, heavy orbs that cast a net of contempt directly at her. It was in that moment that she realized more than anything that Flight 800 could not be permitted to leave the runway.

She pulled back her right arm just as Theo was returning his glance to the front of the line. Finley's fingers curled into a tight, brutally elegant fist that, to anyone around her, became little more than a blur. She clocked Theo on the left corner of his jaw. His body twisted, propelled like some absurd top, so that he ended up facing his attacker. He gathered his senses within a few moments.

"What the fuck is on with you then?" Theo shouted.

Finley's reply was short and devastating. Her first two blows shattered Theo's jaw. She continued to work on the facial bones, machine like, crushing the nasal cartilage. Finley cut her fingers on the edge of Theo's teeth as her fists pounded at his mouth. More cracking sounds followed. The whole attack lasted less than 20 seconds. Alison screamed as others watched in stunned disbelief.

It took three security officers to pull Finley from Theo's unconscious body. They placed her in handcuffs and leg restraints. She erupted with a guttural, primal scream. Finley stared at her fellow passengers, most of who returned to the task of boarding the 747.

"You're all going to die on that plane! You're all going to die!"

She broke free of the men restraining her and lunged toward the crowd.

"You're going to die!"

The air was electric around Finley—a fact she realized too late. The taser pressed against her flesh and, following a moment of searing pain, everything faded to black.

"What do you mean you didn't board it?"

"I didn't board it. It was a doomed flight."

"Really."

The static over the international connection did little to mask Denton Chambers's frustration with Finley.

"And how, precisely, did you arrive at this conclusion?" he asked.

"I just...I just knew it. That's all. Look, why are we even having this discussion?"

"Don't press me, Finley. And to answer your question, we're having this discussion because you freaked out and assaulted a British civilian at a Thai airport, thus creating not one but two international incidents that I am presently trying to address with the Secretary of State and the foreign ambassadors of both nations. And for your information, Flight 800 arrived at Dulles two hours ago without incident."

Finley was silent. The vision had been clear. A failed turbine engine. The shriek as it plunged from the sky and toward the ocean.

"That's not possible. Are you sure?" she asked.

"Of course I'm fucking sure. I had a driver waiting to meet you. Do you have any idea what you've done here?"

"No. I guess I don't. How soon before I'm released?"

"I'm not sure. Soon, I hope. Do you still have it?"

"My bags were confiscated."

"Jesus Christ, Finley."

"I'm sure it'll be returned to me. Don't worry."

"I'm not the one who should worry."

"Yeah."

"I want you to listen to me closely, Finley. You're going to be released, probably within the hour. The detention center is adjacent to the airport. You're going to return to the airport and you're going to board TWA Flight 16 which departs this evening. You're to wait for the boarding announcement. I don't care if the flight is delayed ten minutes. I don't care if it's delayed ten mother-fucking days. You're going to wait for it and you're not going to get shit faced and assault strangers while you wait. Are we clear on this?"

"Crystal."

"Excellent. Though if you don't return with the onion you needn't bother returning at all."

Chambers hung up. Finley stared at the white walls of her prison. It was an unusual room that lacked the metal bars typical of most prison cells. Her body felt stiff from the effects of the taser, and her head throbbed from the hangover. Finley thought about meeting with Dominique for a relaxing cup of tea until she remembered that Dominique was no longer among the living.

The detention room was sparsely furnished, containing only a single wall-mounted bunk, a toilet, and a sink. No windows, not even on the cell door. Two security cameras, mounted at opposite ends of the ceiling and infinitely unreachable, stared accusingly at Finley. She sat on the edge of the bunk and waited. During this time she contemplated her behavior at Don Meuang International.

Had the alcohol she'd consumed triggered a deep-rooted paranoia about air travel, or had the glass onion opened a window into her future? If the latter were true, then how could she explain the safe arrival of Flight 800? What if the vision wasn't specific to that flight but was, rather, a general revelation revealing an unchangeable destiny? There were too many questions and too few answers. But before she could hypothesize further, the door to Finley's cell opened. A round, barrel-chested man in full beard and uniform entered.

"You are free to go. Your bags await you at the front desk of the detention center. A driver will escort you back to Don Meuang. We hope not to see you again."

"Not to worry. You won't."

Finley boarded TWA Flight 16 on schedule. It was a late-model Airbus with less than 500,000 air miles logged. The glass onion remained in her handbag, surrounded by a protective layer of bubble-wrap. She sat down and adjusted the incline of her chair. Her seat was over the left wing of the Airbus. It was a decent seat, roomy and comfortable. Finley peered out the passenger-seat window and watched as the tarmac crew continued with preflight tasks. She placed two fingers of her right hand on the wrist of her left hand. Her pulse rate was normal. She noted, too, that her respiration was average. She was not perspiring. There was absolutely nothing to worry about.

Denton Chambers decided to personally meet Finley at the Dulles arrivals gate. He was flanked by three additional agents. Denton held a black attaché that was handcuffed to his left hand. He briefly addressed his crew.

"I don't want any fuck ups," he said. "She steps off plane and you pull her aside. You pull her aside and you transfer the object into my briefcase. We depart, quickly and smoothly. We drive the briefcase to The Hut. Any questions?"

Denton and his crew watched as the Airbus taxied toward the gate. Minutes later the passengers began to disembark. The men waited and watched patiently. Then impatiently. It appeared that Finley was not among the exiting travelers.

"Wait here," Denton said.

He approached the flight crew.

"Where's Finley Finlay? Is there anyone else on board the plane?"

Far, far away, in a hotel room in Bangkok, Finley Finlay sat curled in a ball on a worn-out mattress. She considered phoning Denton Chambers and knew it was the right thing to do. But she also knew that Denton would be furious. Well beyond furious.

"But I had no choice," Finley whispered to herself.

The vision was clear, just as it had been clear the first time she experienced it. A blown jet engine. Her own death. Finley could not remain aboard Flight 16 just as she could not board Flight 800. And yet both flights had reached their destinations. Without incident. Without fatalities.

Her hotel room phone rang. On the twenty-fourth ring, Finley reluctantly picked up the receiver.

"How did you know where to find me?"

"I've a better idea: I'll ask the questions," Denton said. "A flight attendant mentioned that you stepped off Flight 16 shortly before take-off and never returned. So I'm just curious; was the on-flight meal not to your liking? Or were you hoping for a different movie; a romantic comedy, perhaps? I mean, what the fuck, Finley?"

"I couldn't stay on that flight. It was a doomed flight."

"You've lost it, agent Finley. You're suspended as of this moment. Stay where you are. Do not leave your hotel room. Do you understand me? Do not leave your room. I'll put Oppenheimer on the next flight out. You'll release the onion to him."

"Don't. You don't have to do this."

"I've been patient, Finley; more than patient. Your paranoia is jeopardizing this project. You do see that, don't you?"

"What I saw," she said, her voice trembling, "what I experienced wasn't paranoia. The plane's engine caught fire. Exploded. I was killed."

"But none of that happened. Not Flight 800. Not Flight 16. Your self-proclaimed visions are the product of a warped imagination."

"You don't know that. If I had been on either flight…"

"I'm not going to debate you, Finley, and I'm sure as fuck not interested in an abstract discussion about fate or predetermined destiny. Take a Valium; take several. Stay put."

"I'll fly back with Otis?"

"I don't think so. No. In fact, I want you to have as little contact with Oppenheimer as possible."

"But…"

"This is how it's going to go down: Otis arrives at your hotel. He knocks on the door to your room. You open the door. You do not speak to him. You do not make eye contact with him. You hand him the prize and you close the door. Otis returns alone."

"What about me?"

"Assuming you've found the real deal, I can probably reinstate you, provided you're able to pass a psychological profile and medical clearance. Nothing heavy. No field work. You've been in the field too long. If it turns out that you've wasted everyone's time, your life isn't going to be worth much. I guess you know that."

"Yeah. I guess. It just…it just sounds like you're taking this personally," Finley said.

"Personally? Well, fuck yes, Finley, I guess I'm taking it personally. It affects me. It affects me and it affects Oppenheimer, Caloway, Johanson, and everyone else assigned to this goddam project. It affects us all. I've lost sleep. My marriage is in the toilet. I haven't seen my kids in so long I've forgotten their genders. And your ineptitude has, of late, become a steady stream of frustration. So yes, I'm taking it personally."

"I'm sorry," Finley said. It was the first time in recent memory that she'd said the words and actually meant them.

"Fuck sorry. Look, at this point, your job is so easy a fucking panda could do it. No mission. No air travel. No nothing. Just sit and wait for Otis to arrive. Can you handle that?"

Finley was silent.

"Can you handle that, agent Finley?"

"Yes. Of course."

"Excellent. Now take a pill and sit the fuck down; read a book, watch TV, or listen to the radio. Do whatever is it you like to do; just don't leave your room. We all need this to end Finley. We need this goddam scavenger hunt to fucking end. Do you see that? We're all disposable. If that means you go down, then you go down, girl. I won't change my directions for you or for anyone. Sit the fuck tight; Otis will be there before morning."

He slammed the phone down and swore violently. Moments later he dialed Otis.

When he saw the 202 number displayed on the phone, Otis considered not answering. He'd been enjoying his time home with Elise; it had been too long since they'd had anything resembling a real relationship. But he also knew that Denton's persistence was unequalled.

It was a brief, albeit frustrating, exchange.

"Goddammit. Why me?" Otis asked. "Send someone else."

"I don't want to send anyone else," Denton said. "I want this done and done right. I know it's a pain in the ass but you're a vital part of this. Besides, if it's true, if Finley really has it..."

"I know. I know."

"Good. I'll have a taxi at your door in twenty minutes."

The most difficult part was devising a plausible reason for his sudden departure. As far as Elise knew, Otis was a writer; a moderately successful novelist. He concocted an excuse about his agent and an opportunity with Scribner's that required a face-to-face meeting. It sounded stupid, and he felt stupid saying it.

"Anyway," he said, "We've the Rome trip on the horizon."

"Yes," Elise smiled. "It'll be nice to take a break from treating patients for a while."

Otis arrived at Dulles one hour after Denton's call and boarded a private jet to Don Meuang International. He arrived, tired and pissed off, at Finley Finlay's hotel nine hours after speaking with Denton.

"Finley," he said, and knocked on the door.

Silence.

He tried the door knob; it was unlocked. Otis entered cautiously and with his gun drawn.

A quick check of the room, and Otis realized that he was alone. The envelope on the coffee table was addressed to him. Its contents included a metal key and a short note on which was written the address of a local bus terminal and a locker number.

The trip to the bus station took seventy-five minutes. He opened locker 236 and found yet another note:

Otis, I'm so sorry to have fucked with you like this. I needed to buy a bit of time. I'm sure you understand. I figure there's a fifty-fifty chance that Chambers wants me dead. While I don't think you'd pull the trigger, I can't be sure, and I don't intend to hang around to find out. I've taken the onion with me. Assure Denton that, once I'm somewhere safe, I'll arrange for its delivery. Tell him I'm sorry, but soon he'll have his prize.

"Goddammit, Finley," Otis said, and slammed the locker door shut.

It was raining in Washington DC when Otis and Denton met the following evening.

"So what, we just, we're just supposed to wait for a package to arrive via FedEx?"

"I...I really don't know, sir."

"By now she's living under an alias and could be anywhere. Fuck!"

"Where would she go? Finley…I don't know her that well, but I know human nature. We go to what's familiar. I'll pull her dossier, find out where she's been, where she's from."

"The sooner we find her, the sooner we can put this fucking project behind us," Denton said. "Christ, I'm beginning to sound like a broken record."

"Yes sir."

"I can't believe she thought I'd want her dead. I'm not a monster, am I, Otis?"

"Of course not."

"Roughed up, maybe. Smacked around. But dead? She must think I'm fucking Adolf Hitler or something. Find her, Okay?"

"Okay."

"Good. Until we know otherwise, let's assume Finley has the real deal. Put everyone on this. I want her found ASAP. Dispatch Calloway to Bangkok; I wouldn't put it past Finley to still be there. She's been too afraid to fly."

Otis stood silent for a moment.

"Was there something else?" Denton asked.

"I realize the timing on this is bad, but I was going to request a few weeks leave. Elise and I have planned a trip to Rome and—"

"It'll have to wait. I'm sorry, Otis; we're too close now."

"What would you suggest I tell her?"

"I don't know. Tell her…tell her you're going to be doing a multi-city promotional signing. Tell her it's in your contract. She'll understand, yes?"

"I really don't know, sir."

"Well then how the fuck do you expect me to know, Otis? We're all fucked. Fucking Reagan and his screwball beliefs. Fuck us Otis. Fuck us every one."

12   November 1996: Finley at Sea

The waters on which the *Kingdom's Treasure* sailed, on her berth to New Guinea, were unusually calm. The setting sun melted into the South China Sea with a Dali-esque surrealism. Finley Finlay was indifferent to the picturesque moment. She stood on the deck of the fishing vessel in quiet solitude and slowly erased her existence. Bit by bit, her identity slowly disappeared beneath blue waves. Photographs. Credit cards. US passport. The documents that validated her life were released. She no longer needed them. Finley possessed everything necessary to begin a new life, thanks in large part to Dominique Hartley, whose decaying (and unidentifiable) body was still days from being discovered.

Finley held all of the main components of Dominique's life. A quick dye job and a pair of dollar eyeglasses helped pull off the illusion. And there was plenty of cash to go around. Dominique turned out to have a surprising amount of cash in her hotel room. Plus, during her years on the GO project, Finley had amassed a small fortune through falsified receipts and unabashed theft. She understood the importance of lying and the art of lying low. Once in Australia, she'd burn Dominique's papers and assume yet another identity. It was comically easy. She knew this, just as she knew Denton Chambers knew it.

The glass onion would find its way to a safe location. Away from the GO team. Away from every human being on earth. She would hide it, and she alone would know its location. A bit of insurance in the unlikely event of discovery.

Finley was down to a single bag containing only essentials. A change of clothes. Cash. Toothbrush. Deodorant. The onion. Two pistols and a complement of bullets. She'd smashed her cell phone before boarding the ship and burned her other belongings.

The only objectionable aspect of her new life was the smell. The air all around Finley stunk of rotting fish. It wasn't that the boat was transporting anything rancid; the smell resided in the bows of the vessel itself. To the men who earned their livelihood aboard

Kingdom's Treasure, the scent was marginal, even pleasant. But to an outsider like Finley the odor was a constant assault on the nasal passages. She did her best to cope, often reminding herself that anonymity, not comfort, was the objective of her passage.

Captain Jamello and his crew paid Finley little mind, having been well compensated for the courtesy. The captain watched from a distance as Finley released a handful of photographs, the last symbols of her past. They floated on the water for several seconds before slipping beneath the current.

Jamello approached Finley, but remained several feet distant.

"Bad memories?" he asked.

"You might say that, Jamello. Though it's not really any of your concern."

Captain Jamello tugged on the whiskers of his white, pointed beard. His dark skin shone against the glowing moon.

"Maybe not my concern. But I tell you, I been on the ocean many years. Many years. You think you the first human cargo we transport? Nothing matter with running."

"What makes you think I'm running?"

"Everyone running. You. Me. Fish in the ocean. We all running whether we know it or not."

"You're a smart man, Mr. Jamello."

"Like I say. Running okay. Sometimes you got to. Rabbit doesn't run, gonna get eaten by the fox."

"And the fox?"

"Fox don't run, gonna get caught in the hunt. Everybody know that."

"Where's home, Jamello?"

"This vessel home. Long time now. Before that, Dominican Republic. Lot of rabbits there. Lot of foxes. Lot of running."

Jamello removed a pipe from his pocket and struck a match. The cherry tobacco aroma wafted across the deck reminding Finley of her early childhood and a foster family she barely remembered.

"I've only started running," Finley confessed. "And honestly, my days of running are likely numbered."

"You think you gonna be found?" Jamello asked.

"That's up to you, isn't it?"

Jamello stared into Finley's eyes assuring her there was no cause for concern.

"You gonna have a nice time, wherever the waters might carry you."

"That's the plan."

"Go on an' get yourself something to eat from the galley. Better yet, tell Mr. Karim to fix you a meal. Tell him I said."

"Thanks. I may do that."

Jamello nodded and walked toward the ship's bow before making his way toward the tiny navigation room. Finley turned her gaze to the moon and the stars and wondered about Captain Jamello and the tales he could likely tell.

In the distance Finley saw the running lights of a commercial jet as it shot across the sky. The image of a burning jet engine was still fresh in her mind and Finley decided she would never fly again. Any destination she might desire was accessible via train or ship.

Nearly 30,000 feet above Finley, Flight 137 continued its journey north. The A320-100 was, in aviation production terms, a rare bird. During its production, Airbus completed only 21 of the A320-100, half of which were owned and operated by British Airways.

At 10:37 p.m. an engine warning light flashed in the cockpit of the transpacific flight. The jet continued on course as veteran Captain McCall Douglas radioed air traffic control of a malfunctioning high-pressure compressor. The CFM International turbofan engine was throttled back to compensate for the malfunctioning compressor. The reverberations caused a significant albeit brief amount of turbulence and a large fireball to erupt from the engine. Passengers screamed at the sight of the flames, but the engine was quickly switched off and plane continued on its destination. One of the engine's 24-gauge metal retaining bolts, no larger than an index finger and which had been improperly fastened during the jet's most recent scheduled maintenance, was ripped loose from the engine's low-pressure shaft. It skirted momentarily on the inner-rim of the two-spool engine like a lazy ballerina and was caught in the slowing fan blades. Seconds later the small bolt dropped from the sky.

Onboard the *Kingdom's Treasure*, Captain Jamello stood at the wheel of his ship and smiled. He stared ahead, but not at the sea. His eyes were transfixed on Finley. He studied her hair, skin, and face, backlit by the moonlight. Whatever burden she'd faced, Jamello believed she'd overcome it. She was free.

The captain returned his attention to matters of sea. When he saw Finley a short while later, she was seated on the ship's deck. Her legs were twisted to the side and her right arm was behind her back. It was an unnatural posture, even among the intoxicated, and there'd been no smell of alcohol on Finley's breath when they spoke. Hers was an unconscious pose.

The 24-gauge retaining bolt of the Airbus A320-100 had descended 30,000-feet and accelerated to 172 miles per hour before striking the back of Finley's head ripping through her brain as surely as if a gun had been placed against her skull and fired. Finley never knew she was gone.

Two days later the *Kingdom's Treasure* docked in the western port of Sarmi. The captain and crew enjoyed a brief stay on the island before setting sail back to Thailand. There was no mention of their female passenger. Before weighting her body and dropping it into the Celebes Sea, Captain Jamello and his crew unearthed the bankrolls Finley was carrying. They divided the cash, convinced that the best course of action was for Finley to simply disappear. The death of a US citizen aboard a Thai commercial fishing vessel would likely result in an international investigation of Jamello, and the captain had a number of skeletons in his closet that he preferred remained hidden.

Her body sank unceremoniously in the tropical waters.

Finley's handbag was also tossed overboard. Jamello unwrapped the glass onion from its bubble-wrap tomb. He eyed it curiously and drew back his right hand like a baseball pitcher. But instead of casting the onion out to sea, he simply deposited it in his jacket pocket. He later placed it on a shelf in his private quarters, alongside a weathered copy of *Moby Dick* and adjacent to a rotting wooden plaque that read: "The sea is both savage and mysterious. You never know on what path the waters will take you or what you'll find when you arrive."

13   December 1996, Denton and Aliya at the Coffee Shop

November blew into Washington with cold arctic winds and a frost that sent residents in the DC-Virgina-Maryland area scrambling for their winter attire. The cherry blossoms would have to endure much worse before their spring rebirth. Denton Chambers was accustomed to the area's unpredictable weather, and he kept proper attire for any change both at home and at the office. He sat, toasty and warm, in a comfortable lounge chair and sipped hot cocoa. The coffee shop on K Street had been around for several years, and Denton visited often. The woman seated across his table stared down and scribbled numbers on a half-dozen forms.

"They don't make it easy, do they?" Denton said.

"No. Fucking expense reports. Between the paperwork and the internal audits, I'm lucky to see a goddam dime reimbursed."

"It's not so bad."

"Not for you. Of course, we run a bit tighter ship than your group of Armani-wearing treasure hunters."

"There's no denying it."

"I assume you've asked to meet with me because you need a favor."

Denton placed his drink on the table and his body posture changed to a less-relaxed position.

"Why do you have to be like that, Aliya?"

She finished one form and turned it over, pausing to answer Denton's question.

"I'm like this, Denton, because I know you. You aren't the type to ring someone up for a drink without an ulterior motive."

"My motives are hardly ulterior."

Aliya pushed her jet-black hair aside and stared up at her ex-lover.

"You know, there's a reason why the bureau and the agency don't mesh. Too much bullshit and too little transparency. Please, just tell me what you want."

Denton bit softly on the inside of his lower lip. It was a habit that surfaced during moments of stress or frustration. Lately the inside his mouth was looking like a tattered newspaper.

"One of my agents is AWOL. You know her. Finley."

"Finley Finlay? She always seemed so...stable."

"She's lost it, and now she's gone off the map."

"Just write her off."

"It's not that simple. I've good reason to believe she has the key to this whole fucking project."

"I'm listening."

"She used the red phone."

"She used the red phone?"

"Yup."

"Before or after she went bonkers?"

"Before...I think."

Aliya stared across the table at Denton, vaguely recalling the attraction they once shared.

"What can the bureau do?"

"I want her on the list."

"What list?"

"You know what list."

"You want Finley Finlay placed on the FBI's 10-most-wanted list."

"Yes."

"And...just how high up the list would you like her to be?"

"Hmmm...number one?"

"I don't see it happening."

"Five?"

"Have you seen the top 10 lately? David Alex Alvarez was just added yesterday."

"Who's David Alex Alvarez?"

"You really don't keep up on current events. Three months ago Alvarez, an LA gangbanger, shot and killed four people, execution style, in Baldwin Park, California. Two of the victims were sisters, ages 12 and 9. He also wounded three others. You're telling me you want him bumped and replaced with your rogue agent?"

"Could you...could you put her at number 10 on the list? Maybe bump Thang Nguyen for a few months."

"Thang Nguyen?"

"Yes. I do read the bureau's lists, Aliya."

Aliya pushed her remaining paperwork in Denton's direction and stood up.

"Fill these out. Make sure you don't fuck up the math. I need to make a phone call."

Denton stared at the forms and began sorting through an assortment of crumpled receipts. He scratched his head and tried to make sense of it all. A few minutes later Aliya returned.

"Have you finished?"

"I've noticed a trend here. You seem to be spending a lot of time at the airport Hilton."

"Don't be a jealous prick, Denton; it doesn't suit you."

"Just an observation is all."

"If you must know, we're conducting a search into an electronics importing scheme."

"You have good news for me?"

"I think so. I think it's fucking fantastic news for you. Finley Finlay has been added to the FBI's ten-most-wanted list. You're going to need to write a bio and a back story ASAP. We need something to give the media, and I doubt very much you want to publicize your glass onion campaign."

"It's all been emailed to you already," Denton said. "I owe you, Aliya. I owe you big time for this one."

"Goddam right you do," Aliya said. "You can start by never fucking phoning me again."

"Seriously. Why the hating?"

She ignored the question, gathered her paperwork and her coat, and left without looking back. A gust of wind shot into the café. It was going to be a cold winter.

14 December 24, 1996: Denton

Following his meeting with Aliya, Denton Chambers was convinced that by Christmas Eve he'd have both Finley and the glass onion in his possession.

On December 24, he awoke at 6:00 p.m. with chills and body aches for the third consecutive day. He had the flu, and was certain that he picked it up on the crowded Orange Line while shopping for holiday gifts in Tyson's Corner.

The flu for Christmas.

But no Finley.

No onion.

The wife and kids were in Gaithersburg visiting relatives—he insisted they carry on without him. His body temperature rose and fell like the sweep hand of a clock. Feeling dehydrated, Denton left the comfort of his warm bed and staggered to the kitchen. There he mixed a remedy consisting of equal parts ginger ale, Theraflu, and whiskey and nearly gagged while downing it. Denton stared into the living room at the brightly colored lights that adorned the family's Christmas tree. The room swayed slightly in hues of green and red as Denton wobbled back upstairs to the bedroom.

Finley and the glass onion. It would, Denton thought, have been a wonderful Christmas present. His homespun tonic soon kicked in and Denton slipped into a deep sleep. As Christmas morning approached, he was oblivious to the fact that Finley Finlay was no longer among the living. Denton was equally unaware that the much-desired glass object she claimed to own was even closer than he could have possibly imagined.

15 January 1997: Sarah's Funeral; Archie and Reginald

Sarah Singleton was dead. The schoolgirl turned spy turned proprietor turned diplomat was no longer among the living. The funeral was small and private. Sarah outlived many of her contemporaries; those who might say farewell were either involved in loftier pursuits and matters of state or were in failing health. They knew she'd understand.

But there were mourners. Family members. Current and former employees of Singleton House. Local merchants. Regional government associates who regarded Lady Sarah as a local celebrity. Archie Huntsman was among those who offered their last respects. He smiled, nodded, and did his best to offer condolences to Sarah's surviving relatives.

Huntsman looked thin, tired, and old. His suit hung loosely on his body; both had seen better days. He walked toward a corner of the room, away from the small crowd. Huntsman was more than a bit surprised to see Reginald Middleton approach.

"The problem with this job is it never stops aging you beyond your years," Reginald said, shaking Archie's hand.

"You're looking well," Archie said.

"I'm surviving, which is more than can be said for some. You heard the news about Ferris?"

"Prostate cancer, wasn't it?"

"Poor bastard left behind three kids and a grieving widow," Reginald said.

"Right. So are you here on official business or are you among the mourning?"

"Jesus Christ, Archie. That's callous even by your standards."

"I only mean to say, well, you're a long way from Lambeth is all."

"Let's walk," Reginald said.

Archie and Reginald stepped outside into the cold afternoon air and headed along a sidewalk for one block before resting at a metro stop.

"Periodically I like to review the status of SIS special projects." Reginald said. "To be perfectly honest, Archie, it's not something I enjoy but it's become a necessary evil given current budget allocations. I'm sure you understand."

"I can assure you, Reginald, you'll find no disparities in the funds allocated to Project M."

"Your bookkeeping skills are without par; no one doubts that. Sometimes, Archie, I wonder why you didn't pursue a position in the financial department. Lately there've been a number of solid positions in accounts receivable."

Reginald cracked his knuckles and stared at the gray winter sky.

"Sir, if this is about results…"

"No. Nothing like that, old boy. Look, to be brutally honest, I'm a bit disappointed that you assigned Tad Dewhurst to the states."

"Tad Dewhurst? You asked me to put him on this assignment."

"I asked you to put him on an island. In fucking no-man's land. Perhaps I was somewhat unclear about that."

"With all due respect, Reginald, he's stationed in Topeka, Kansas. It's not exactly the Seychelles."

"I must admit, I don't know much about US geography. This place, Topeka, is it bad?"

"It literally means 'to dig good potatoes.' You may draw your own conclusions."

"Blimey. Well, I suppose that's all right. I'd still prefer that you reassign him somewhere a bit more…oppressive. Damascus. Ranipet."

"I'll work on it. But you know how it is; you go where the lead takes you."

"Ten years now."

"Quite."

"You understand, Huntsman, that you were the right man to oversee this project."

"I understand. But SIS can't exactly be overjoyed with my paucity of results. A decade of resources and we're still no closer. But you know as well as I do, there's a fair chance this is a bloody snipe hunt despite our wishes to believe otherwise."

"The American team is still fully engaged in the onion's retrieval."

"That hardly validates our efforts, sir."

"No, but neither does it invalidate them; remember that. Lord knows other nations may be searching. I don't want to think about it in North Korea's hands. Anyway, I'm off to Lancaster Commons. Some bloody CCI agent has filed a sexual harassment grievance with the board. God, sometimes I really miss the bloody Cold War era. You'd best get yourself indoors before you catch pneumonia. Do give my condolences to Lady Sarah's family."

"Of course."

"Oh, and mind what I said about Tad Dewhurst."

"I shall."

That evening, Archie accessed the master database to Project M. He rewrote the specifics of Tad Dewhurst's profile, virtually relocating him to Central Africa. However, he purposely forgot to alter the specific assignment registries. Archie knew that Reginald never performed more than a superficial staff audit. He, or anyone else who accessed the central M file, would assume that Dewhurst had been reassigned. Loyalty to queen and country notwithstanding, Archie had no intention of reassigning Tad despite orders. One of Archie's greatest strengths was his ability to maintain objectivity; he understood the need for a solid agent in the US, and Tad fit the bill.

Archie saved and closed the file then logged out of the SIS system. As snow showers blanketed the city, he sat next to a cozy fire and enjoyed a cup of Earl Gray and a warm raspberry crumpet in Sarah Singleton's honor. To do less would have been criminal.

16   March 1997: Tad and Yu; Topeka, KS

Tad Dewhurst stared out a dirty bedroom window and frowned.

Lately, it seemed that frowning was all he was capable of doing. Like so many others in pursuit of the glass onion, Tad was tired. He'd gotten lazy and had fallen out of his daily routines. His once clean-shaven face wore a perpetual five-o'clock shadow. His skin was dry and his nails had not been entrusted to a manicurist in months. Tad's wardrobe, once a point of pride, had grown wrinkled, faded, and stale. His weight was high, his esteem low, and he doubted very much he could run an 8-minute mile. Worst of all, his prized collection of silk ties had lost their brilliance; they were stained with coffee, wine, or food.

This wasn't at all what Tad expected from love. And the thirty-seven-year-old special services agent was most certainly in love.

It was March in Topeka and the temperature a brisk 17 degrees. The winds and cloud cover were precursors to another heavy snowfall. Tad was weary of snow, cold weather, and the nothingness Topeka had to offer. He was out of synch with his assignment and drinking too much scotch whiskey.

Soft footsteps approached from outside. Tad caught the saccharine scent of her perfume as she reached the front door and he remembered why he was able to tolerate this otherwise cold and unforgiving month. Yu Song had arrived.

Quickly he shoved the empty bottles of scotch underneath the bed. There was no time to shave, no time to do much of anything. Tad tucked in his shirt and pressed the palm of his hand against his hair in a twelfth-hour attempt to look presentable.

Yu's smile greeted Tad as he unlocked the door.

"Come inside," he said, pulling her in.

Yu eyed Tad curiously as he closed the door and the pair embraced.

"Are you okay?"

"Of course. Of course."

"What's wrong? Are you not pleased to see me?"

"Quite the opposite."

"You're an absolute mess. You and your home."

"Please don't call this place my home. Anyway, you know how it is," Tad said. "Surveillance, investigation. The deadly combo."

"I don't like this at all," Yu said, removing her coat and placing it on the back of a chair. "This assignment is killing you."

"Come on, love. Don't be like that. Let's have us a drink. Let's celebrate."

She sniffed the interior air.

"Seems you've had enough to drink for both of us. Tad, what's going on?"

"What's going on is, I'm still here. Still in Kansas. I mean, at least bloody Dorothy was given a respite to Oz. But I'm still here. I must apologize for having overlooked our rendezvous."

"Is that what it's become? A rendezvous?" Yu asked, and undid the zipper on her dress.

"Not like that. You know I don't mean it like that. It's good to see you again. How long?"

"Just tonight. The orchestra is performing at the recreation center tonight for one concert before traveling to Los Angeles."

"Shouldn't you, you know, be somewhere else right about now?"

"I told the music director I wasn't feeling well. We were all allotted a brief respite from rehearsals."

"What's the program?" Tad asked.

"The usual. Mozart. Only the popular material, of course. Nothing obscure or exciting for the masses."

"Right. The renowned Chinese composer Wolfgang Amadeus Mozart. Doesn't it bother you that your touring company only performs the work of Germans?"

"I'm pleased to be with the symphony, to tour and see the United States and other countries. There are many in China, many of my peers, who long for the opportunity I've been given."

"Lots of competition for violin first chair?"

"Silly. You know I play the cello."

Yu smiled lightly and fell onto the bed. Tad sat on the bed next to her and she untucked his shirt. He ran his hands through Yu's shoulder-length black locks.

"Your hair is lovely as always. May I have it? It'll keep me warm on cold winter nights."

"Silly. I'm letting it grow. We've talked about it before."

"You've never looked better," he said.

"I wish I could say the same about you."

"You really have no idea what it's like to be here. I feel as though I'm little more than a treaded tire being driven nonstop across unpaved highway, waiting for but never finding an off-ramp. But..."

"But...?" Yu asked. She laid back and spread her thighs wide.

"Later," Tad said.

"Your spirits may be down, but I see something else is on the rise."

He smiled and moved into position atop her. Yu flinched as Tad held her arms back. It had been far too long for both of them. Outside, the snow began to blanket Interstate 70.

Afternoon faded to evening as Tad and Yu sat by a fire and watched the snow which continued to cover the city.

"So," he said, "tell me a story."

"A happy story or a sad story?"

"Doesn't matter. I enjoy your voice; it's like sweet berries atop a sugary bowl of cereal."

"You won't like this story."

"I might."

"We were in Prague last month for a series of performances. One afternoon I decided to split from my friends and explore the city on my own. I stepped onto a commuter bus. The buses aren't like the ones in Beijing or the states. They're old, usually reconditioned things that smell like urine and emissions on the inside."

"That's actually not too far off from the buses in London," Tad said.

"The driver of the bus was Saudi, mid-50s. Thick head of hair and a long face with an exceptional nose. It was the kind of nose sculptors would want to reference."

Tad lit a cigarette and remained silent.

"You shouldn't smoke."

"Without vices the world would be a boring place. Where were you headed on your bus trip in Prague?"

"I wasn't going anywhere particular. Just around. The bus was just a place to be. To sit and think or not think. You kill a man, the bus is a good place to go for respite."

"Had you killed a man?"

"Don't be silly. That's your lifestyle not mine. I'm merely stating that a bus is a good place to retreat to. So this bus is rolling along and I'm half asleep, notes on sheet music dancing in my lazy head. If I open my eyes, I can see the driver's reflection in the rear view. Just his profile, really. He's focused on the road and sipping coffee from a cup that looks as weathered as his vehicle. His face is solemn. He starts to wipe his eyes. Dust or allergies thinks I. Maybe gnats. But then I realize he's crying."

"Why was he crying?" Tad asked.

"Well, that was the question. No one else seemed to have noticed. His lips began to move but he wasn't speaking to anyone. So I asked myself: Why is this driver crying and whispering to himself? I studied his lips, his words, and you know what?"

"What?"

"He was praying."

"Jesus."

"Not quite. It was then I noticed the wires. There were wires beneath his sweater but two were visible along the nape of his neck. I had to exit the bus at once. I did not want to be a casualty to this man's religious and political beliefs. It would be easy enough for me to depart the vehicle, but I couldn't exactly leave behind the other passengers who rode along oblivious that their driver was on a suicide bombing mission."

"Well, that's a tough acorn to crack," Tad said. "Personally, I'd have jumped off and left everyone else to their fate."

"That's because you're heartless and a man," Yu said. "I really had one recourse. Any idea?"

"Kill the driver?"

"I'm a cellist, silly. I hijacked the bus."

"You hijacked the bus. How the bloody hell did you hijack a bus?"

"I thought about what you might have done in the same situation. When I approached the driver, I told him I was armed and was prepared to kill him unless he stopped the bus and let everyone disembark."

"You did that?"

"I had to. Actually, I think he was relieved. After the passengers exited I rode along with the driver for another mile or so. We talked and I said a prayer for him in Mandarin."

"Did he still go through with his plan?"

"Yes. A shopping district. I heard the explosion a few minutes later."

"Wouldn't it have been better to just, I don't know, persuade him not to go through with it?"

"This man wasn't a lone fanatic possessed of a death wish. I'm certain he was a cog in a much larger machine. If he failed to complete the task, someone else would have done it. Perhaps they'd have strapped the explosives onto a woman or child."

"Great story."

"I never said it would be great. It is what it is. Why don't you tell me a story?"

"Very well. Permit me to regale you with a witty tale. A story of love, intrigue, betrayal, and revenge. But be forewarned, it has a twist at the end."

"Let me guess," Yu said, "It's the story of Tad Dewhurst."

"Once upon a time there was a handsome and intelligent man. After excelling through university, he found employ with the British government. His star shone brightly, and the handsome and intelligent man's career ascended quickly. But an ill-fated courtship with the sibling of an SIS overlord ended his roller coaster career ride, and the handsome and intelligent man found himself relocated to a dark and dreary city filled with unimaginative folk whose greatest ambition is to dine at Sub-Way.

"He was given an impossible task—to find a glass needle in a planet-sized haystack. By chance he met another soul, like himself— a passionate, lyrical soul with a desire to accomplish greatness. Although they lived on opposite sides of the globe, the pair met regularly, though over the years those meetings became less frequent. And the onion of glass, an object of much desire, remained lost to the ages."

"I thought you said this story had a twist," Yu said.

He rose from the floor and stepped across the room, returning a moment later with a small wooden box.

"So it does," Tad said.

Yu watched Tad curiously as he sat down next to her by the fire.

"What are you on about now?" she said.

"You're starting to sound positively British. I like that."

He peeled back the lid of the box. She eyed its contents curiously.

"Is this a joke?" she asked.

"No joke."

"How…where did you find this?"

"It isn't important. What matters is what we do next," Tad said.

"What are you telling me? Are you telling me this is it?"

"Yes."

She removed the onion from the box and held it in her hands. The fire reflected against the sculpted glass though the onion felt cold to the touch. Yu eyed the object with suspicious caution.

"Where did you find this?" she asked again.

"I found it. That's all that matters. It's mine. Ours."

"If it's genuine, you'll be knighted. They'll write hymns in your honor and your name will be known to school children across the UK."

"I don't want hymns or knighthood," Tad said. "I have no intention of surrendering this gem to my beloved monarchy."

"What then?"

"I've already spoken, on condition of anonymity of course, to several private, obscenely wealthy individuals who are quite interested in taking possession," Tad said. "You and I can live quite comfortably."

"That really wouldn't work though, would it? I mean, you can't just disappear. People in your profession don't do that."

"On the contrary. Vanishing acts are commonplace for those like me."

"Your government will want to know what's become of you. My government will ask the same question of me. In time, we'd be found out."

"I don't think so."

"What makes you so sure?" Yu asked. "Have you seen the future?"

"As a matter of fact, I have."

He pressed Yu's hands tight against the talisman.

"You may feel a bit of a jolt at first, but it isn't painful."

She was gone for a moment. Tad gazed at her with excitement and anticipation.

"What did you see?" he asked.

She smiled softly.

"You. Me. Happy ever after."

"Yes."

Tad removed the glass onion from Yu's hands and returned it to its mahogany coffin. He quickly sealed the lid.

"We've talked about doing this for years. And now it's within our grasp."

The fire's shadows betrayed Yu's smile and Tad saw in her eyes genuine concern.

"What's the matter?" he asked.

"What if...what if it's wrong?"

"I've had the onion for...some time now. I've held it each night, asking myself the same question. And each night, I've been shown the same vision. The same vision of you and me."

"Happy ever after?"

"Happy ever after. It's destiny, and destiny cannot be altered."

"And if I walk out of here right now and never return?" Yu asked.

"You won't. The future is what it is."

Yu began to speak but paused and instead drank from a half-empty bottle of Merlot.

"Do you remember the first time we met?" she asked.

"Of course. We met in a shopping district not far from here. You were sorting through a box of vintage *Saturday Evening Post* magazines."

"Was I? I don't remember that."

"Yes. You were looking for a particular Rockwell cover."

"That's right. The baseball cover; the one with the rainstorm. You tricked me into loving you that very evening."

"Tricked you? I merely wooed you with my polished British charm and sophistication."

"Do you remember what I said to you that evening, the first evening we made love?" Yu asked. "I told you this would end badly. I didn't need a glass talisman to know this."

"But it hasn't ended badly, nor is it going to. You can see that now."

"I don't know. What you're proposing scares me. You have a responsibility; we both do."

"Strewth! Screw responsibility. I've given enough of my soul and body to queen and country. Listen to me. Do you want to spend your life traveling from city to miserable city?"

"I enjoy touring. You know that."

"That isn't what I mean. You saw the vision just as I did. A cabin in the woods. A fresh blanket of snow. A comfortable fire. You and me happily ever after. You saw it," Tad said.

"I...yes. I saw it."

"It's your destiny. It's our destiny."

"Happily ever after?"

"Happily ever after. You can even bring along your cello."

The dying fire masked a faint smile that washed across Yu's face and quickly vanished.

The following morning Tad woke alone. There was no note; it wasn't Yu's style to leave notes. Tad reached underneath the bed and retrieved a half-empty bottle of Cutty Sark and pried open the cap. He drank deep from the bottle before staggering out of bed. While waiting for the shower water to heat up, Tad stared at a small map of the US that hung from the bathroom door. He drew an imaginary line from Kansas to California. There was still much to do.

At 3:37 p.m. Pacific Standard Time, Northwest Flight 931 arrived at Los Angeles International and taxied to terminal 27B. A total of 187 passengers soon disembarked including 27 members of the Beijing Symphonic Touring Company. Yu Song was not among them.

The violent rain that soaked the Beijing streets did little to interfere with air traffic. Fan Li awaited Yu Song's arrival. He chain smoked. When he wasn't smoking, Fan busied himself by cleaning the lenses of his eyeglasses compulsively. Fan stood away from the crowd that watched passengers funnel frantically through the airport's main exit. He stared across a sea of faces but could not find Yu Song, expertly polished lenses notwithstanding. Only when he paused to light another smoke did Fan realize that Yu was standing beside him. He flinched in surprise.

"You're early. Cigarette?" Fan said.

Yu nodded. She inhaled deeply and closed her eyes. It felt good to be back in Beijing, a cigarette in her hand. But Fan seemed uncomfortable.

"What's wrong? Am I in trouble again?"

"There have been some changes in the Ministry of late," Fan said.

"What sort of changes?"

Fan escorted Yu to his car without addressing the question.

17 March 1997: Yu Song and Wai Chun

"As you know," Wai Chun said, "my predecessor was a tolerant man. However, you shall soon discover that I lack this particular character trait. Tolerance is a weakness. A cancer. You recognize, of course, your own failings within this department."

Lu paused, taken aback at the comment. For years she worked diligently to establish herself within the Ministry.

"I was not aware that I had failed," Lu said with tempered defiance.

"Naturally. You believe that your prior service record speaks for itself. Indeed, it does. You attended the People's Public Security School and graduated in the top one percent of the class. Your work within the Ministry of State Security has not been without merits. But your reputation is largely built upon a single intelligence coup. You know that of which I speak?"

"I would disagree with your assessment, but I believe you are speaking of my counterintelligence work that resulted in a month-long compromise in the security system of the Federal Aviation Administration's central computer system."

"Yes. An impressive, albeit short-lived, advantage to the People's Republic. Unfortunately, your more recent cultivations have yielded few, if any, crops. It is my personal belief that you have lost not only your objectivity but your loyalty toward the Ministry."

"That is not the case," Yu said and stood up.

"Be seated. Your position with the Beijing Symphonic Touring Company gives you immediate access to a variety of sources within the United States. You choose to spend your time copulating with a British Intelligence agent."

"As you are doubtless aware, the agent of whom you speak is on assignment to retrieve the glass onion. I act under direct orders from Sun Tang."

"Yes, my deposed predecessor. I've read Sun Tang's reports, and while I find them questionable at best, I nonetheless understand the importance of locating this absurd glass object. It is, however, a single component of the Ministry's work. Never forget this, Yu. Do not wrap yourself so tightly around this rainbow or the fools who chase it."

"I understand," Yu said.

"You love this man? This SIS operative?"

"Do not mistake love with the sordid requirements of espionage, Wai Chun."

"I'm pleased to hear this. You may continue to romance this British spy you have come to know. But do not allow your mind to lend itself to illusion as to where your loyalties must lie."

"My loyalties are with the People's Republic of China, as always."

"Of course. Please remain seated."

Wai Chun stepped out of the small, damp room without speaking. Yu studied her surroundings. Aside from a small side-table, the chair on which she sat was the only furniture in the room. There were no windows and the room was lit by a single overhead lamp. A large portrait of Mao hung on the wall in front of her. Mao's eyes stared back at Yu with silent accusation.

Yu closed her eyes and meditated. Though she cared for Tad, Yu's devotion was to her own country. Tad's sophomoric concept of "happily ever after" paled in comparison to Yu's loyalty to the China Republic. Despite her growing contempt for Wai Chun, Yu knew that she had little choice but to disclose to the director everything Tad had shared with her.

Several minutes elapsed before Wai Chun returned to the room, accompanied by a petite teenage female dressed in black with a white overcoat. She carried a small leather handbag which she sat on a table next to Yu. Wai Chun made no attempt at introductions as Yu studied the younger woman's smooth, flawless face.

"As you will doubtless recall from your years at the Security School, it is the finer details that distinguish a good operative from one who is without equal. Details such as fingernail quality, gum line, or in your case, hair length."

"Excuse me?" Yu asked, as Wai's teenage assistant removed scissors and a brush from her attaché.

"I noticed it the moment we met. Your hair is well beyond regulation length."

"Yes, well, I'm letting it grow. Surely, given my position with the orchestra…"

Wai shook his head disapprovingly and the young cosmetologist began her task.

"These matters cannot be taken lightly. Do not allow the vanity of Westerners to be your downfall. Do you understand?"

"I…of course," Yu said.

She was unaware that she'd bitten through her inside lower lip until she tasted blood.

"Very good. I trust your British companion has made no forward strides in his search."

Yu remained silent a moment and stared mournfully at the freshly cut hair that lined the floor. She refused to give Wai Chun the satisfaction of tears. Two words, spoken earlier by Tad, entered her mind.

Screw responsibility.

"No forward strides," she said.

"Not at all surprising," Wai said. "After Miako has finished with you, be sure to complete your reports. I've noticed that your record keeping of late has been slipshod. Documentation is a crucial aspect of your position. Do not be dismissive regarding your responsibilities to the Ministry, Yu Song."

"Of course. Thank you, Wai Chun."

Wai Chun left the room. Yu stared at Miako with disdain, though the stylist seemed oblivious. Tad's words continued to echo in Yu's mind; the blood on her tongue tasted strangely sweet.

Later that afternoon, Yu logged onto the Ministry's reporting database and completed her weekly report. Her documentation was specific, precise, and largely fiction.

18   April 1997: Tad: A Phone Call

Tad Dewhurst sat in the dark, lonely room, a cell phone in one hand, the glass onion in the other.

"Despite what you or I would otherwise like to believe, the fact is I'm washed up," he said. "My career with SIS is a joke. This assignment has been a joke. Okay, so I fucked Reginald Middleton's sister. It was ten bloody years ago. We were in a relationship for Christ's sake! It ended. These things happen. How was I to know the bastard would crucify me over it?"

His fingers caressed the shiny talisman as he stared out into the evening sky.

"One day I'm going to send that pompous ass a resignation letter by way of a Polaroid of me with the onion. Quite honestly it's more than a minor blessing that I've found it. It's a major fucking miracle, actually."

He drank from a freshly opened bottle of 1992 Mount Langi Ghiran Cabernet Merlot and walked across his mattress. The wine was too warm, but was otherwise inspiring.

"Okay, I don't think it's news that I'm feeling more than a bit insecure about Yu. It's not that I distrust her. But, I mean, look at her. Young. Talented. Beautiful. I wouldn't believe it possible for us to last except...well... I've seen it. I've *seen* it."

He tightened his grip on the glass onion and revisited its familiar visions. Snow. A cabin in the woods. He and Yu happy together. As Tad stared out his bedroom window he watched a young couple walk hand in hand across the street.

"I mean, how do you refute this? And yet....and yet I have doubts. Bad dreams. Nightmares that contradict everything I've been shown. It probably doesn't help that I'm a paranoid, insecure bastard. Fuck. Anyway, as long as the vision remains unchanged, there's nothing to worry about. Right?"

The other end of the phone was silent and Tad found solace knowing this. He'd learned the technique during a six-week mandatory psychiatric coaching session during his agency training.

At the time he scoffed at the method. But in the ensuing years, Tad often spoke into a dead phone as a means of sorting through a complex dilemma. The quandary Tad pondered was unlike anything he'd faced before. The mysterious glass onion provided a comfortable degree of assurance. With it, he saw events that were yet to unfold. It served as a glass security blanket to suppress his anxiety and emerging concerns.

Yet Tad was acutely aware that very soon he would be without it; Cardone Bud Craxone was anxiously waiting to take possession.

19 April 1997: Cardone Bud Craxone

The morning air wafted through open French windows and into a pastel-colored bedroom as seagulls screamed in the distance. Ivory white Egyptian cotton sheets, thread count 800, were pushed aside and a pair of bare feet stepped onto an antique silver marble floor crafted in Venice in 1898. The sun rose lazily above the Atlantic as waves crashed madly against the shore. The bare feet found a pair of slippers hand-crafted in Milan, and walked slowly toward a wide oak door that once adorned the Baltimore residence of Edgar Allan Poe. A freshly manicured hand undid a trio of custom-made Wenzhou Libaijia deadbolt locks. He savored the aroma of fresh-brewed espresso and descended a gold spiral staircase formerly owned by William Randolph Hearst.

Slowly he walked past the servant quarters toward the main kitchen where the espresso and a hard roll with currant jelly awaited. Within moments both were consumed. He inhaled deeply and smiled a comfortable smile that belonged to him and few others. Cardone Bud Craxone was awake.

"It's a good day to be alive," Bud said, as Casi Milanasi entered through an adjacent glass door.

"You say that every morning," Casi said, wrapping a towel around her naked waist. "You really should try the pool today; the water is magnificent."

"Perhaps. We'll see how I feel after the treatment."

"Goddammed chemo," Casi said.

"It's the goddamed chemo that's kept me alive, my dear."

"That and a lust for life unparalleled by anyone alive since the dawn of creation."

"You flatter me. Not that it isn't true. Immeasurable wealth is not without its perks."

"Is that why you're going to throw away $500 million on a glass ball?"

Bud paused, taken aback by the question.

"Where did you hear that? Who told you that?"

"You talk in your sleep too much. I've said so before. So it's true?"

"It isn't a ball. It's an onion. A glass onion," Bud said, feeling slightly defensive by the impromptu Q&A.

"Seriously? John Lennon must be rolling in his grave," Casi said.

"What are you talking about? I think at times you forget I'm twice your age."

"In 1968 The Beatles released a double-album commonly known as *The White Album*."

"Not a very imaginative title."

"It was supposed to be called *A Doll's House*, but that's another story. The album cover is entirely white, hence its unofficial title. One of the more memorable tracks is a John Lennon song called Glass Onion. Kind of an absurdist little tune containing references to other Beatles tracks. I'll play it for you if you'd like."

"No. That's quite unnecessary. Casi, are you aware that for years both the US and England have been searching for this object?" Bud asked.

"No, I wasn't aware of that. But it doesn't surprise me. Big governments with disposable revenue often squander it on foolish endeavors."

"I know where it is."

"That doesn't surprise me either," Casi said. "In your sleep, you mentioned this thing could predict future events."

"That's precisely why the heads of government so desperately want it recovered."

"And you? Do you want to see the future?"

"Not especially," Bud said. "As for this glass charm, I intend to have my people dissect it. There's most certainly a way to extract and repurpose its energies. The munitions market will be disrupted as never before. And with my Middle East connections my return on investment will make its $500 million price tag seem like pocket change."

"You'd sell something like that to the Saudis?"

"It hardly seems right to discriminate or favor one empire over another."

"What if it's bogus? A fake?"

"That would not bode well for Tad Dewhurst."

"Who's Tad Dewhurst?"

"Tad Dewhurst is a bumbling, over-the-hill SIS operative stationed in the US. Astonishingly, he's had the remarkable fortune of finding that which seemingly could not be found. However, he's become disillusioned and jaded by the politics that have dictated his fortunes, or lack thereof, so he's decided to sell the onion outright rather than present it to his superiors. He isn't too far removed from the mercenaries I dealt with in Uganda in the 1970s. The only difference is a middle-class British accent. Tad is selling and we're buying."

"When and where?"

"Those details have yet to be fleshed out, but I suspect soon. Now be a love and help me upstairs so I can get dressed, won't you? Today is my final treatment; I'd prefer to arrive with dignity, and there's nothing so dignified as punctuality. Which reminds me— have Miguel prepare the copter. We'll make better time if we fly."

"I want to see it. I need to know…things."

"Yes, I thought you might."

"You know my family's history. I need to know if cancer is something I'll have to look forward to as well."

"Of course. Though I don't need a magic trinket to know that you have a long life ahead of you. I've survived this disease, and you've got at least twice my verve and vigor."

"Thank you. You're a sweet man," Casi said quietly.

Bud's words were comforting, but as far as Casi was concerned, the acquisition of the glass onion couldn't happen quickly enough.

Three weeks after his final chemotherapy session, Cardone Bud Craxone phoned Tad Dewhurst. Tad glanced at the number displayed on his cell and recognized it at once. He tapped his fingers against the phone and reluctantly answered.

"Hello," he said in a voice barely above a whisper.

"Mr. Dewhurst, we have unfinished business. I hope you have not been avoiding my calls."

"No, not at all."

"I would suspect that someone in your position would be anxious to complete his pending transactions."

"Someone like me?"

"You're about to become an obscenely wealthy man. A man

without a country and a traitor to your own queen, but a wealthy traitor nonetheless."

"You may be surprised to hear this, but loyalty to the monarchy is highly overrated."

"I'm certain that it is. And all the more reason that we conclude our business."

"The thing of it is, Mr. Craxone…the thing of it is, I need more time."

"I'm a man who does not like to be kept waiting," Bud said.

"I can appreciate that. Seriously though, I need a little more time. I'll contact you."

"You have other interested parties? Competing offers?"

"No. Nothing like that. Personal matters. Trust me."

"You are being presented with a unique opportunity, Mr. Dewhurst. I suggest you resolve whatever 'personal' issues you're facing, and we make the exchange. As I said, I don't like to be kept waiting."

"I'll be in touch," Tad said.

"You're making a momentous error in judgment," Bud said.

Tad ended the call without a retort and promptly dislodged the battery from his cell phone. He then removed the phone's SIM card and cut it into thin strips, which he flushed down the toilet.

Little mattered to Tad of late. Certainly not the carrot of wealth dangling from Craxone's fingers. Over the last few days the bright future the onion revealed was beginning to trouble Tad. The landscape remained consistent: A cabin in the woods, blanketed by winter snow; Yu Sung and a cozy fireplace. But other elements— emotions—were clouding the topography: Frustration, anger, hostility. He didn't know how to interpret these, nor did Tad understand their presence in a future that had previously seemed so simple and perfect.

He donned a pair of latex gloves and began the arduous, albeit necessary, task of wiping down his apartment. For several hours Tad removed his fingerprints from door knobs, faucets, walls, countertops, and drawer handles. He vacuumed every room and flushed the vacuum bag's contents. He was determined to leave no trace of his presence.

Although unaware of Bud's plans for the glass onion, Tad suspected that the astute munitions developer would doubtless be searching for him. Bud's reputation was well known, and his information network vast. His contacts ranged from top US government officials and east coast crime bosses to street thugs willing to kill simply to gain Bud's loyalty. He was resourceful, confident, and tough.

In many ways Tad admired Bud, which was perhaps why he contacted him initially. But whether consciously aware of it or not, Tad was at war with himself. The heart and mind could not reach a truce—one longed to be with Yu while the other believed it impossible. The glass onion had become a crutch to help soothe his troubled mind.

It was, he concluded, necessary to flee Topeka and relocate to the remote north, far away from cell phone towers and monetary offers. Somewhere a cabin awaited his arrival.

He tapped an ATM and withdrew most of his savings. It wasn't much; certainly not enough to provide long-term self-sustainability, let alone support for both he and Yu. Tad still intended to sell the onion to Craxone, provided the old man was still alive and interested when that time arrived. Regardless, there would always be interested parties. Tad pacified his wallet knowing that, when the time was right, he would part with the glass object for unlimited currency. At present too many variables and shadows remained; he simply could not let go of it yet.

Tad threw his suitcases into the trunk of his car, fueled up at a nearby Arco station, and began driving north toward an uncertain destiny viewed through layers of glass.

20   May 1997: Archie and Reginald in Lambeth

Archie Middleton had seen better days. As he sat in the office of Reginald Huntsman, several entered his mind:

September 10, 1991: a minor car accident on London's Bridesboro Bridge. Although the damage to his vehicle was minimal, Archie strained his back and later required surgery and six months of intense physical therapy.

June 5, 1995: a gunshot wound to the abdomen that resulted while single-handedly foiling an attempted armored car heist in Fultonshire.

October 17, 1988: on the first night of a long-planned trip to Tokyo, Archie spent several hours in a hotel room vomiting mussels and clams.

He would have welcomed any of those days now; Reginald wasn't about to make this easy.

"This does not bode well at all now does it Archie?" Reginald said.

"No sir. I suppose it bodes poorly at best." Archie replied.

"I'm just not following this, Archie. You told me you'd transferred Tad to Central Africa months ago. His profile in the CKS system also confirmed this. Are you telling me he was never reassigned?"

"Yes."

"Might I inquire as to why the bloody hell not?"

"Because, Reginald, we needed an operative in the states and, regardless of your personal vendetta against him, Tad was the best man for the assignment."

"Don't push me, Archie."

"I wouldn't think to, sir. You trusted me to head this project and to make the right decisions. It was the right decision to place Tad in the states."

"Except that now he's vanished. Without a trace."

"Well, yes. Apparently he has."

"How long has Tad been MIA?"

"Three weeks."

"Christ," Reginald said. "Weren't you conducting weekly updates by phone or e-mail?"

"The frequency of our contact with Tad, with all the agents on the project, has dwindled over the years," Archie said. "Since there's been nothing to report, I mean."

"At this moment, Tad could be anywhere on the planet," Reginald said. "I suppose he might have met with foul play. If nothing else, that would at least give us closure. Have you checked his residence?"

"Yes, we had it checked this morning. No Tad. No nothing."

"The flat was wiped clean?"

"It sparkled. We found a partial print on an interior refrigerator door handle. It's a match."

"Christ. Have you tried GPS?"

"No GPS. Tad, most of the crew actually, joined SIS prior to mandatory GPS implanting. His cell phone included a GPS locator, but we haven't been able to obtain a signal. Most likely he destroyed the phone."

"It isn't like an SIS operative to simply vanish," Reginald said. "Not anymore, anyway."

"What do you mean?" Archie asked.

"It happened a lot back in the day. Lot more than we'd care to admit. Sullivan. Blynn. The Asher twins. Gainesborough. They bought and sold state secrets like rabid Wall Street traders and vanished without a trace. It was all a game to them. JIC had its head up its ass for a long time. Thankfully that era is little more than a bad memory. Tad's clearance level, what is it?"

"It isn't high. 6-F, if I'm not mistaken."

"That's good. If he has flipped, he'd have little of value to offer," Reginald said.

"Of course if he found it...the onion I mean..."

"Don't be preposterous, Archie. Dewhurst couldn't find his dick if it was staring him in the face. Just...just have a squad search a five-hundred mile radius of Topeka. Drag the local streams and rivers, assuming there are any."

"Right. Anything else?"

"There is one other thing, Archie. If you ever fucking pull this kind of bullocks again I'll have you transferred to the ISC secretary pool faster than you can say Buckingham-fucking Palace. Is that quite understood?"

"Quite," Archie said, taking his coat and hat.

21 Philadelphia, January 27, 2009: Otis (still) on the Ben Franklin

His hands were beyond numb, but it didn't matter. They'd been beyond numb before. It was nothing a bit of R&R, a Camel, and a tall glass of Jack Daniels couldn't cure. Otis Oppenheimer stared at the crushed Camel filters at his feet. There were plenty of smokes. The missing liquid component would have to wait.

The moon remained eclipsed beneath thick black clouds. It was only a matter of time before the snow would fall. Several hundred feet beneath him, twin barges drifted slowly on the icy Delaware River, invisible but for a few cabin lights. He adjusted the small audio device, which was still set to record mode.

"I remember once in high school meeting with a guidance counselor during career planning week. It was the school district's way of preparing teens for adulthood. Everyone was given a booklet containing dozens of questions. *Do you enjoy math? Are you a fan of geography? Do you like pulling the wings off butterflies?* Your answers were supposedly indicative of your ideal career.

"My guidance counselor was named Linda Kincaid. She was a big woman in her late 40s. Not fat big. Big frame. Big head. A big mop of Jet-black hair that flowed half-way down her big back. Her hands were massive, and they reminded me of giant claws. She could probably catch lake fish barehanded.

"There was a lot of discussion during career-planning week. Everyone was asked to contemplate what they wanted to do post-graduation. I discovered secret-agent fiction and espionage films at a young age. I devoured it like candy. More than that, I wanted in."

Otis cupped his hands and fired up another Camel. The nicotine produced artificial warmth, a strange placebo effect that took the edge off the bitter wind gusts.

"I was direct, and maybe my naiveté was a mistake. In hindsight, I should have simply nodded in agreement when Kincaid explained that a robust profession as an offshore rig crewman loomed on the horizon. Instead I spoke in acronym: KBG, CIA, SIS,

OCP. I rambled on about and international intelligence and counterintelligence measures in the wake of the Cold War to a woman who barely knew my name. She stared at me with bewildered annoyance.

"Many years later I saw her again. I was on assignment in Toronto, assisting a senior agent, just a few weeks before Reagan's obsession with psychics ruined my life. The agency called it pseudo assassination—the killing of an elected official without resorting to murder. The target was an old-school US Senator from South Carolina named Jacoby Keefer. He'd made a lot of enemies within the Executive branch. The incriminating evidence we left behind destroyed Keefer's stellar career before he reached Canadian customs.

"There are no coincidences. As such, I knew it wasn't happenstance when I spotted Linda Kincaid in the lobby of our hotel. The years had been unkind to my former guidance counselor. Her face was sunken, and her skin wore a coat of age spots. One aspect that remained unchanged was her head. It was still large. A conspicuous piñata. We were stuck in Toronto for the weekend, so I decided to do a bit of investigating."

An unusually gusty wind whipped across the Ben Franklin Bridge. The smoke from his Camel blew into Otis' face and he snapped his eyes shut. When they reopened, Otis saw a silhouetted couple approaching on the walkway. The duo was distant, and in the darkness Otis could determine little more than gender.

The male was a tall adolescent youth with bright red shoulder-length hair. His female companion was shapely and a full foot shorter in height. Both wore denim jeans and wool coats. Both were twenty-one at most. And both gazed curiously at Otis as their paths crossed.

"You'll get cancer," the red-headed male cautioned.

"What's your name?" Otis asked.

"I'm Simak. And this is Donder."

"Donder?" Otis asked. "Like the reindeer?"

"Yeah," Donder said. "Like the reindeer."

"That's rough."

"My mom is a bit fanatical when it comes to Christmas. I'm majoring in maternal homicide at Devry, so it'll all work out in the end."

"You're still a long way from South Street," Otis said.

"What makes you think we're headed there?" Simak asked.

"This time of night, you're either going to South Street or Olde City, and neither of you look the Olde City type. No offense."

"Nice."

"So what's your story?" Donder asked.

"My story?"

"Well-dressed, middle-age, chain-smoking white male, alone at night on a bridge."

"You forgot to include *handsome*."

"Right. You get dumped? Something like that?"

"Something like that," Otis said.

"That sucks. Are you going to jump?"

"What's the point of jumping?" Otis said.

Otis studied the features of Donder's face. High cheekbones, a softly curved jaw, and full lips. Her eyes were wide, curious blue orbs. A patch of black hair peaked out from beneath a green and orange knitted cap. She looked distinctly familiar, but Otis couldn't quite place it.

"Can I bum a smoke?" Simak said.

"It happens that I'm especially in need of nicotine, but I'll tell you what let's do. You give me the whiskey bottle you're carrying inside your coat and I'll give you a pair of crisp, hundred-dollar bills. "

"It's not exactly full," Simak said, retrieving the half-empty bottle of bourbon.

"Didn't suspect it would be," Otis said.

He removed the wallet from his inner-jacket pocket and presented the bills to Donder, whose silent smile smacked of familiarity.

"Enjoy it in good health," Simak said, passing the bottle to Otis' waiting hand.

"I intend to. And if you live on the Jersey side, use that money to take a fuckin' cab ride home. Don't walk through Camden at this hour for Christ's sake."

Without realizing it, Otis had changed from an interesting stranger to just another parent. An awkward silence enveloped the trio. It was broken by the shriek of a siren as an ambulance raced eastward across the bridge.

"C'mon Dond, let's go," Simak said. "Josie's party isn't gonna last all night."

"Take care," Donder said to Otis as the couple continued across the walkway toward Philadelphia.

"You too," Otis said, nodding.

He watched for a moment as the pair stumbled along the narrow walkway toward their destination. Donder suddenly turned and ran back toward him. Otis stared blankly at the girl for a moment.

Donder removed her wool mittens, which were white with sky-blue polka dots. She placed them in Otis' hands. Her fingers felt warm and blanket soft.

"I don't exactly know what you're doing up here on such a cold night, but I think you need these more than I do."

"No, it's okay," Otis said.

"You'll find they're quite warm; I knitted them myself. Sorry they're a bit on the girly side, but I doubt anyone will notice."

Donder waved goodbye and scooted ahead to catch up with Simak. Within moments they were gone. Only then was Otis aware that Donder reminded him of his own daughter, Karrie. The realization that he would likely never see Karrie again tore at Otis' heart like alcohol on an open wound. Otis stared at the mittens for a full minute before placing them over his cold hands. He pressed them to his face for warmth and caught a faint clean scent. Otis shut his eyes and inhaled deeply. It was a pleasant aroma. Not at all like alcohol or tobacco or gunpowder.

He placed the mittens in his jacket pocket and took a long drink from the bottle.

"Linda Kincaid had fallen on hard times. Her career in academia ended abruptly following charges of discrimination and racial profiling. She stumbled through life falling in and out of alcoholism before expatriating to Canada where she found employment writing technical manuals for an electronics manufacturer. Estranged from her family, Linda lived a solitary existence. Her sole companion was a cat named Scruffles. She collected debt the way some collect postage stamps. She also collected postage stamps. I actually felt badly for her.

"I thought about doing something poignant. Perhaps a letter or a mysterious encrypted note. But I realized she was too far gone, too beaten down by the world, for it to matter. I guess I was too young and optimistic to understand it, really. That kind of realization would arrive later, after the GO project and the shit I've been through since. After Karrie. After Elise. In the end I decided to help Kincaid with an electronic transfer of funds from Senator (soon to be ex-Senator) Keefer's overseas account. Nothing extraordinary. Just enough to ensure her financial independence during the retirement years. It seemed like a decent plan, but she died of alcohol-related liver failure less than a year later. So much for good intentions."

Otis half-collapsed on the concrete walkway of the Ben Franklin Bridge and pressed his back against the metal safety railing. He removed the blue and white mittens, the first gift he'd received in years, from his coat pocket and slid them over his hands. The wind kicked up and a stream of orange ash blew from the tip of his cigarette, singing the left mitten

"Goddammit," he said, and took another drink.

22   Denver, November 1997: Tad and Yu, a Cabin in the Woods

Four a.m. and Tad Dewhurst was wide awake while Yu Song slept soundly beneath soft flannel sheets that smelled faintly of Christmas. Her chest rose and fell gently, as gently as the flakes outside busy covering the cold earth with a fresh blanket of snow. It was the first significant snowfall in the three weeks since Yu first arrived.

The cabin was a cozy, romantic dwelling, complete with a fireplace, wood-burning stove, Jacuzzi, and a spectacular mountain view. They were deep in the wilderness, far away from society, cell phone towers, and espionage. It was exactly as Tad expected.

He arrived ahead of Yu by two weeks. During that time he purchased numerous supplies for their stay. The massive basement storage freezer was filled to maximum capacity with Ahi tuna, wild-caught salmon, and a variety of meats and vegetables. The pantry shelves were stocked with enough canned goods and grains to survive several seasons. There was no shortage of beverages. Wine, beer, and other spirits were in abundance.

It was a temporary home. A winter retreat where they could live, love, and plan a future together. Immeasurable wealth loomed on the horizon. Tad knew that financial independence was a mere phone call away. He simply needed to finish his business with Bud Craxone. He assured Yu (and himself) that the deal was nearly done.

During their months apart, Tad had become increasingly doubtful of the picture-perfect future the onion painted. Time and again, however, the glass talisman's vision remained unchanged. It appeared that Yu and Tad were destined for happiness, despite Tad's flailing self-confidence. Still, he found himself unable to sleep through the cold winter nights, even with Yu by his side. He typically woke at 3:00 a.m. and sat alone by the fireplace until dawn, cradling the glass onion with desperation.

There was also something different about Yu. It wasn't simply that her hair was significantly shorter. She seemed troubled, but Tad's attempts to broach the subject were met with resistance. Yu was also growing anxious about Tad's increasing indecision to relinquish the onion to Bud Craxone.

"I'm beginning to have my doubts," Yu said, earlier that evening.

"About us?" Tad asked.

"Not about us. About you, and your obsession with that glass ball."

"My only obsession is you. You know that."

"Once upon a time, perhaps. I need to know that you're going to follow through with the plans we've made."

"Of course. You know I will. It's just...it's complicated."

"What is complicated? You have a buyer. Where is the complication?"

"It's not that simple. You know, we're cut off here. No telly. No wireless. It's twenty miles to the nearest payphone in Shankton. Besides, I thought you liked it here."

"Whether I like it here or not isn't the issue."

"What then? What's the issue?" Tad asked.

"Let it go. Stop looking for answers to questions you already know the answer to," Yu said, and turned away.

At 8:00 a.m. Tad made coffee for Yu, who was still sleep. Without a sound he quietly left the cozy cabin and drove to Shankton, keeping one hand on the wheel and one hand on the onion. In his mind's eye, Tad saw what appeared to be a small colored dot. It looked like a balloon being viewed from a faraway shore. A bright, red balloon.

"I think you'll agree that the offer is more than fair," Bud Craxone said.

"It's less, considerably less, than what we previously discussed," Tad said.

"Yes, well, that ship has sailed. Still, if you have other, more agreeable offers on the table..."

Tad's silence was broken only by static on the line.

"Naturally, I'm in negotiations with others. However, I'd prefer dealing with you," he said.

"Of course you would. Understand, Mr. Dewhurst, I'm not a

man who likes to be kept waiting, and you have, I'm sure you'll agree, postponed this exchange for a significant amount of time."

"Any delays have been…necessary."

"Very well," Bud said. "Let's negotiate."

The negotiations were swift. Both men possessed something desperately wanted by the other. Bud had grand designs for the glass onion, while Tad looked forward an $8.5 million bounty and lifelong fiscal freedom. There were details to work out and matters of trust to confront. They agreed to meet on December 1.

Before returning to the secluded cabin he and Yu shared, Tad made several stops. He purchased baguettes, a variety of imported cheeses, and a $125 bottle of ice wine. As he unpacked the goods, he presented Yu with a dozen red roses.

Yu uncorked the wine.

"What is this? What are we celebrating?" she asked.

"This is a precursor. Do you know what that means?"

Yu shook her head.

"A precursor is a sign of things to come. In this case, our life together far from the snow and ice of Colorado. Soon we leave for Europe."

"How soon?"

"Two weeks."

"Two weeks," Yu said, smiling. "You're sure?"

"I'm sure."

They kissed and toasted to their future. Tad closed his eyes as the wine reached his palette. It was sweet, though he couldn't fully shake the image of a colorful red balloon. Tad was convinced it meant something, and that the answer lay within the glass onion. He had 14 days to figure it out.

Horace Finnegan sat quietly in the southeast corner of the Third Street branch of the Miami Public Library. A hard rain continued to sweep across the entire state of Florida as tropical storm Allan crept up the east coast. Horace stared out at the deluge momentarily before returning his attention to Conan-Doyle. It was nearly noon. At 12:15 p.m. Horace was joined at his reading table.

"Hello Bud," he whispered, without looking up.

"How's the leg?" Bud said.

"You know. It's always worse whenever it rains. Fucking

steel rods."

"You fared better than Plimster."

"Plimster's dead."

"Like I said, you fared better than he did."

"Small comfort in that on days like these."

Horace adjusted his eyeglasses and returned to *The Red-headed League*.

"Are you interested in a job?" Bud asked.

"I'm always interested in working for you," Horace said, and continued reading.

Bud reached across the table and closed Horace's book. Agitated, Horace stared across the table.

"You could lose an arm," Horace said, though he spoke with a soft smile.

"I'll keep that in mind. First, you should realize this isn't some Mickey Mouse proposition. You stand to make a considerable amount of money."

"How considerable?"

"Six figures considerable."

"So who's body do I have to break? I'm not a young man anymore you know."

"Nothing like that," Bud said. "This requires more brain than brawn. It's a missing person type of situation, in a manner of speaking."

"In that a person is missing?"

Bud handed Horace an envelope containing a one-page bio and head shot.

"This looks official," Horace said.

"It should. It's straight from the SIS personnel records. The schmuck in the photo is named Tad Dewhurst. Mr. Dewhurst and I have a pending business exchange. I need to know where he's hiding out."

"It's a big planet."

"He's in Colorado in a remote area near Shankton."

"Never heard of it."

"You wouldn't have. Nonetheless, Mr. Dewhurst is there—or in the vicinity. Find out exactly where."

"Not a problem," Horace said.

"You have less than 2 weeks."

"You know me, Bud. We have a history together. I'll find this prick for you, five days tops."

Bud rose from the table and handed an envelope to Horace.

"Always did like your style, Horace. Consider this a down payment. By the way, the league isn't real. It's a red-herring. You'll see."

"Thanks a lot, fucko," Horace said, as Bud walked toward the exit.

In his sixty-three years, Horace Finnegan had seen many cities in the US and abroad. He preferred warm weather climates but was often subjected to cold, wet weather. The combination produced a pain sensation that caused him to limp. On days like these, Horace lamented many of his life decisions. The money was always good, but money in and of itself, he discovered, wasn't the end all on the path to happiness.

Among everything else, Horace valued loyalty. He'd served Bud Craxone for many years and did so gladly. Horace was a contract-man who had worked for many employers, but Bud was like family. He tried to keep this in mind and work past the pain.

On the first day of his arrival in Colorado there was little to do. The majority of the day was consumed at Denver International Airport because the car rental agencies were short on vehicles. Ever persuasive, particularly with a fat wallet in hand, Horace convinced the assistant manager at the Avis kiosk to lend him his personal vehicle. The interior of the '93 Bronco smelled of chewing tobacco, black licorice, and burnt motor oil. By nightfall Horace was still en route to Shankton. He slept in a motel in nearby Elkthrope and awoke the following morning with flea bites on both legs. Horace quickly showered and dressed before continuing his trek to Shankton.

Throughout the day, Horace made numerous inquiries about Tad Dewhurst. It helped that there was little more to Shankton than a handful of retail merchants, all crowded together on what was laughably known by natives as the town's business district. He presented a 3 x 5 head shot of Tad to Allen Kligermann, Shankton's sole barkeep.

"I seen him here a few days ago, yeah," Kligermann said. "Instant dislike. Fucking limey comes in here and uses the payphone in the back of the room. Then he asks me if I sell Boddington's."

"I'm guessing you don't."

"Fuck that lager shit. You're looking for this guy?"

"You could say that. Know where he's residing?"

"Maybe, but I'm not exactly the fucking American Red Cross, if you catch my drift."

Horace slid a bill across the bar to Kligermann. He held the currency toward the light and checked its watermark.

"Hundred bucks," he said, and pocketed the money. "Shit. For a hundred bucks I'll draw you a goddam map or drive you there myself."

Once upon a time Tad Dewhurst found solace not in a glass bottle but in an onion of glass. It was simple; he merely held the object in his hands and saw his heart's desire become reality. He and Yu and a lifetime of happiness. The visions helped Tad to overcome deep-seated insecurities and trust issues that tended to grip his heart like a drowning man clinging to driftwood. His psyche was soothed by onion's comforting imagery.

Then the red balloon had appeared.

It began as little more than a dot, a blemish on an otherwise Kodak-perfect photo. The red balloon dangled atop the onion's visions, distant but gradually floating closer and taking on greater prominence. He didn't understand its significance and was powerless to control the balloon. Before long there were many balloons of various sizes. Each bright red, each as abstract in meaning as its predecessor.

Tad struggled with this in the days leading to his exchange with Bud Craxone. The balloon imagery was, he ultimately reasoned, symbolic of the freedom he and Yu would soon celebrate. There was one other explanation, but Tad pushed it far away from his mind.

Like most of the men and women in his profession, Tad Dewhurst was possessed of an uncanny attention to detail, even in the remote wilderness. Certain sounds and scents were specific to the woods surrounding the cabin. The cracking of snow from a trio of deer that appeared daily just prior to dawn. The claws of a raccoon struggling against the cabin's cedar shingles. The lingering scent of cooked Italian sausage from a faraway campsite. The position of the moon and its effect on the shadows it cast. The rhythmic tapping of the woodpecker that dwelled in the oak tree adjacent to the cabin's kitchen. The tap-tap of pine cones that smacked against glass windows on windy evenings. Within a few days Tad knew every sound, sight, and smell that belonged in the woods.

And which didn't.

He placed the glass onion in its protective wooden box and stepped across the dark room toward the back door. Tad glanced at the red light of the microwave's clock which read 2:23 and he laced his shoestrings. Before stepping outside he retrieved a small handgun from a kitchen drawer.

The moon was mostly lost to clouds but Tad's vision had already adjusted to the darkness. He treaded lightly atop the bed of snow without a sound, unlike the SUV parked in the distance. Tad was aware of the vehicle's presence before he saw it. The cracking of frozen snow beneath its massive tires was sufficient to rouse suspicion. Tad continued to silently advance upon his prey, guided by the smell of engine oil and cigarettes.

Within the confines of his vehicle, Horace Finnegan maintained a silent vigil. The map given to him earlier was accurate insofar as it brought him to a remote cabin. Horace was determined to report Tad's location to Bud but he'd yet to make a positive ID. The most he'd seen was the slender form of Yu several hours earlier before the lights in the cabin went dark. Still jetlagged, he struggled to overcome exhaustion with nicotine, Advil, and a large thermos of black coffee that was lukewarm at best. He needed a hot bath, a soft bed, and hard liquor.

Horace closed his eyes for a brief moment and passed a hand atop his thin hair, which he combed across his head from left to right. The air felt momentarily chill. Horace opened his eyes, suddenly aware that he was no longer alone.

"Ta, gov," Tad said, sitting comfortably in the passenger seat of the SUV. "Smells a bit ripe in here."

Horace made a grab for the .38 in his coat pocket but quickly reconsidered as the cold steel of Tad's weapon pressed tightly against his neck.

"You don't mind do you?" Tad said, and snagged a cigarette from Horace.

"Help yourself, Mr. Dewhurst."

"You see," Tad said lighting up, "this is a problem. I mean, you obviously know me yet I have no idea who you are."

"You seem clever enough. I'm sure you can use your big British brain to arrive at an answer," Horace said.

"Indeed. We can rule out British Intelligence. You haven't the accent, physique, grooming, or intelligence. We can also rule out domestic agencies for the aforementioned reasons. From the look of your hands, you've spent a considerable number of years engaged in physical labor, poor sodding bastard. A bit on the brawny side, and you're packing heat. Whose payroll you on then?"

"Fuck off, limey bastard," Horace managed.

"Okay. Okay, I can appreciate that. You've been found out and you're embarrassed. I'm embarrassed for you, old boy. It happens though. The question is, what do we do about it?"

Horace offered no answer.

"Here's one potential scenario: We step outside the cozy confines of your vehicle. We walk several hundred yards to the east where I kill you execution style. I'd prefer an outcome that's a bit less violent, perhaps one in which you're still breathing. Though to be perfectly honest, it's not a priority for me—I think the 'limey bastard' comment is sinking into my big British brain."

"Do your worst, or at least try. You're soft."

"Really."

"Really. Too many years spent stuffing your face. A disgrace, even by UK standards."

"Doubtless you're here on behalf of Bud Craxone."

Horace remained silent, but was betrayed by an involuntary facial twitch.

"It makes little difference what you know," he said.

"I'm glad you feel that way," Tad said. "I think it means Bud had better sweeten his offer again."

"Are you familiar with the phrase 'stand and deliver'?"

"Some kind of sexual fetish?"

"Not even close."

Tad confiscated Horace's weapons—three handguns, a switchblade, a sawed-off shotgun, and a stun gun—as well as his wallet and cell phone.

"You're a dead man, Mr. Dewhurst."

"The rumors of my death are highly exaggerated. I want you to give a message to your employer. Think you can do that?"

"I'll consider it."

"Good man."

Minutes later, as snow began to fall, Tad watched Horace back the SUV up and then slowly pull away. He walked back toward the cabin and stepped inside. Tad placed Horace's former belongings on the kitchen counter and stepped into the living room. Smoldering fireplace embers cast a light crimson glow throughout the room.

"You're awake," he said to Yu, who sat in a lounge chair with her back to Tad. "Is everything okay?"

"Yes," she said softly.

Tad stepped around to face her.

"What are you doing?" he asked.

She returned the glass onion to its protective casing.

"Looking for answers. Just like you."

"What sort of answers did you find? Did you see the red balloons?"

"No. I didn't see any balloons, red or otherwise."

"Doesn't matter. There's been a change in plan."

"What do you mean?"

"I think Bud Craxone is or was planning a double-cross."

"A disloyal Mafioso arms dealer. Who'd have thought?"

"It's okay. The business will still be sorted out in the end. What did the onion show you?"

Yu was silent, and she turned away.

Tad removed the object hastily from its box and closed his eyes. A strange dizziness overtook Tad as he stared past the wall of red balloons that had clouded his vision of events to come. He felt like a small boy peaking behind a velvet curtain that was reserved for adults committing adult activities.

After a few minutes his eyes opened. The caterpillar's cocoon that had been Tad's world was no more. In its wake was brilliant, butterfly awareness.

"This is how it's always been?" he asked.

"No," Yu said. "Not always."

"You know, years ago when I agreed to this assignment the Ministry conducted an orientation outlining the dangers of relationships. It all sounded too Ian Fleming to me but attendance was mandatory. The topic of Lesson 24 was personal relationships, which the Ministry frowns upon. Do you know why the Ministry doesn't encourage its agents to develop close personal relationships in the field?"

"No," Yu said softly.

"Apparently working in the field for a lengthy period of time can have a profound effect on the psyche. An otherwise competent operative can easily lose objectivity and fail to see obvious red flags, Yu. Christ. Is Yu even your real name?"

"Yes."

"All this time, you've played me. Goddammit."

"It's not like that," she said. "If it was, I'd have taken the glass onion long ago. We both know there were many opportunities."

"Months ago you, when you first stared into it, you lead me to believe that we shared the same vision. A vision of this cabin, of us, together. Together for the long term. That was all fabrication, wasn't it?"

"Nothing is as black and white as you're choosing to paint it," Yu said.

"Tell me. Paint a canvas for me using your most elaborate color palette."

"I wasn't certain of any of this until now. You yourself saw the vision of what's to come."

"All this time. All this time."

"As a self-involved opportunist, I wouldn't expect you to understand this, but my loyalties to the state surpass whatever feelings I have for you. For a time I had forgotten my place within the People's Republic. I let my heart lead me here on this fanciful whim of yours and the promise of a dream that would never be fulfilled."

"What are you talking about?"

"Don't act so glib. We both know that you have no intention of selling the glass onion to Bud Craxone or to anyone else. You own it. Rather, it owns you."

"That's absurd."

"Is it? I've lost count of the number of nights you've sat lying awake, fingers pressed against that glass orb just as you're doing now. You've forgotten how to function, little Gollum, how to be a man. Your life is little more than a phantom existence based on false visions assembled by your own tormented will."

"And you, the good little Communist, I suppose you stand to receive the hero's welcome for delivering this valuable prize to your commanders."

"In matters of state there's little use for such personal glory;

you'd know this if you were a better agent and a better listener. What matters, all that matters, is that my actions are harmonious with my country. You tried to lead me astray of this, to choose a personal indulgence over obligation to the state. Again, I don't expect you to understand. Your loyalty is limited to the nation of Tad Dewhurst."

"My loyalty *was* to us."

"You must understand," Yu said with matter-of-fact objectivity and took aim at Tad's forehead, "that this is not a personal attack upon you. The glass onion is far more important than the emotional attachments of two, or even two-hundred, souls."

"What are you going to do, kill me?" Tad asked, smiling.

"You're going to place the glass onion on the floor and you're going to walk to the corner of the room where you will face the wall. I'd prefer not to shoot you, but I won't allow you to compromise my objective."

"Have it your way."

Tad leaned down and placed the glass onion on the cabin's hardwood floor as instructed. He rose, slowly then dove unexpectedly in Yu's direction. She fired wildly, six clips in half as many seconds, and was knocked to the ground. She felt his warm blood against her arms but Tad was still very much alive.

He wrenched the weapon from her hands and clenched its barrel. Tad's attack was savage and swift. The metal handle shattered bone and teeth. Yu was unconscious within seconds, but the thrashing continued for long minutes.

He howled, heartbroken and enraged beyond comprehension. Tad felt sickened by his actions even as he continued to hammer at Yu's flesh. Suddenly he felt a strange déjà vu as the world seemed to slow to half-speed. He watched as dozens of droplets of blood floated across the air. Different shapes and sizes, they nonetheless floated in shimmering crimson backlit by glowing fireplace embers. So much red, like a balloon-filled sky. Tad felt euphoric as he blacked out.

Consciousness returned within minutes and Tad staggered to his feet. Yu was unrecognizable. Her cold body was as devoid of color as it was of life. The gun was still pressed against his right hand, adhered by a layer of drying blood. He threw the weapon to the floor and retrieved the glass onion.

Tad coughed, suddenly aware of the hole in his stomach. He

pressed his left hand against the wound and felt the warm, sticky wetness. He was determined not to bleed to death. For a brief moment he stared at the glass onion, but the tell-all talisman offered no answers.

It was snowing heavily. An inch of fresh powder lay atop the walk. He staggered toward his vehicle but stumbled to the ground. Tad protected the glass onion with both hands. His keys skidded across a foot-deep mound of snow and vanished. He searched on all fours, digging and clawing through the frozen landscape, but was unable to find the key ring. The pure white snow was soon stained red.

"God-fucking-dammit!" he said, and fell backward in exhaustion.

Tad momentarily regained his stamina and rose to his feet. He stumbled along, determined to reach the main road where he was certain he'd find help. But there was no moon to guide him. The storm reduced visibility to near zero, and Tad was nearing blood-loss-induced shock. His sense of direction was gone, and he staggered deeper into the wild.

When he became too weak to walk, Tad crawled.

Eventually he stopped to rest against a massive pine tree. Tad's hands were frostbitten and numb. There was no warmth to be found, though he continued clinging to the glass onion in hopes it would offer a respite from his worsening dilemma. There was, however, only blackness.

They arrived at dawn with little regard for stealth. A small fleet of jeeps flanked by a snowmobile piloted by Bud Craxone. His face was strained and tired, a combination of jet-lag and chemotherapy. The crew of twenty included Horace Finnegan, who ignored the pain in his leg as he stepped out of his vehicle and stared at the falling snow with disgust.

The men gathered around Bud like football players in a huddle.

"Two targets. One male, one female. I don't care who you take out, but I don't want any random firing. The object I'm seeking is useless if it's shattered into a thousand glass fragments."

Bud placed a foam plug into each ear.

"Can't stand the sound of gunfire," he said. "Take careful aim. Preferably head shots; more reliable than a hit to the torso. Go."

The men surrounded the cabin and rushed the doors. Bud anxiously waited for the inevitable explosion of gunfire.

And waited.

After a few minutes one of the men signaled him. Bud trod through the snow and entered the cabin via its front door.

"Jesus Christ," Bud said, and stepped toward Yu's body. "I didn't know the limey had it in him."

"Love can bring out hidden qualities in a man," Horace said.

Bud stared at the gun, caked with dry blood and flesh.

"Like this? So this is love," Bud said.

"I'm not talking about the love between two people."

"No. No, I don't suppose you are."

In the hours that followed, Bud's crew performed a meticulous inspection of the cabin. They looked in drawers and on shelves. Beneath beds and behind furniture. Paneling was torn from walls in hopes of discovering a hidden vault. And of course Yu's body was searched. There was no sign of Tad Dewhurst aside from a faint trail of blood that ended at the cabin's back door. Horace and Bud stepped outside.

"Vehicle hasn't been moved," Horace said. "Maybe he walked outta here. Wouldn't have gotten far without medical attention."

"Astute observation," Bud said. "Rally the boys, won't you?"

Within minutes, Bud's hired hands began scouring the woods. In many areas the snow, which continued to fall, was knee deep. After an hour, the crew returned with little more than fatigue to show for their labors.

"I appreciate your efforts. As always, you can expect to be well compensated. If you're cold, I suggest you stand by the fire for a while before we pack up."

One of the gunmen, a short, round fellow with glasses and a thick red beard, looked side to side.

"Um, excuse me, Mr. Craxone," he said. "What fire?"

Bud glanced at Horace who stood in the main doorway of the cabin. He lit a match and dropped it on a gasoline soaked floor then stepped away as a twenty-foot wall of flame ignited behind him.

"As I was saying," Bud said.

23   Miami, March 1998: Bud and Casi

Barefoot and draped in soft linens, Casi and Bud walked hand in hand across the warm Miami sand. The air was light and the ocean mist unusually mild. They eyed a trio of school-age children who ran along the distant shoreline chasing gulls and singing songs.

"Do you remember a time when life was carefree?" Casi asked.

"Once," Bud said, "a long time ago."

"Tell me."

"It was a glorious moment. I was ten years old. My parents lived in a two-story duplex in Columbus with an attic that they converted into a rumpus room for me and my friends."

"That's a silly word," Casi said.

"What is?"

"Rumpus room."

"It's quite new to the English language, actually, and dates back only to 1939. Whereas rumpus has been around for several centuries."

"Always the master of minutia. What sort of rumpusing did you and your friends do in this room of yours?"

"We hung out, trading baseball cards and listening to *Dragnet* or *True Stories of the FBI*. The offerings were slim because the radio-drama was dying its slow death."

Bud tried to stop the words from spilling out, but it was too late.

"I'm sorry," he said.

"You didn't do anything wrong. There's no need to apologize."

"There was an opportunity and I let it slip away. In hindsight, I shouldn't have sent Horace. It was a job for someone younger; Kanada perhaps."

"Horace is a good man, and a good friend."

"True. But he's old and his reflexes have slowed."

"Sweetie, we're all old," Casi said.

"Too true."

They walked in silence for a while.

"I am sorry," Bud said, clasping Casi's hand a bit tighter. "It's goddam criminal.

"I so desperately wanted to see the future. Turns out I didn't need to. Anyway, you've done quite well with the chemo treatments. Hopefully I'll be as fortunate."

"You will."

"We'll see."

"It's still out there somewhere."

"A tiny glass ball on a big blue marble," Casi said, humming softly. "Perhaps some squirrels are getting the inside scoop on an acorn harvest."

"Let's go home," Bud said.

The couple walked toward their beachfront property, kicking sand and humming songs like children. Carefree, if only for the moment.

24   April 5, 1986: A Toast

On the evening after being introduced to Ronald Reagan, operatives Otis Oppenheimer, Billings Smith, and Key Reilly met at the Centre Bar on F Street in Georgetown. It was a loud, one-room dive crammed with college-agers enchanted by Depeche Mode, The Cure, and any other flavor-of-the-month British pop band specializing in songs about teen angst. The agents found a corner booth and purchased several bottles. They drank heavily in celebration of their new appointment and good fortune. As the spirits flowed and the evening wore on, Otis, who consumed the least alcohol, seemed mired in depression.

"Whassup, Oppy? You're positively morose?" Reilly asked.

"Did you notice what he did? Rather, what he *didn't* do?" Otis said.

"What *who* didn't do?" Smith asked.

"The old man. The Commander-in-Chief. El Presidente."

"What the fuck are you talking about?"

"It's a simple question," Otis said.

"No. I mean, I guess not. What *didn't* he do?"

"Look back."

Billings and Key looked over their shoulders.

"No. I mean he—Reagan—never looked back. He committed us to this project. He smiled and waved and walked toward the White House parlor doors and never looked back. Not once."

"He waved? I don't remember that."

"Maybe he didn't wave. But he didn't look back, either. You don't find that a bit unsettling?"

"So the man doesn't like to turn a shoulder. Maybe he's got arthritis. What's the problem?"

"It's not natural; not given the situation."

"You think it's a bad omen?" Billings asked.

"It leaves me feeling skeptical is all," Otis said, shaking his head.

"You're overanalyzing," Key said. "You probably think Oswald didn't act alone in Dallas."

Billings and Key toasted to the memory of JFK.

"We've been given an impossible assignment," Otis said. "Do either of you realize the enormity of what we've been tasked to do?"

"Job security," Reilly said. "And speaking of which…"

He retrieved two white circular pills from a small bottle kept in his inner jacket pocket.

"Listen, Otis, I don't think any of us doubt the vastness of this assignment. Like any other job, it is what it is. You do it and use whatever means necessary to keep your sanity. Case in point," Reilly said, popping the pills into his mouth and downing them with a glass of scotch.

"You should go easy with that shit," Otis said.

"Yeah, and you shouldn't worry so much about whether a senile actor-turned- US President looks backward before entering a building. Christ."

25 March 1, 1988: Otis and Emma – An Awkward Pause

The early years of the US Glass Onion initiative were turbulent, confusing times for all involved in the project. Although twelve staff agents were recruited, the Reagan administration granted the team sufficient funding to accelerate the retrieval by recruiting up to two-hundred freelance operatives to search for the elusive treasured object.

Otis Oppenheimer was initially assigned to the DC-Metro area and spent much of his time at a satellite office in Alexandria. It was located on the second floor of a crowded, awkward building fronted as an office-supply shop that offered a single variety of rubber band, manufactured in India and packaged and sold in bundles of 50,000. Alexandria Rubber Band Supply's only customer was a 75-year-old man from Herndon named Beaumont Blevins. Beaumont was obsessed with constructing the world's largest rubber-band ball. His monthly transaction, which he conducted between noon and 12:30 p.m. on the first Monday of each month, consisted of a single box of rubber bands. The fanatical senior stood at the counter on March 1, 1988, and scraped through his wallet oblivious to Otis, who entered the shop and quickly vanished into a back room marked "private."

Otis passed through the security door and completed the required voice, retina, fingerprint, and DNA scans. He walked to the second floor and stumbled into the crowded office of Emma Johanson.

"If I ever get like that," Otis said, "promise you'll put two bullets into me."

"Like what?" Emma Johanson asked.

"The rubber-band enthusiast is here."

"Mr. Blevins?" Emma said with a note of sadness.

"What's wrong?"

"Did you know he's dying from advanced throat cancer? Never once smoked."

"Do you know him?"

"No."

"Then how do you...oh, the psychic thing. May I ask you a question?"

"It varies," Emma said.

"It varies?"

"You were about to ask me what it's like to be like me. It varies. Everyone radiates a different vibe. Beaumont Blevins, the old man downstairs, transmits an unusually strong signal."

"So it's like you're a radio and everyone on the planet emits a unique wave?"

"Not quite. And not everyone; very few, actually."

"You ever read me?"

"No. You're blocked."

"What do you mean blocked?"

"To use your radio wave analogy, I've blocked certain signals from entering my mind. Yours. Denton's."

"You can do that?"

"Mostly. Yeah."

"How did you know what I was going to ask you?"

"An educated guess. It's the same question that everyone asks me sooner or later."

"I guess I'm a bit predictable," Otis said. "Um, what's with all the boxes? You moving?"

"Nothing like that. Ever since your team started outsourcing its search efforts I've been inundated with onions of glass."

"Isn't that a good thing?"

"You'd think so. But no, Otis, it's not good at all. Your boss, Denton Chambers, is having all this shit shipped to me for psychic analysis. I'm not a machine."

"What exactly do you do?"

"What do I do?"

"I'm not being a smart ass; I honestly don't understand what you do."

"No, it's a fair question. I guess I try to find answers where there are no obvious answers. It's my sad task to determine which, if any, of the glass onions contained in these hundred-plus boxes is the genuine artifact."

"How do you make that determination?" Otis asked.

"I'll show you. Hand me one of the boxes."

"Which one?"

"Doesn't matter."

Otis pulled a package at random from the shelf. Moments later, the box unpacked, Emma held a glass onion in her hands.

"Are you going to close your eyes?" Otis asked.

"Why would I close my eyes?"

"Isn't that, um, what psychics typically do? You close your eyes and have some sort of clairvoyant experience?"

"That's complete Hollywood-grade bullshit."

"Do you need me to sit perfectly still and stuff?"

"No. Just kick back."

Several minutes passed during which neither Emma nor Otis spoke. He spent this time studying the boxes, the smallest of which was a palm-sized jewelry container and the largest of which was a sizeable suitcase. The majority of the packages contained US postal cancellations though Otis noticed several boxes with international postmarks.

"This particular object," Emma said, "has an interesting history, though it's clearly neither a glass onion nor the prize we're seeking. The glass was hand-blown in Louisville two summers ago at a Renaissance fair and given to a woman named Joan Waul in lieu of an engagement ring."

"Serious?"

"Ring phobia. There's probably a term for that in DSM-III; not sure. Anyway, the offering didn't go over well, and the engagement ended suddenly when Joan professed her love for another woman."

"Renaissance fairs and lesbians," Otis said. "Typical."

"Enjoy," Emma said, and tossed the glass object to Otis. "Anyway, that was a rather easy analysis. Most reads are more involved and can take days, or weeks, to assess. There's usually a considerable amount of resultant mental fatigue as well."

"That sucks."

"Can't be helped," Emma said.

"You feel like grabbing some lunch?" Otis asked.

"It's like you're reading my mind," she said, smiling.

"From a fundamental perspective, the glass onion initiative was flawed from its onset," Emma said, and sipped the remains of a tall Long Island iced tea.

Their table was a crowded mass of plates and glasses. Otis signaled the waitress and she promptly returned with fresh drinks in hand.

"Flawed how?" Otis asked.

"Well, think about it. Reagan green-lit this multi-million-dollar project after consulting with Julian Copeland. Copeland has been the Presidential spiritual advisor for many, many years."

"Is there a 'but' to this?"

"But, in the world of legitimate psychic science, Julian's a flake. She's a hack."

"Has anyone told the Reagans?"

"It's not that simple. You don't just walk up to Ronald Reagan and verbally bitch-slap a psychic they love and revere. Not to say it's never been tried. A year ago, give or take, Amelio Kirkpatrick, an auditor with the Treasury Department, provided the Reagans with a 48-page report outlining Copeland's financial dealings. These ranged from questionable to outright fraudulent. Shortly after delivering his report to the President and First Lady, Amelio was transferred to an overseas office."

"That doesn't sound so bad."

"In the Congo."

"Oh."

"Trust me," Emma said, "There are roads you don't want to travel."

"But how did she, Copeland I mean, get in so tight with the Oval Office?"

"A wealthy republican upbringing helped. She worked briefly as a motivational speaker and spring-boarded into the spiritual arts. Anyway, I have it on good authority that she's a fraud."

"Your source?"

Emma stared at Otis without answering.

"Oh," he said.

"I met her while working security at a White House gala where we exchanged a handshake. In that brief moment I learned that she flunked out of community college in year one, had been divorced five times, abused cocaine daily, and lacked anything resembling a conscience much less precognition."

"All that from a handshake," Otis said.

"Yup. It's my blessing and curse."

"I've always wanted to ask this. Could you give me a demo?" Otis said, extending his right hand across the table.

"Otis."

"I know earlier you said that you've blocked me and all."

"Better let's not travel this road."

"How bad could it be?"

Emma eyed Otis suspiciously.

"Your hand isn't covered in something sticky is it?"

"No."

"No hidden joy-buzzers?"

"No. No tricks."

"Really, I'd rather not." Otis did not move his hand or alter his gaze.

Reluctantly Emma leaned forward and grasped Otis' hand. A moment later her head began to bob uncontrollably and her body trembled in spasm. Otis released his grip.

"Are you okay?" He asked with genuine concern.

"Sure," Emma said, smiling. "Just messing with you is all."

"Fuck."

"Shall I tell you what dark and dirty random secrets I've learned about you?"

"Enlighten me."

"When you were seven years old you snuck underneath the porch and tried to burn down your house. Your favorite TV shows are *Room 222* and *Mary Hartman, Mary Hartman*. You idolize Truman Capote and secretly long to be a journalist. Your wife…"

"I'm not married," Otis said. "But you already knew that."

Emma was silent.

"Oh. You're talking about the future, aren't you? Emma, what about my wife? Tell me what you've seen."

Otis grabbed Emma's hands.

"Tell me what you've seen; please."

"Your wife. She's…she's beautiful. That's all I know."

Otis released his hold on Emma.

"Sorry. It's just that…it sounded so ominous. I've had…relationship issues. The work doesn't bode well for long-term companionship," he said.

"I understand," Emma said, and quietly sipped her drink.

She averted Otis' gaze for a few moments and an awkward silence developed.

"I should probably get back to the office," Emma finally said and reached for the check.

"I'll take that," Otis said.

"No. I insist."

She placed two crisp fifty-dollar bills on the table and stood up.

"Don't worry about anything I told you," Emma said. "Seriously."

"What's to worry? I have a beautiful wife in my future."

"That's right. A beautiful wife."

Emma and Otis parted ways as a light afternoon rain began to blanket the streets of Washington.

26   September 13, 1993: Elise

Mickey Solomon had a ten-second head start. It wasn't much, but Mickey was a fast sprinter. He also knew the neighborhood better than most, certainly better than Otis Oppenheimer. Still, ten seconds wasn't much, and Mickey knew that men like Otis were skilled in the art of pursuit.

He darted across two lanes of traffic toward Fifteenth Street and Hacksway, twisting and turning like a marionette, moving in whatever way it took to keep from wiping out on the rain-soaked streets. He knew better than to look back. The echo of Otis' heels on the concrete sidewalk was a grim reminder that the ten-second gap was closing.

The elderly couple leaving Mason's Pharmacy never stood a chance. They fumbled with an umbrella as Mickey turned the corner and uprooted them with the force of a raging bull. Mickey skidded to the ground and tore the denim of his jeans and the skin of his right knee. Two seconds later he was on his feet. But Otis was two seconds closer. Otis glanced at the confused elderly couple and continued to pursue Solomon. He took little joy in chasing Mickey, but it needed to be done.

Eventually Mickey began to gain the advantage. Years of cigarettes and alcohol use were taking a toll on Otis. He continued to give chase, but his intensity waned. Mickey turned left into a cavernous alley on Southampton that he knew well. He smiled, confident that freedom was moments away. From prior experience, he knew it was a simple matter to grab the bottom-most rung of the fire escape ladder. He would then climb to the roof and sprint to the opposite end of the building. After losing Otis, Mickey would quickly double-back to the bar, grab his belongings, and leave town for a few days.

The escape plan had one flaw: the fire escape ladder had been raised and was beyond his grasp. By the time he realized this, Mickey was too far into the alley to back out. As Otis' shadow fell atop Mickey, the con man's smile was quickly replaced with dread.

"Nowhere to go," Otis said, breathless. "You son of a bitch."

"I'm sorry," Mickey said. "You know how it is."

"I know how it is? This is Armani," Otis said, and removed his jacket. "It's ruined."

He dropped the jacket to the ground, wiped the rain from his brow, and rolled up his shirtsleeves.

"Tell me how it is," he said. "Tell me."

Mickey tried to answer, but Otis dealt a blow to his thorax that sent him reeling. He fell backward onto the pavement.

"I always wondered, how does this guy do it?" Otis said. "Twenty-two-year-old high-school dropout. How is he so well connected that he's able to provide me with solid leads?"

"Otis, I—"

"Shut up. I mean, I work for the nation's leading intelligence network and can't generate leads like these. So how is it that a guy like Mickey Solomon—an uneducated weasel like Mickey Solomon who spends his hours pouring drinks for low-life scumbags—pulls this off? We both know the answer to that question, right Mickey?"

Mickey tried to stand but Otis kicked him in the chest. And when Mickey cried out, Otis kicked him a second time.

"How many months have I spent following bogus leads because I believed that you actually had some inside connection to all of this? I don't like being made the fool."

"Occupational hazard," Mickey managed.

"So is this," Otis said.

He kicked at Mickey a third time, but the con-man grabbed hold of Otis' leg and pulled forward. Otis stumbled clumsily and fell to the ground. He felt something snap. Mickey staggered to his feet and scurried away. Otis quickly regained his composure but his right leg could no longer bear weight. He hopped out of the alley and swore. There was of course, no sign of Mickey. If he was smart, there never would be again.

Otis pressed his back against the front door of a nearby row home and sank to the stoop. The rain continued its deluge as Otis discovered his cell phone was no longer functional.

"Goddammit," he said and stared at the worthless device as a shadow fell slowly across him.

"You don't look like the homeless guy who usually crashes here," Elise said.

Otis glanced at the stranger standing above him. She wore orange and green Asics cross-trainers. Baggy sweatpants and a green anorak rendered her shapeless. Her face was partially buried beneath the hood of the jacket and was somewhat lost to shadow. Her full lips reflected against the streetlamps and a lock of shoulder-length hair revealed itself.

"I'm not homeless," Otis answered.

"I didn't think you were. Nonetheless, you're blocking my entry."

"Name's Otis, not nonetheless, although that would be a creative parental choice. If you can help me to stand, I'll be out of your way."

"You're obviously hurt, Otis. At least come in out of the rain and rest a while."

"No rest for the wicked, but perhaps I can use a phone. What's your name?"

"Perhaps," Elise said, and extended a hand in Otis' direction. Otis smiled a wide smile that wasn't at all dampened by the pain or the weather.

It was an unusual beginning, but it was a beginning nonetheless.

Otis and Elise were married in July 1994 at a private ceremony in Washington, DC. The reception which followed was an intimate affair. Those in attendance included several of Otis' GO colleagues—Denton Chambers, Billings Smith, Key Reilly, and Brad Calloway. They stood close together huddled at the bar. Emma Johanson was also there, alone and adorned in a stylish black and orange Donna Karin ankle-length dress and a sad expression that Key's clumsy jokes and a second Long Island couldn't shake.

It was an unorthodox homecoming for the members of the GO team whose days and months were typically spent alone in search of an elusive glass prize. Otis approached the bar but was sidetracked by Denton Chambers.

"Congratulations, Otis. She's one hell of a beautiful woman," Denton said, as they retreated to a quiet corner.

"Thanks. I'm glad you could attend."

"Wouldn't have missed it. How confident are you regarding your alias?"

"Right to business then."

"It isn't like that. You know the agency's policy on interpersonal relationships," Denton said.

"Section 23, paragraph 9. I've also passed the aliasing certification course."

"Look, it's—"

"Twice."

"Otis, it's no big deal if she learns you're with the agency; just be sure not to divulge specifics. She cleared all background screens with flying colors."

Otis sighed and looked at the ground.

"Don't act hurt. You know that everyone undergoes screening; it's my job."

They stood in silence for a moment.

"I know you're only doing your job," Otis said. "But you might have picked a more appropriate venue during which to wax poetic about office protocol. Excuse me."

Otis walked back to the bar. He ordered tequila and lit a cigarette.

"You okay?" Emma asked quietly.

"I'm okay. Anyway, you were right," Otis said.

"I was right? What was I right about?"

"You made a prediction."

"I don't make predictions. Fraudulent TV psychics make predictions. I have visions of what's to come."

"Not trying to insult your profession. Five years ago you told me I'd have a beautiful wife. And here we are today, and there's Elise; my beautiful wife."

"That's right."

"So sullen. What's going on?"

"You should seriously consider transferring to another assignment."

"Is that your personal or professional opinion, Emma?"

"A pinnacle moment in Dickens' *A Christmas Carol* occurs when the Spirit of Christmas Present looks at Tiny Tim's chair and warns of the boy's impending death. 'I see an empty chair if these shadows remain unchanged.'"

"What are you telling me?"

"You're seven years into this assignment. Seven years. It's going to chew you up and spit you out. You, all of you, the plural you, but especially you, Otis, the nice guy with the beautiful wife. You need to walk away from it."

"Doesn't work that way; you know that. How long before the

plug is pulled on Glass Onion?"

"Look, a lot of the visions are blurry. This assignment is going to continue for a long time. It'll consume Key first; it bodes poorly for Billings also. Lots more civilian casualties. There's going to be considerable physical and emotional fallout; none of you are immune."

"Immunity is easier to procure than you might imagine," Otis said, and tipped his glass.

Toward the end of the evening, Otis and Elise bade good evening to their family and friends. It was a short drive to Dulles International. They boarded a red-eye bound for Hawaii and slept on the flight. Their time on the island of Maui passed slowly. For Otis the world of spies and espionage was replaced by sun, sand, snorkeling, and Elise's smile.

On the final morning of their getaway, Elise and Otis awoke early and walked to the beach. They sat on the sand close to the water and waited for the sun to rise over the Pacific.

"You look so downtrodden," she said. "Like you've lost your best friend."

"No. Nothing like that. Not looking forward to returning to DC."

"We'll come back to the islands."

"I know."

"Besides, aren't you looking forward to your upcoming tour?"

"My tour? Oh, right; I forgot."

More than anything, Otis regretted not being upfront with Elise at the onset. His own personal paradox was that he hated lying, but was unable to be completely honest with Elise. As far as she and the rest of the public were concerned, Otis was a moderately successful criminology writer and historian who guest lectured at colleges nationwide. It was a sleek cover. The agency maintained its own printing division and a small collection of ghost writers who penned the works that others would claim as their own. Otis knew that he wasn't the first field operative to be handed a writer's life, though the knowledge offered little consolation to the troubled agent.

"There are worse jobs," Elise said, as the sun began to reveal its hidden face.

"Yeah, I suppose there are. I suppose so," Otis said.

27   January 26, 2009: The Long Day

The bottom of the glass coffee pot was lined with a burn circle. Otis poured the last of the liquid into a ceramic mug but found it undrinkable. He'd been up all night and was desperate for caffeine and sleep, though neither seemed possible. Like the Italian Market merchants who, a few blocks to the west, readied their shops for the restaurant sous chefs in search of the best produce, fish, cheese, and meat, Otis had much to do.

He fumbled through the apartment, stepped into the bathroom, and ran hot water. The vanity was cluttered with perfume bottles, lipstick tubes, and hair brushes. Otis found a toothbrush and saturated it with liquid soap. He scrubbed beneath his nails with practiced skill. The red crust slowly began to fragment and wash away. He hadn't expected there would be so much blood.

Otis stared at himself in the mirror, barely recognizing the reflection that stared back. He looked ancient. A tired, sad man trapped on a high-wire with no visible means of escape and no safety net on which to rely.

"Little matter," he said, and phoned for a clean-up crew.

He hadn't intended to kill Mickey Solomon. The bitterness he felt toward Mickey had subsided over the years. If anything, he felt strangely in Mickey's debt—without Mickey, Otis and Elise would likely have never met.

But it had been a particularly difficult week. The agency was abuzz with news of a massive influx of federal money allocated to the GO Project. Any thoughts that GO would be going away, or that Otis would be reassigned, were crushed following an interoffice memo from Denton Chambers received only days earlier. The project was securely funded through December 2020.

Otis arrived at 829 South Second Street following a tip from a street vendor he knew and trusted. He was restless and hoped that an evening of poker would help alleviate the tedium. Otis was taken aback when the loft door opened and he stood face to face with Mickey Solomon. For a brief moment Mickey stood and tried to place Otis. Hindered by years of narcotics abuse, Mickey's mind slowly processed events from his past.

He suddenly realized that Jack the Ripper had returned. Mickey shoved the door closed, his pulse racing with fright. His efforts were fruitless and Otis easily pushed forward. Once inside, he turned the deadbolt. They were three flights up with nowhere to go.

"You looking for a card game, mister?" Mickey asked, feigning ignorance of his unanticipated guest.

"Not a very good poker face, Mickey. Not very good at all."

Otis walked across the floor to a back room where six men, all white and all in their mid-twenties, eyed him suspiciously.

"Game's over," Otis said quietly. "You boys go on home now."

A beefy man with buzz-cut hair and a dark complexion placed his playing hand face down on the table and stood up.

"Good man," Otis said.

"I ain't leaving. You are."

He lunged at Otis with outstretched arms. A simple tripping move knocked the adversary off balance. As he stumbled forward, Otis grabbed the man's right arm at the wrist and bicep. A soft popping sound was immediately followed by shrieks of pain.

"Unless anyone else would prefer a dislocated humerus, I suggest you men leave now," Otis said. "And take this crybaby with you."

They scurried away like rats and dragged along their wounded companion.

"Just the two of us now," Otis said and smiled.

"What do you want?" Mickey asked.

"It's been a long time," Otis said. Fifteen, almost sixteen years. To be perfectly honest, I never thought I'd see you again. Can't say that I wanted to."

"Yeah, well, the feeling's mutual."

"Listen to me. What happened before is ancient history. Now what say we sit down at this table, pour some drinks, and play a bit of five-card draw."

"You're serious," Mickey said.

"Yes," Otis said, grinning. "Now sit down and deal or I swear to God I'll blow your mother-fucking head off."

Mickey smiled nervously and complied.

For the next several hours, the men drank and played cards.

They talked, but the conversation was nothing beyond superficial—cars, movies, music, real estate. At 3:59 a.m. the game ended abruptly with Otis ahead nearly ten grand.

"You son of a bitch. You've been throwing the game, haven't you?"

"Don't be ridiculous."

Otis reached across the table and poured a glass of scotch. Mickey's perspiration, against his baking soda white complexion, was unmistakable.

"Here's my theory, and please, feel free to dispute it: You've been throwing this game because you're hoping that a happy Otis, a winning Otis, would take mercy on the poor Mickey mouse."

"You're tired and drunk. The combination is making you paranoid," Mickey said with surprising calm, though his hands shook nervously.

"I told you hours ago, any bad blood between you and me is history. But this…"

"I've been straight with you," Mickey insisted.

Otis reached across the table and overturned three cards.

"Three kings. You gave up three kings on your last hand. Tell me again how you've been playing straight."

"Look, I haven't done anything here."

"That isn't true. You goddam well know that isn't true, Mickey. You've ruined everything. You know, I just…I just wanted to play for a few hours. Have a bit of normalcy in my life. That's all. But even that's been denied me."

"I'm sorry. I thought you'd want to win. How do I…how do I make this right?"

Otis pulled Mickey across the table and shoved him to the floor.

"You can't. You can't fucking 'make this right.'"

"Don't!" Mickey said.

"I've spent more than half my existence in a futile search for a fucking glass ball. It's poisoned friends and colleagues. I barely know my wife and daughter. My entire life is a goddam lie. Do you have any idea what that's like?"

Mickey was barely able to utter a syllable against the onslaught of violence that followed. Otis took his time, time being the one thing he still had.

By 5:00 a.m. Otis was exhausted. The blood beneath his nails was thick and dry. He sat and rested on a black leather sofa and stared at the dead man once known as Mickey Solomon. Otis took little comfort in what he'd done, but little comfort was still better than none at all. He closed his eyes and slept for thirty-seven minutes as morning and a light snowstorm arrived.

The clean-up squad arrived shortly after 9:00 a.m. and Otis ushered them toward their task. Rudy Fernandez, a veteran cleaner who previously worked with Otis on numerous assignments, placed a mid-sized suitcase next to the corpse.

"Jesus Christ, Oppenheimer, you look worse than your friend here," Rudy said.

"I feel worse, too," Otis said, and lit a cigarette.

"I should fucking hope so. You probably shouldn't smoke in here while we're working," Rudy cautioned.

"There's a lot a man should and shouldn't do," Otis said.

Fernandez, a soft, candy bar of a man in his 50s with a handlebar moustache and penciled-in eyebrows, undid the clasps on the suitcase and began prepping for the clean-up.

"At least take it into the next room," he said.

"Not to worry. I don't much care for the smell of ammonia, so unless you need a John Hancock…"

"No, we're good. I don't suppose there's a coffee maker in the kitchen."

"There is, along with a bag of free-trade roast from Kenya. Half-and-half in the fridge is organic."

"It's the little, unexpected perks that make this more than just a job," Rudy said, sliding a pair of latex gloves onto his hands as Otis left the flat.

The morning Philly air was cold and a dusting of fresh white powder did little to help the working class commute. Otis hadn't spoken with Elise or Karrie in nearly two weeks. He knew better than to speak with them while intoxicated, but he was feeling particularly alone in the world. It would be okay provided he could remember to keep the call short and the conversation light.

Otis rang Elise's cell but the phone forwarded straight to voice mail. He tried the home line. Lupe Rosa, who cleaned the Oppenheimer's three-bedroom Bethesda home each week, answered on the fourth ring.

"Um, good morning Lupe," Otis said.

"Hello Mr. Otis, good morning. How are you?"

"I'm fine, Lupe. Um, why are you answering the phone?"

"I always answer the phone when Mrs. Otis and Karrie are away."

"Oh. Where is Karrie?" Otis asked, speaking slowly and enunciating each word for clarity.

Otis sat on the frozen concrete stairs of the Strike Three bar, a tiny dive located on Second Street just south of Washington. He sat and waited and watched as morning traffic eked south. Eventually 10:00 a.m. arrived and the establishment opened. Otis staggered in and placed a hundred on the bar. Molly Maguire, who was barely of legal drinking age, stood behind the bar and eyed Otis suspiciously.

"I can't change that," she said.

"No need. Bourbon on the rocks, and keep it coming."

Molly snatched the money and held it to a lamp next to the cash register.

"Don't worry, it's real enough," Otis said.

She returned a moment later and placed a bottle and a glass in front of Otis.

"We won't have ice for another 20 minutes or so."

"That's okay."

Otis poured a drink and salivated at the scent of the liquor. He flipped open his cell and dialed Emma's office phone. She answered on the first ring.

"Let me ask you a question," he said.

"Otis?"

"Yeah, it's me. I hope this isn't bad timing. Can't be helped."

"I'm mired in requisition forms. What's up?"

"Elise is leaving me. She's off with Karrie looking at property in Gaithersburg."

"Otis. I'm sorry."

"It's okay. I mean, it's not like I've been there…well…ever."

"You could still work it out. For Karrie's sake at least."

"Actually I feel like our split is in everyone's best interest, Karrie's in particular."

"I'm so sorry."

"It okay. Listen, there's something that's been in the back of my mind for a while."

"I'm listening," Emma said.

"Right. A while back you had a vision."

"I have visions all the time, Otis. It's what I do."

"This one was related to me. You told me you saw a beautiful wife in my future."

"Otis, that was a long time ago."

"I know. The thing is I always sensed that you were, I don't know, being less than honest with me."

"I'm not sure that I understand."

"Let me phrase it this way: Did you, do you, know how it's all going to end?"

"All what?"

"Elise and I; this assignment; everything."

"Otis, this isn't the sort of thing you casually discuss in a phone call."

"Not sure when I'll be in the DC area. Can you…can you just tell me."

Emma replied slowly and clearly, as if reading a well-rehearsed speech.

"You'll never see Elise again. Your cleaning lady gave you a bogus story; she was paid quite well to do this. Your wife and daughter have been residing in Hammerfest, Norway for several weeks. They've renounced their citizenship and have no intention of returning to the US. Elise has filed for divorce on grounds of abandonment. You will receive the paperwork on February 2."

"How sure are you of all this? I mean, is this a psychic hunch? Are you fucking with me? I'm very tired, Emma. Very tired."

"I told you, I don't make hunches. It is what it is, Otis. I'm sorry."

"You've known about this since…"

"I've known about it for some time."

"Jesus Christ. I'm too fucking tired for this, Emma. Why didn't you tell me? Why didn't you tell me this years ago?"

"There are some who consider me gifted, though I've always felt my ability to be more of a curse than a blessing. It isn't my job to steer the lives of others so they can make all the right choices."

"Much easier to break the news after the fact?"

"Maybe...never mind."

"Tell me," Otis said.

"Maybe if you had told her who you are, what you do. I never really understood the need to live a double-life."

"Let me ask you something. Do you moonlight as a fucking marriage counselor when the psychic work is slow? Anyway, you know the rules regarding disclosures to civilians."

"The rules have become relaxed. You know this. Besides, rules sometimes need to be broken."

"You should consider practicing what you preach."

"I'm sorry, Otis."

"If you knew all this, about Elise and Karrie, did you also know that we, you and I, would be having the conversation we're having now?"

"Yes," Emma said softly.

"Right. Then you probably know how this call ends."

"Yes. It ends with you hanging up on me."

"You're good, Emma; you're an asset to the agency," Otis said, and ended the call.

Otis collapsed the phone and returned it to his inside jacket pocket. He watched Molly the bartender as she mindlessly rinsed and towel dried a half-dozen dirty glasses.

"I won't be needing this," Otis said, and slid his glass in Molly's direction.

He grabbed the neck of the bottle and took a long swallow.

"I admire your gusto," Molly said.

Otis staggered out of the dive just before noon and headed toward South Street. He pissed and then vomited in an alley on Catherine Street, oblivious to curious onlookers who passed by. He inhaled the cold air and stood upright.

He phoned Emma again.

"What do you want?"

"Tell me just one thing," Otis said. "You do know what I'm going to ask, right?"

"I don't have a clue nor do I really care," Emma said, flatly.

"Will we find it?"

"As I recall, you found it once before, and you let it slip away."

"Just tell me. Will we find it again?"

"Yes. You will find it. I don't know when, so don't ask. But yes, Otis, you'll find your glass onion. It will show you truths that may be difficult to accept. Beyond that, I'm as in the dark as you."

"Okay. Thanks."

"Don't fucking call me again," Emma said with tears in her voice and hung up.

Otis closed the phone and smiled to the extent his facial muscles could pull together a smile. At that moment, he knew that everything would be okay. It didn't matter that Elise was gone. Theirs had been a marriage built upon a life Otis didn't possess, a man he never was. Life without Elise, and especially without Karrie, would be nearly pointless. Nearly, but not entirely. He would complete his assignment and transition to a new project and a new life following a very long vacation.

He continued on foot toward South Street, stopping to grab a Coke and cheese steak with fried peppers from a street vendor. A short walk to Pine Street followed and Otis dusted the snow off a park bench and sat down to eat. It was the first time in too long a time that food actually tasted like food. Otis told himself that everything was going to be okay as he slowly crawled back toward sobriety. In a way, losing Elise, the beautiful Elise, took a lot of weight from Otis' shoulders. He felt taller.

He considered phoning Denton Chambers but quickly reconsidered. Emma didn't say when the onion would be found; it could be months or years. If Denton wanted to know Emma's mind, he could make inquiries of his own. It would be Otis' task to plant the seed, nothing more.

Otis finished eating and squeezed the foil wrapper into a ball that he threw onto the ground. A man dressed in a tall trench-coat approached.

"That's a hundred-fifty-dollar fine, mister," a voice, vaguely familiar, remarked.

"I'll be sure to add littering to my hobbies list. Long time."

"It's a small world after all," Brad Calloway said. "Hello Otis."

"Brad," Otis said, nodding.

"Let's find someplace warm and dry to talk. That is, unless you prefer freezing your balls on a park bench."

The walk along Penn's Landing toward the *Mousholu* was long, and the cold wind was an uninvited guest that refused to leave.

"This is why I could never pull an east coast gig," Brad Calloway said.

He shoved both hands deep into the pockets of his wool coat and sucked vigorously on a filterless Camel.

"Like anything else, it just takes some getting used to," Otis said.

Ignoring a sign that read "Closed for Renovations," the men approached the permanently docked vessel and ascended its gang plank. Otis and Brad walked along the deck and stared across the Delaware River at adjacent Camden. They stepped through a narrow opening and into a cozy dining area where the air was toasty and warm with the faint scent of cherries jubilee. The room was mostly empty but for a small collection of agency men and women sitting at a corner table. Aside from a few new faces, Otis and Brad recognized the lot.

"The woman with the big hair, pale complexion, and huge grin is Wari Sappo," Otis said lightly.

"Sounds familiar."

"She won the Kreuger Award for Outstanding Excellence in the field of espionage two years running."

Brad glanced in Wari's direction.

"As I recall, she made a rep on the backs of her fellow agents. She's not exactly fucking angelic, Otis."

"What's she doing in Philly?"

"Fuck if I know. Probably passing through from New York to DC. Or maybe she's working a job or screwing over someone."

"I suppose. Speaking of passing through, what brings you here?"

Brad removed a Polaroid from his shirt pocket. The body of Mickey Solomon was barely recognizable, was barely a body in the traditional sense.

"Where did you get that?"

"I had a late breakfast with Rudy. I swear to God, you've never seen a man put away so many flapjacks."

"Not exactly by the book. The Polaroids I mean."

"Man's got to have a hobby, especially in this line of work. Here, take it."

"No, that's okay."

"You'll sleep better. Take the fucking photo."

Otis snatched the small glossy from Brad's fingers and began tearing it into small strips which he tore into smaller pieces.

"You're a paranoid fucker," Brad said.

"Paranoia doesn't enter into it."

A waiter approached their table.

"Club soda," Otis said.

"I'll have the same," Brad said, "but throw an obscene amount of scotch into the glass."

The waiter nodded and stepped away.

"Listen, it's no coincidence I ran into you."

"I figured as much," Otis said.

"The fact is I've been running a bit of a side business. I mean, can you blame me? We're not exactly getting rich stuck on this goddam assignment, whereas treacherous fucks like Wari Sappo are pulling down six-figure bonuses."

"Wari Sappo got a six-figure bonus?" Otis said, staring across the room at her.

"Rumor has it."

"Jesus Christ. No wonder she's always smiling. Tell me about this side project you're working."

"I won't bore you with the sordid details. The less you know, the better. Trust me."

"Some type of embezzlement scheme?" Otis asked. "Political blackmail?"

"Nothing so pedestrian. Listen, I need your help."

"Okay."

"Today."

"Just tell me where to aim and who to shoot."

"I'm serious, Otis."

"So am I."

"Good man. How's Elise?"

"Eh. Best not to ask."

"For real?"

Otis remained silent.

"I'm sorry, man."

"S'okay. I only found out today. Still don't quite know what's going on."

"She know you're with the company?"

"You think that makes a difference?"

"I don't know. Maybe."

"Emma implied as much."

"The psychic wonder?"

"I guess neither of you give a fuck about policy."

"Don't lecture me about policy. This isn't the fucking boy scouts, Otis. There are some secrets we don't share, and there are some we do share. Your problem is you have too much integrity for this job."

"Tell that to Mickey Solomon," Otis said, glancing at the torn Polaroid. "Poor son of a bitch thought he was doing me a favor."

"Work is different. I'd put a bullet through the head of my priest if I thought it would get me one step closer to the fucking onion."

"They let men like you have priests? That's fucked up," Otis asked.

Several hours later and as evening began its descent over the city of Philadelphia, Brad and Otis arrived in a slum neighborhood north of the city. The block was mixed with rusted twenty-year-old trucks and station wagons, a few on concrete blocks. At least three vehicles wore bright-orange restraint boots, locked onto the front tires by traffic enforcement personnel. The showroom-new black Toyota hybrid in which Brad and Otis traveled couldn't have looked more conspicuous.

Brad parked on the corner and removed a small, black nylon bag from the glove compartment.

"What ya got?" Otis asked.

"The truth is, we're in a bad neighborhood. As such, we're likely to encounter a bit of hostility. There's a vest in the back seat; put it on."

"What about you?"

"I'm wearing more protection than a frat boy in a sorority house that's been fumigated with Spanish fly," Brad said.

"You've never actually been in a sorority house before, have you?"

Brad unzipped the black bag and removed a syringe and two small glass bottles filled with a dark-blue liquid.

"This is xomamine."

"Never heard of it."

"You wouldn't have. Purely experimental. It's an analgesic derivative that attacks the central nervous system by rending the body's pain centers numb while simultaneously accelerating the mental reflexes. It's quite useful, particularly during altercations."

"You acquired this from the DC lab?"

"No, no. This was strictly a third-party purchase. Give it a go."

"I'll pass."

"More for me," Brad said.

"Enjoy."

Brad filled the syringe and pressed it against his left forearm while Otis fitted the vest.

"Thankfully it's intramuscular," Brad said.

"It's the little things, eh? How long before you're good?"

"A minute," Brad said, and sank into his seat.

Sixty seconds later they exited the car.

"Hundred bucks says it's stolen before we return," Otis said.

"You really have no faith in humanity."

"Seriously, you feeling okay?" Otis said.

"Better than okay; I'm Iron Man."

"Funny, I always pegged you as DC, not Marvel."

"We're going to the third house from the corner. Stay sharp."

Brad handed Otis a white envelope. It was heavy.

"Put this in your jacket pocket."

"What exactly is going on here?"

Brad stopped walking and pulled Otis aside.

"Long time ago you collected two glass fragments. You retained one and gave one to me for safe-keeping. Whatever became of yours?"

"It saved my life once."

"How so?"

"A few years back I had, I don't know, a premonition that caused me to cancel a flight from Pittsburgh to DC. The plane went down and took 136 souls with it."

"Christ."

"I don't know. Could have been a coincidence."

"There are no coincidences. Listen, we're going in here and we're leaving with a notebook…a laptop."

"Okay, I guess. Though I still don't understand what's happening here."

"That little sliver of glass you gave me is driving the notebook's processor."

"You had it forged it into a computer chip?"

"A microprocessor. Imagine the possibilities, Otis. Imagine your premonition on a wide-scale basis. Imagine a machine powered by magic contained within the glass onion."

"Mac or PC?"

"Mac of course."

"How much is this costing you?"

"Don't worry about that. When we enter the house, we'll be walking through the living room toward a bedroom. We'll pass a guy on a sofa; big blubber of a man in his early twenties. Name is Harold Donaldson but he goes by Carp. He'll be watching the 76ers, so he'll be distracted. But he's quick despite his ridiculous size. There'll be two men in the bedroom; both are early twenties and both are tall, skinny sons of bitches. Fucking Amazons aren't as tall as these two. The bald guy is Leon Jefferson. He'll be packing a .45, safety off; the stupid fuck keeps it in a fanny pack. Can you fucking believe that? The other one, Gordy Ginsberg, has a ridiculously large afro; you'd swear the guy stepped out of a *Fat Albert* cartoon."

"I love that show."

"Me too. Prior to 1980, Bill Cosby was a fucking genius. Anyway, Ginsberg is the brain and he's unarmed. If things go south, put a gun to his head but do not shoot. He may be our ticket outta here."

"So basically, keep my trigger finger itchy but exercise caution," Otis said.

"Precisely."

"I can do that."

They continued toward their destination. Otis removed a small plastic bottle from his jacket pocket and loosened the lid. He poured a small amount of its powdered contents onto his hands and rubbed them together before screwing the lid shut.

"Perspiration problem?" Brad asked.

"Bit of insurance is all."Brad knocked on the door and it soon buzzed open. Carp, sprawled across the sofa and engrossed in a close game between the Philadelphia 76ers and the Chicago Bulls, sipped a Miller-Lite 40. He turned his glance slowly toward the duo.

"Who's your friend?" Carp asked.

"This is Otis," Brad said. "Otis, say hello to Carp."

"Otis. Good name," Carp said.

"Thanks," Otis said, and extended his right hand.

The men shook briefly and Carp pointed a finger at Brad.

"You can go on back. Have a seat, Mr. Otis."

Otis sank onto a beat-up brown leather recliner as Brad continued toward the bedroom.

"It's nothing personal," Carp said to Otis, and returned his attention to the game.

Otis nodded as his eyes scanned the room. One window, boarded up from the inside. A single archway that lead to the rest of the house. Ceiling-mounted surveillance cameras in the north and west corners. The handle of a gun barely visible beneath a pillow next to Carp.

Instinct told Otis it would end badly. He wanted to feel annoyed at Brad for dragging him along, but his emotional reserve was nearly tapped out.

"Let the chips fall where they will," he whispered.

Carp glanced in Otis' direction.

"You'll want to shut the fuck up while the game is on," he said.

"I'll try to remember that," Otis answered.

Brad stepped into the bedroom and, at the insistence of Leon Jefferson, closed the door. The room was dark but for the glow of computer screens and LED lighting that reflected against Jefferson's shaved head. The room was wall-to-wall technology. Laptops. Desktops. Netbooks. Security cameras and monitors displaying every room of the house as well as the exteriors. Dozens of hand-held peripherals. The floor was a collection of wires, cables, and adaptors. A pair of twin servers stretched floor to ceiling and adorned the far corner of the room. Gordy Ginsberg sat on a bright orange yoga ball and typed frantically at a keyboard.

"Brad Calloway," he said. "Have a seat."

"Last time I was in this room," Brad said, "you had one machine—an old, refurbished Dell PC."

"You could say we've expanded operations," Gordy said.

"What exactly have you expanded into?"

Gordy withdrew his fingers from the keyboard and turned to face Brad.

"That's on a need-to-know basis, and you don't mother-fucking need to know."

"See, there's no need for language like that. Honestly."

"You don't like the way I talk? How about this: Where's my money? Or, put another way, where's my mother-fucking money, mother fucker? Because to be perfectly honest, it don't look like your pockets are overflowing with cash."

Brad turned toward the wall of surveillance monitors.

"You're, um, aware that he's with me," he said, pointing at Otis.

"Is that your accountant?" Gordy said.

"Financial advisor and part-time bodyguard. You don't seriously expect me to carry that sort of money unaccompanied through this neighborhood at night."

Gordy glanced in Leon's direction.

"Bring in mister financial advisor and part-time bodyguard."

"I assume you were successful?" Brad said.

"You asked me to build a notebook using a sliver of glass as the microprocessor. A piece of glass."

"Yes. A very special piece of glass."

"But a piece of glass nonetheless."

"That's right."

"And you expect this machine will somehow magically function? Your CPU is a piece of glass for fuck's sake."

"Never mind," Brad said. "Did you do it?"

"Of course I did it," Gordy said. "I'm a professional."

"What was the end result?"

"The end result?"

"Does it function?"

"It functions. Look around you, idiot. It's fucking life changing."

Gordy removed the notebook from a desk drawer and placed it on the desk next to Brad.

"Steve Jobs would love to get his hands on this fucking piece of machinery."

"I want a demo," Brad said.

"And I want bacon-flavored peanut butter, but that doesn't mean it's gonna happen."

"Listen to me. I'm not paying you a goddam cent until I see what I'm purchasing. If you were in my shoes you'd do the same."

"If I were in your shoes," Gory said, "I'd buy myself a decent pair, and a new suit, cause the mother-fucking polyester look just don't cut it. And the thing of it is, we need to talk renegotiation."

"Renegotiation."

"Did I stutter?" Gordy said.

"Fine. Renegotiation. But not until I see what I'm purchasing."

Gordy opened the laptop lid and booted the machine.

"Sit down, and prepare to have your mother-fucking mind blown away."

From Gordy and Leon's perspective, there was nothing unusual about Brad's user experience. But there was. It began as Brad's pupils became dilated. His pulse rose and dropped erratically and a bead of saliva escaped from the left corner of his mouth. He began to perspire through the ebb and flow of accelerated brain wave activity. Invisible data streams passed through him at rocket-ship speed. He felt faint.

A thin black hand snapped the laptop closed and Brad recoiled his hands away from the keyboard. Brad felt as though he'd touched live current and he struggled not to fall out of his chair.

"What happened? How long have I been sitting here?"

"Twenty, maybe 30 seconds," Gordy said.

"It felt like days."

"I know. Fucking amazing, isn't it? Let's talk price."

Otis entered the room accompanied by Leon who stood close and appeared suspicious.

"Mr. financial advisor and part-time bodyguard. Nice of you to join us," Gordy said. "I hope your pockets are deep."

"Sorry?" Otis asked.

"I told him you're holding the money," Brad said.

"I'm not holding the money. I thought you were holding it."

"No. I gave it to you to hold," Brad insisted. "I'm quite sure."

Gordy stood up and ran a hand through his thick, frizzy hair. Leon took a step back and began unzipping the fanny pack strapped around his waist.

"It's late, and I'm not in a particularly good mood for your bullshit. Therefore, if I don't see a mother fucking wad of money in the next few seconds, you're both going to be shitting blood and leaking brain," he said. "Oh, and you'll also be dead."

"Don't fuck with the man, Otis," Brad said. "Give him the money and let's finish this."

"Fine," Otis said.

He felt the barrel of Leon's .45 pressed against his lower back.

"No funny business," Leon said.

"Do I look stupid?"

Otis slowly reached into his inner jacket pocket and removed a thick business-size envelope.

"Here," he said, and tossed it toward the table. The throw was short, and the envelope landed on the floor.

Brad, still somewhat foggy, nonetheless recognized the strategic advantage Otis' action afforded. With Leon kneeling down, Otis could easily knock him off balance and put two bullets in his skull in as few seconds. Otis inhaled deeply, mentally preparing for the deed at hand.

Unfortunately, the opportunity never arose.

Otis collapsed to the ground as Leon, smelling double-cross, suddenly and violently smashed his weapon against the back of the agent's head. He struggled to maintain consciousness against a room that quickly became a distant blur. He smelled sulfur, and his taste buds were overwrought with the sensation of spoiled milk. Otis was unable to recognize himself, much less Brad, Gordy, and Leon.

The blackness was quick to consume him.

His ears felt a tremendous pressure, as if he were being pulled beneath the ocean to submarine depths. The gunshots that followed snapped like far-distant bottle rockets. Unconsciousness was no longer a state to be feared but, rather, a welcome friend.

His return to the waking world was no less dizzying, no less agonizing. Otis rubbed his right hand against the fresh lump on the back of his skull. The blackness threatened its return but was kept at bay by the scent of ammonium carbonate.

"We now resume our regularly scheduled program," Brad said.

Brad was driving faster than usual and approaching the city skyline. He nearly fishtailed while turning onto Woodley Street. He reduced speed and steered into a vacant school parking lot. The car drifted slowly toward the back of the lot. Brad killed the lights and engine.

"What the fuck happened?" Otis asked.

"After your stunt, which, don't get me wrong—it was a good stunt—but after it failed, I was left with little recourse but to take matters into my own hands. Best way out of that room was via Gordy. Thanks, by the way, for taking care of Carp."

"The hand powder worked. I was worried that he might have been immune to its effects."

"After Leon sacked you, he turned his gun's sight on me. I grabbed the laptop and ripped Gordy from his chair. The room was dark enough, and I was fast enough. So we were at an impasse. Except…"

"Except?"

"Two problems."

"Two problems are better than three problems," Otis said.

"Look down."

Otis glanced at the floor mat and reached for the laptop.

"The bullet shattered the glass microprocessor. It's fucking wasted."

"Jesus Christ. I guess Leon was a better shot than we suspected."

"Which brings us to problem numero dos."

Brad removed a red-stained hand from his side.

"You told me you were wearing a vest," Otis said.

"Yeah, I kind of lied about that. Figured you'd need it more than me."

"Goddammit Brad."

Otis dialed 911 on his cell but Brad snagged the phone from his hand and disconnected the call. He placed the phone on the car's dashboard.

"I'm fine. It's just a flesh wound."

"You've been shot."

"Grazed. Don't be so dramatic. Besides, the xomamine is still working. I feel nothing."

"What became of Leon and Gordy?" Otis asked.

"You already know the answer to that. No great losses there. Fucking shame about the laptop though."

"What did you see?"

"It was beyond words."

Otis stared at the empty school building and briefly flashed back to the carefree days of middle school.

"Every day is like school. Every day you learn something new," Otis said.

"I know what you're wondering," Brad said. "You want to know why I didn't simply take the glass to the R&D team. I might ask you the same question."

"You might," Otis said. "But I wasn't trying to construct a super-computer with a glass microprocessor."

"Yeah. There's that. Listen, you and I both know that if I'd have approached Denton he'd have confiscated the glass."

"So this super-computer idea, were you planning to change the world?"

"Fuck that. I would have used it for personal gain, obviously. And here I am now, bleeding like a goddam fountain in the front seat of a stolen car."

"It's a flesh wound. Right?"

Brad's voice waned. "Listen, we've been duped. We've all been duped. You. Me. Key. Billings. There's only one way off this bus. If you're smart you'll walk away. Get the fuck out now while you can."

Otis retrieved his phone. It was wet and warm with blood.

"Do not phone 911. Otis, don't make me smash your goddam phone."

"You need an ambulance."

"Listen, I want to talk with you for a minute."

"A minute. Then we ring for help."

"You've somehow managed to eke out a life despite this fucking whore of an assignment. This whole Elise business, you have to make matters right."

"That isn't likely going to happen."

"Goddamit, at least try. Fucking try, Otis."

"Okay, Brad. Okay."

"I fucked those guys up."

"Gordy and Leon?"

"Yeah," Brad said, a satisfied grin stretched across his tired face. "Fucked them up beyond belief."

"Good man."

Brad extended his arms and took hold of the steering wheel. His skin was pale and his lips powder white. He arched his head backward and slipped into shock.

"Goddammit!" Otis said.

He dialed 911 but closed the phone before an operator picked up. Otis had seen death enough to know when a life was beyond saving. He removed Brad's wallet and stripped it of cash, credit cards, and a half-dozen IDs.

Several hundred miles south, Denton Chambers sat behind a large oak desk and sipped a tall latte. He reviewed a spreadsheet containing the names, salaries, and expense reports of active GO agents during the prior twelve months. The budget and allocation season was at hand, and with a new administration entering the White House, the weeks ahead would typically include many sleepless nights. Recent sources of revenue, however, provided Denton with a sense of relief he'd not seen since the Reagan years.

He glanced at the incoming call on his cell and picked up.

"Hello Brad. You'll be pleased to know that as a result of recent funding we'll be adding several new agents to the project's ranks. With any luck this may be our final year on this goddam assignment."

"Denton, it's Otis."

"Otis? What's going on?"

"Brad is dead. His body is lying in a black Honda in the parking lot of Gooding Elementary in north Philly. I don't have the exact address but I'm sure you can Google it."

"What's happened?"

"It's a long story, and I'm too fucking tired to go into it right now. The short version is that Brad was shot. Just...just send in a crew to retrieve the body before daybreak. Probably wouldn't be good for a bunch of elementary school brats to see this. It's a hell of a thing. I never did find out why he hated LA so goddam much."

"What the fuck are you talking about?"

"Nothing."

"Get yourself to 30th Street Station and onto a Metroliner. I want you back in DC for a debriefing."

"Yeah. I'll get right on that, Denton," Otis said, ending the call.

He removed the SIM card then tossed the phone through a storm grate. Otis walked toward Broad Street and hailed a taxi. Sitting in the heavy southbound traffic, he thought about Brad's final words of advice.

He tried to keep it civil. Otis felt an initial shock that his call to Elise hadn't gone straight to voice mail, that she was actually speaking with him. The shock wore off quickly enough. Her voice was overflowing with indifference. How long, he wondered, had it been this way. It was becoming quickly apparent that Elise had no intention of returning to the United States. There were so many questions.

"What happened to us?" Otis said.

"You failed me. You failed Karrie. You failed us all."

She answered his queries in the past tense, and he knew it was over.

"I know I let you down. Can't we still fix this? How did we become broken beyond fixing?" he asked.

"It's was a long time in coming. You were never there."

"I should have been honest with you about my work."

"That would have been like placing a Band-Aid on a severed limb. I've known about your association with the agency for some time."

Otis was silent.

"For Christ's sake, Otis, you were a novelist who never wrote, never took notes or kept a journal. You never visited a library. Never read. You were never home. We didn't even own an ink-jet printer. To be honest, I didn't know who you were or where you drew a paycheck for a long time. Eventually I hired an investigator. Maybe I should have been relieved that you weren't having an affair."

"You had me investigated?"

"Don't act so violated. Isn't that what you people do every day?"

"None of this should matter. If you knew how I earned a wage then you also should have understood nature of the work. The less you know about me the better."

"The less I know about you? Listen to what you're asking of me."

"That isn't what I meant."

"It is what it is. The divorce papers are at the house. Anything else that needs to be discussed should be done via my attorney in the states."

"Who do you think you're talking to? I have friends in the State Department. Kerrie will be back here with me where she belongs faster than you can suture a wound."

"I'd have expected better of you than threats, Otis. You'll never see Kerrie again."

"Forgive me. My marriage is collapsing, and I just watched a friend die," Otis said.

"I'm sorry for your losses. Otis…"

"Yes?"

"Don't call me again."

The taxi pulled up to the intersection of Sixth and South. Otis paid the fare and walked half a block to a bar called Fusion.

The stylish, semi-upscale joint sprawled both floors of a former row house. The Fusion staff and clientele resembled extras from a generation-zero fashion shoot: twenty-something men in black denim, fitted Gap tees, and Dr. Martin's. Young women in black minis, leather boots, thigh-highs, and sleeveless sweaters or backless blouses. The music was loud but not overbearing, ranging from 1960s psychedelic underground to mainstream modern pop and rock. Otis instantly hated the place.

Otis walked past the bar to the men's room. He closed and locked the door behind him, washed his hands, splashed cold water on his face, and made a futile attempt to brush his teeth clean with an index finger. The reflection that stared back, a face of frustration, anger, and exhaustion, seemed even less familiar than it had just hours earlier. He considered punching the mirror but decided that emotional pain was sufficient suffering. No need, Otis reasoned, to add self-inflicted physical injury to his growing list.

He ascended the stairs to the second story. It was darker upstairs. Black walls and black plush carpet. Acid jazz and ambient sounds. Slightly less crowded. Otis found a small corner table and light a cigarette. He ordered beer with a scotch chaser and gave the waitress two-hundred dollars.

"Keep half for yourself. And don't let me get thirsty," Otis said.

The evening crept slowly by and Otis sank into an inebriated state. The shadowed faces that surrounded him reminded Otis just how dark the world was and how alone he was in it. The thought of resignation crept into his head. But there was no resigning from the assignment. Even if insubordinate, Otis reasoned that Denton would be reluctant to remove him from the GO team. The government had invested too many years and too many miles in Otis Oppenheimer to let him walk away. Dismissal would require extreme measures.

He took a head count of those in his immediate vicinity. Otis had enough firepower to kill nearly everyone. He pointed at each patron with his right index finger in a mock group assassination.

"The problem," he said to the waitress as she refreshed his drinks, "is that regardless of what actions I choose, it's a lose-lose situation."

"Sorry?"

"You see, I could take out everyone in this room, but where would that get me? More blood on my hands. Incarcerated or on the run? Neither scenario is desirable."

"I don't suppose they would be."

"How do you get fired from a job you can't get fired from?"

"That's easy, and best of all you don't need to resort to killing strangers."

"I'm all ears," Otis said, and light a cigarette.

"I've done this many times, so believe me when I tell you that it works. The trick is to stop showing up."

"That's...that's fucking brilliant."

"It works. You may think you're irreplaceable, but you know what, no one is. We're all interchangeable like blocks in a kid's puzzle box."

Otis paused on the suggestion as his thoughts turned to Kerrie and Elise.

"What's your name?"

"Pillar."

"I think...I think my family may have taken your advice, Pillar."

"That sucks. But, sometimes everyone needs to start over."

"Maybe so. I've spent half of my life searching for something that can't or doesn't want to be found."

"It may be time to call off the bloodhounds," Pillar said.

"You're too wise for your age," Otis said and stood up." I'd appreciate it if you'd make sure no one takes my table or appropriates my cigarettes while I'm gone."

"Just promise me you're not going to embark on a murderous rampage."

"I make no promises," Otis said, smiling and barely recognizing what it felt like to smile. "Okay, I promise."

He staggered toward the men's room as Pillar resumed her tasks. The room was standard fare, consisting of a toilet, a urinal, and an ornate porcelain sink. Otis closed and locked the stall door and sat on the floor next to the toilet. Within the men's room, the bar music was reduced to a muted, rhythmic bass line. Otis leaned against the wall and felt the pulse of the music. It was a dangerously relaxing sensation and his eyes were soon shut tight.

His respite from the waking world was short lived due to twenty-one-year-old Derick Hanson. The typically reserved Derick had spent the evening downing glasses of Yeungling beer with his friends. His sobriety and politesse were both awry. He stood and pounded a fist against the stall door.

"Open the fucking door, man! I gotta take a dump! C'mon, man!"

Otis rose from the floor and brushed a hand against his jacket and slacks while Derick continued to scream and swear.

"Just a second," Otis said.

"I've been waiting ten minutes. Hurry up, fucko!"

Otis slowly unlocked the stall door. He then kicked the door open wide. Its edge clocked Derick in the face, shattering his nasal septum. He dropped to his knees amidst a fury of blood and pain. Otis stepped toward him and leaned over.

"I'm sorry, was I fast enough for you?"

"You brof my fucking node," Derick said. His garbled voice was faint and growing fainter.

"Yes, I suppose I did. You'll want to see a doctor, quite soon I'd imagine."

While Otis slowly straightened his jacket and washed up, Derick obligingly succumbed to unconsciousness. Otis met Pillar as he left the men's room.

"I thought you might have left without saying goodbye," Pillar said.

"No such luck. A drunkard seems to have taken a nasty fall in the men's room. I tried to help him, but he may need an ambulance."

"Oh," she said.

Otis returned to his table and watched as Pillar summoned aid for Derick Hanson. He stared at the collection of glass objects on his table.

Shot glass.

Beer glass.

Glass beer bottle.

Glass ashtray.

In the middle of these objects, nearly invisible in the darkness, sat the prize of prizes. Otis' body twitched and his eyes widened with a cartoonish exaggeration that would have inspired illustrators from the Warner Brothers animation department. He was sober enough to know that he wasn't hallucinating.

Pillar approached his table.

"This object wasn't at my table before. Where did it come from?"

"I really don't know. It's pretty. Is it glass?"

"What do you mean you really don't know? Either you know or you don't know."

"Then I don't know. I've never seen it before."

"You're sure? Think, Pillar. Someone was here. Someone left this here."

"It's been kind of slow tonight. I didn't see anyone near your table. Look around."

"You must not have looked very closely. This didn't just materialize out of the thin fucking air."

"You don't have to be a dick," Pillar said.

"I'm sorry. It's just…it's been a long day."

Pillar stared quizzically at the object.

"What is it?" she asked.

"Someone's twisted idea of a joke."

"It isn't very funny."

"No. It isn't."

Pillar stepped away from Otis, and he sank further into his chair. His mind racing, Otis reached the logical conclusion that he'd been duped. Somehow his privacy had been compromised. The object before him was obviously a fraud. He was being made the fool.

Except that it was chipped.

The imperfections in the glass were unmistakable. Otis removed a handkerchief from his pants pocket and carefully lifted the onion from the table. The weight felt right. It looked right.

He sighed and smiled. The world in which he'd spent the last two decades of his life was about to change for the better. The quest for the elusive glass onion was at an end. The price the glass onion had exacted was heavy. The talisman had claimed his youth, his career, his wife and daughter, his self-respect, and the souls of several colleagues. The time was at hand to reclaim all that he could.

He placed the glass onion back onto the table. As there was no one to share in the celebration, Otis raised a glass and silently toasted his own good fortune. He then held the prized object intent on reaping the reward. It would, he realized, be impossible not to risk a glimpse.

"You fucking owe me," he whispered.

The glass onion appeared to welcome the query. A soft white glow surrounded Otis' worn fingertips, and he found it impossible to loosen his grip. Otis closed his eyes as his grasp tightened and the rough edge of the onion, the chipped section, cut his right hand.

The visions that followed were as black and white and soundless as early motion pictures. But there was no mistaking their meaning; the message was as clear as it was devastating: Otis Oppenheimer would spend the rest of his considerably long life alone and in search of the glass onion. The hunt would take him to unique and far-away lands. He would climb Everest and explore the caves of the Pacific Ocean. He would see Tunisia and the Great Pyramids. He would survive a near-fatal car collision in Lima, Peru. But beyond the current moment in time, never again would he see or possess the glass onion. His was an inescapable predetermined future.

Otis opened his eyes and, upon adjusting to the darkness, stared down at the table. His hands were cupped and one was bleeding. The emptiness he felt in his soul was mirrored by the contents, or lack thereof, on the table. His longed-for possession was gone as though it had never existed. He scanned the area around him then dropped to the floor and crawled beneath his table. He searched the tables next to his, bumping into strangers. With each passing moment his desperation escalated.

He staggered to the bar and caught sight of Pillar.

"Where is it?" he asked. "You saw it. Where did it go?"

"Listen, you're starting to creep me out. Maybe you should consider, you know, hailing a taxi and calling it a night."

"Goddammit," Otis said.

He tottered back to his table and continued the search. There was no urgency, no panic. And no hope. Otis already knew that the search would end in disappointment. The young patrons who momentarily found Otis an interesting curiosity soon returned to socializing with one another. Resigned to his fate, Otis sat and sipped on his loss until last call. He was finally, completely, bereft.

South Street was still a kaleidoscope of social activity at 2:00 a.m. as Otis walked east toward Front Street. Police on horseback monitored the street activity at every corner in anticipation of drug- and alcohol-inspired fights that were the sad status quo in the city of brotherly love. Otis pushed his way through the wall of humanity and headed north on Fifth Street where life consisted of alley rats the size of footballs and forgotten vagrants huddled beneath cardboard or dirty blankets.

He crossed St. James Court and approached Walnut Street and Independence Hall. Following the September 11 attacks the block-long historic structure and birthplace of a nation's freedom changed radically. Much of its majesty was replaced by waist-high metal fencing designed to dissuade terrorist attacks. Otis recalled seeing the barricades years ago. He still considered them a symbol of fear, a psychological victory for America's enemies.

Psychological victories. He wondered who had scored one on him tonight; the list of possibilities was long and inscrutable.

Several blocks later Otis approached the Christ Church Cemetery. He stopped to gaze at various headstones, which date back to the early 1800s, before continuing along with no actual destination. Otis turned East onto Arch Street. At Fourth and Arch, he stepped into the intersection toward the path of an oncoming SUV driven by fifty-four-year-old Anton Sherman, who was returning from a bachelor's party in Camden. Anton wailed on the vehicle's horn and swerved hard to avoid hitting Otis. The passenger side-view mirror clipped Otis' right shoulder. He staggered but maintained his footing as the vehicle and its inebriated driver sped away.

"Didn't hurt," he said, and proceeded through the intersection.

If the glass onion's visions were accurate, Otis concluded that, like the seasons, his life was preordained. As such, it couldn't be changed. Not even by him. Otis saw little reason not to test the theory.

He continued on foot toward the Ben Franklin Bridge where, within a few minutes, he stood at the entranceway of the eastbound pedestrian walkway. It was locked, as it was locked each night at

11:00 p.m. But as many others had done before him, Otis scaled the fence and proceeded up the narrow walkway.

He reached midpoint, several hundred feet above the river, within a few minutes. Otis stopped. He felt more sober than he'd felt in months.

He began to tell his spy-issue tale into a cheap spy-issue tape recorder. He bummed a smoke from a couple walking from Camden. He froze. He felt good and sorry for himself for a long time.

The chip and the blood had sealed the deal. Were it not for the chip in the glass onion, were it not for the cut on his hand, he could have continued to live the lie that he'd lived for so many years. The fairytale of an ending. Not a certain kind of ending, but an ending. A day of rest, a fucking Sabbath for Christ's sake.

But there was the cut. He could not deny the physicality of it. There it fucking was. And here he was. Was it all just bullshit? Was he just bullshit? Or had he stepped beyond the veil? Was he a goddam super hero?

"Why not?" he said.

Otis removed his coat and placed it carefully on the walkway. Who the fuck knew, and it was a damn nice coat. Then he turned, took a deep and long inhale of the Philly atmosphere, and prepared to step over the concrete railing and into the Delaware River. It had been a long day but it would soon be over.

Or not.

28 Philadelphia, January 27, 2009: Otis Atop the Ben Franklin (Reprise)

As he sat on the ledge of the guardrail of the pedestrian walkway of the Ben Franklin Bridge, Otis realized that, although unlikely, it was possible he could survive the free-fall into the Delaware River independent of the future visions revealed by the glass onion. He would accomplish nothing (aside from ruining a very expensive Armani suit). A more definitive acid test would involve a gun, a bullet, and his brain, but Otis was reluctant to resort to this option.

There was also the possibility that the incident at the bar—the entire vision—had been a byproduct of his bourbon-altered brain. Otis loathed his assignment but was at the same time married to it. What if he were wrong? What if it had been an attack on his conscious mind by his subconscious? What if the wound on his hand had been subconsciously self-inflicted? He couldn't rule out the possibility even though he knew in his heart that what happened had, in fact, happened.

Otis continued to ponder the gun, bullet, and brain solution. In the interim he decided to dictate an audio account of what were likely to be his final moments. He fumbled with the portable necklace recorder that he'd worn for years but had never found useful.

By 3:30 a.m. Otis was physically and emotionally exhausted. The bourbon he'd purchased earlier from Simak was nearly gone, although a sufficient number of cigarettes still remained. Otis took comfort in the white mittens given to him earlier by Donder, but he saw little else in his life worthy of celebration.

"Where do we go from here?" he asked. "More tell-all confessionals and dirty secrets revealed? What's left to reveal? More advice for the uninformed? I've none to offer."

He opened his wallet and removed a handful of photographs of Elise and Kerrie. He dropped the photos over the railing and watched as they fluttered and floated toward the river's surface.

"Going…going…gone," he said, with no emotion.

Otis removed other items from his wallet. Credit cards. Photo IDs. One by one he sent them over the edge. He threw his cash in the air. The bills were caught in an updraft and floated above his head and toward the westbound lanes of the bridge. Lastly Otis dropped his wallet.

"It appears I have little choice," he said. "The question remains: am I a free man or a slave to a ball of glass? Is my destiny predetermined or can I change it? Best to settle these questions right here, right now. To those I leave behind let me just say…"

He paused and realized that he was leaving none behind; none who would notice he was gone anyway.

Otis removed his mittens and sat on the cold concrete walkway. He removed his pistol from its holster. He checked the cartridge and switched off the safety. He placed the barrel of the gun against his lips. It felt surprisingly, comfortingly warm. He opened his mouth and leaned his head back slightly. The bullet would travel through the roof of his mouth and exit through the lower quadrant of his brain. He wrapped his right index finger around the trigger and squeezed once. Then twice. Then thrice.

The gun would not fire.

He examined the weapon, removing and replacing the cartridge and firing pin and ruling out any possible mechanical issues. Still it would not discharge. Disgusted, he hurled the firearm into the river and stood up. He emptied the bourbon into his mouth and similarly hurled the bottle southward into the Delaware.

"God-fucking-dammit," Otis said.

He slipped the mittens over his hands, buttoned his jacket, and began the long march down the crosswalk toward Philadelphia.

29   Epilogue: 1966: Weybridge, UK

He was in the sunroom again.

Whenever he wasn't running round with the band mates all across the world without her, he was likely holed up in that cramped little sunroom. She knew he was going to leave her and Jules, knew it, and didn't know what she'd do, who she'd be, if she wasn't Mrs. Him. Cynthia had lost countless hours agonizing over how she might hold onto what was clearly slipping away. It seemed a happy ending would be impossible.

And then, one day, a small cardboard parcel arrived in the mail. It was addressed to her. The real her—not the her that served as an extension of Him. Within the box was a small glass sphere, a little onion, and tied to its stem was a simple little cardboard tag containing a simple little request.

"HOLD ME."

Cynthia thought of Lewis Carroll and wonderment of Alice's adventures. She so badly wanted to hold something, or for something to hold her.

She carried the parcel to the kitchen, where she knew she would be uninterrupted. They liked her best in the kitchen—cooking and keeping busy, leaving Him alone. His creativity was at its zenith in the company of solitude. Solitude and a cache of amphetamines. Cynthia gently lifted the glass onion from its box and placed both hands around it.

In an instant she saw two stories.

In the first story, she stood in the driveway and rolled the little onion like a bowling ball down toward the street. It bobbed and weaved, eventually spiraling its way into a distant gutter. She started to cry. She and Jules no longer resided here at Kenwood. No longer was the castle theirs to share, for the only key in their possession belonged to a used piece of Samsonite luggage. Cynthia's life was never the same again. No stability. She was nothing and young Jules lost all importance to the world.

In the second story, she carried the little onion into the sunroom. She stepped in. She interrupted Him.

She.

Interrupted.

Him.

She closed the lid on the upright piano and placed the object in front of Him, and said, "HOLD THIS!" She was firm of conviction. And He, who was now so bored with her, was, for the moment, intrigued. He gently closed the pad in which He'd been writing, picked up the orb, and shut His eyes. He held it for several minutes, and slowly a smile washed across His face. He opened His eyes, set aside the onion, and took her hands. "I love you and our son," He said, "Thank you for this. It will be okay now."

The two stories abruptly ended. The images that seemed to play inside the glass onion faded to film credit black. Cynthia placed the onion in the silverware drawer and began to make a trifle. She made good trifle, and He had quite the sweet tooth. He would grab the biggest spoon He could find and eat right from the glass dish. Always the rapscallion.

As she worked, the two visions played over and over in her mind, and with them, a question arose.

What would He see?

Her head spun 'round and 'round trying to arrive at an answer. Finally, the trifle done, she lifted the little glass ball from the drawer.

"What will He see?" she whispered, and this is what she saw as the little onion revealed itself once more:

Cynthia saw herself and Jules, and they glowed as if they were angels in His life. They stood backstage, and as He came off the stage, He ran to hold them both. He ran right past the screaming girls who desperately wanted Him. The image dissolved from a concert stage to an auditorium and Julian's graduation. They were still together. They embraced and He was so happy. Backstage again, several years later, at Julian's first live performance. They watched him play the beat up Rickenbacker 325, overjoyed at their child's success. The image dissolved into soft blue water. They were much older. Still together, they relaxed on a beautiful beach in South Hampton along with Julian and his wife and children. She gazed at her wonderful famous husband and realized that His old eyes were filled with gentle tears. And then, quick as that, she saw Him step out of the vision, open His eyes, release the onion, and clasp her hands.

"I love you and our son," He said. "Thank you for this. It will be okay now. I want to come with you, my darling, but I feel so inspired. I've had a vision of our lives, you and our son. I must write this song—this song of our lives. It's in my head. The whole bloody thing is bursting to come out. I've got this whole song about you and Jules. I have to write it."

So much sorrow. So much contention. All of it could be washed away like muddy water. He simply needed to open His eyes, or have them opened for Him. He would see that she and Jules were real, that they mattered. They were His key to ultimate satisfaction.

Cynthia felt a sudden electric jolt and she instantly opened her clasped hand. As the onion dropped to the floor her reverie faded, albeit slightly. She was weeping with joy. She dropped to the floor, relieved that the onion had survived its plummet. Oh my God, how important this little glass trinket was! Someone had sent her the gift of magic. Someone wanted her to save her life.

She pushed open the door of the solarium. He was sketching and turned a bit away from her intrusion.

"Here," she said, "hold this."

He looked up at her askance, and then down at the object in her hand. He arched an eyebrow quizzically and extended a hand.

"Both hands!" she barked.

He looked up again, the way a little boy looks up at his mommy, and slowly reached His hands to take the object from her.

Although she saw nothing in the glass as He held it, she saw the vision wash over Him. She turned away, momentarily distracted by the vast collection of objects aligning the shelves in the room. Her eyes fixated on the mortar and pestle, which so often aided His efforts to attain the perfect altered state. When she looked back, He was both smiling and weeping.

He put the onion down on the cushion next to Him. He looked up at her and reached to take her hands.

"Thank you. It will be okay now," He said.

"I'm so, oh sweetheart, I'm so... I made you a trifle," she said.

His eyes were off her. He retrieved pen and pad.

"I'm so grateful for this, and for the trifle too, but I've got to write down these song lyrics first. It's in my head. The whole bloody thing is bursting to come out. I've got this whole song. Can't you see that?"

He spoke with urgency.

"Yes," Cynthia said, as she turned to go, "I understand, and I know what you've got to do. I'll be waiting."

He started to pen the words, but hesitated. He had to see it again. He needed to be sure the vision was real and not the byproduct of an LSD-imbued mind. He picked up the onion once more and the vision He'd witnessed moments earlier unfolded like a television rerun: They were together. John, Cynthia, and Jules. The perfect nuclear family. But unlike moments earlier, the Machiavellian onion opted to reveal additional details: Together, yes, but without happiness. Always there were fights and jealousies, and not even Kenwood's many rooms could afford Him a moment's peace. In time, all the music He had worked so hard for was gone. In time, He became *he*. An old man in an old house living a bitter life with a bitter wife. Eyes permanently bloodshot from years of substance abuse and nightly tears. While his band mates achieved individual successes, he was never important to anyone again. He was a hero to none, working class or otherwise.

Like storm clouds parting, a second story began to reveal itself to Him. Cynthia was crying. He'd left her and Jules. He saw himself naked and wrapped around the body of an exotic Japanese beauty. He witnessed the birth of a second son, a son born of two equal halves, because He and She understood the world in the way that no others did. The child was the miraculous combination of Their souls. He saw, too, that He would never grow old. His life would end prematurely on the evening of December 8, 1980, on a street in New York. He would die before the story of He and She was supposed to end. But it was enough. It was enough to know that, no matter if she sometimes complained, Yoko really did love John. She loved him beyond herself, beyond anything else in the world. He would leave behind a son, a son born at the perfect time, in the perfect place, from the perfect couple. And that was also okay.

There was no question which path he was about to choose.

John brought his hands up to wipe tearstained eyes as the discarded onion rolled deep into the sofa under the cushions. He didn't notice. The song was calling and calling to him now. It had to be written. He picked up the pencil and the pad and began to scribble...

Looking through a glass onion

Also by David Yurkovich

Fiction

Banana Seat Summer (fall 2014*)*
Iconic (winter 2014)

Graphic Novels

Altercations: The Definitive Edition (fall 2014)
The Broccoli Agenda
Death by Chocolate: Redux
Less Than Heroes

Nonfiction

Mantlo: A Life in Comics

www.ingramcontent.com/pod-product-compliance
Lightning Source LLC
Chambersburg PA
CBHW051434170626
46809CB00006B/2454

* 9 7 8 0 9 7 2 2 6 4 6 2 4 *